Reese's Leap

AN ISLAND MYSTERY

DARCY SCOTT

8-3-2013

TURTLE
POND
PRESS

Also by Darcy Scott
Matinicus—An Island Mystery
Hunter Huntress

Reese's Leap, An Island Mystery
Copyright © 2013 by Darcy Scott
First Edition

ISBN 978-1-938883-34-7

Cover art by Anna Torborg

Book designed and produced by
Maine Authors Publishing
Rockland, Maine
www.maineauthorspublishing.com

For the Island Women, fearless all.
You rock.

It ain't over 'til it's over.
—Yogi Berra

PROLOGUE

July, 1912

Run, baby girl! Mama screams from her grave. *Run!*

And I be fast, too—lickety-split like she always say—rocks and shells cuttin' at my feet as I claw my way up the hill. My breath all hitched and raggedy when I make the rise and creep under them trees that's always so sweet and piney smellin'. My thinkin' trees, Daddy calls 'em.

Through the branches I can see him and Willie bein' marched down to the cove with the others—Willie spittin' and fightin' good as any man though he ain't but six, Daddy gone all quiet as he peeks back to where I'm hid, his eyes catchin' mine like they do, tellin' me to stay put, stay quiet. That he'd be back for me.

Run, girl!

Ain't but a half hour since they come poundin' at the door—the one Mama always said ain't nothin' ever come through but bad news—Daddy awake first, slippin' that old suspender over his shoulder as he picked his way past us in the dark. Willie still hard asleep on the cot, but me, I saw Daddy's back go stiff, his eyes turn hard when he opened up—the faces of them mainland men all twisted and ugly with meanness, lookin' me over like they ate somethin' bad. It was then Mama told me to git.

There's more of 'em movin' up the hill with their torches now, puttin' fire to houses I been in and out of my whole life, laughin' as they step 'round Sally's baby plopped down in the dirt, flappin' her hands and cryin', all big-eyed scared.

I look to the graveyard where our people is buried—a hundred years' worth maybe. Mama laid out just last winter, not a week after bakin' me my nine-years cake. Places in there I know to hide, places I can stay 'til Daddy and them come back, feedin' myself on fish and berries, lyin' in the sun.

Hide! Mama beggin' me now, but my feet don't listen, my eyes still caught on Daddy and Willie and the man pushin' 'em hard toward the boats—Willie cryin', which he don't hardly do no more, even when the cat up and killed her kittens for no reason other than they's gettin' on her nerves.

I'm turnin' to make for the graveyard like she say when I'm took up sudden from behind, a big man-hand slappin' hard over my mouth, hot words whisperin' in my ear. I kick the air, claw to get free—Mama's voice fadin' into Willie's cryin' and the hoarse shouts of ugly men, my heart like to burst 'til the darkness take me down.

Wednesday

Subject: Island Women Week
From: a.jackman@cambridgebooks.com
To: Nora2736@yahoo.com, paddlechick@hellerfamily.net,
Lily@kilabukdesign.com, shelleybelly@aol.com, wildyogathing@yahoo.com

Okay, this is my final email before I see you all on Saturday—promise. And Shelley, what's this shit I hear about you bailing on us to "work on the relationship"? Damn, girl, how can this new man, whom none of us have even met, be worth giving up an entire week on the island? Seriously, put the boy-toy on hold and get packing. Remember our deal? Everyone comes back. Once an Island Woman, always an Island Woman.

Just got off the phone with Margot about the cell service, and yes, it still sucks. And since there's no electricity for charging out here anyway, what do you say we leave the damn things home this time? Lily's idea, actually, and I think it's great. Just putting it out there...

On the plus side, brother Drew has had the propane tanks filled; the gas lights that were on the fritz last year have been replaced; and while the broiler on the stove still goes out any old time it wants, Frosty Frieda and that temperamental pilot light of hers are finally gone, replaced by a brand-new gas fridge. We've got a couple new carts for lugging stuff this year, too—the larger ones that can carry two of the water jugs at once, which means fewer trips from the well up to the Birches. I can hear you all groaning now; just think of it as your aerobic exercise for the week (except for Margot, who will probably hike ten miles and kayak around the island twice each morning before the rest of us are even up).

More good news! As of this week, there are new futons in two of the bedrooms and a new sleeping hammock on the south-facing porch. And we finally tossed the moldy-smelling mattress that was in the Twig and brought in two singles. Still a squirrel problem down there (who wouldn't want to make their nest in that sweet little cottage, right?), so I'm thinking Brit and

Lily should take that since Lily's bringing Gus again. The scent of a dog always keeps them away.

Reminders: It can go from hot to chilly and damp in a matter of minutes out here. Remember last year? So think layers. A bathing suit, if you absolutely must. We'll be totally alone and I, for one, plan to give these lobstermen an eyeful!

As far as dinners go, Saturday night I'm making that Thai Chicken Salad you all liked so much. Margot's taking Sunday, which leaves the rest of you to work out your place in the rotation. Remember you're responsible not only for the meal, but the wine and munchies for cocktail hour (see my last email). There's that supermarket just off the highway and the little gourmet place for provisioning, or you can wait and make a trip later on in the week. As always, bring your own stuff for breakfasts and lunches, etc.

What else? Books, of course. Wine, wine, and more wine. Is there ever enough? And we can always use more candles and lamp oil.

High tide on Saturday is just before two, which is when I'll be at the boat ramp. Please be on time. Seriously. Maneuvering a boat full of people and gear to the island is a lot easier if you don't have to pick your way through rocky ledges in an ebb tide, especially if the fog starts rolling in.

I'm sure you'll let me know if I've forgotten anything. Remember, this week is yours to do whatever, without the distraction of men and other assorted children—hah! Oh, and a caveat to that long list of things I just suggested you bring? Remember it's a good half-mile slog from dock to house, and the only person schlepping your stuff will be you. Guaranteed.

Have to run; got a new author coming in for a reading.

Island Women rule!

Adria

Sunday

GIL

"It wasn't much of a friendship to begin with, and now—well."

No idea where Duggan's going with this, so I say nothing. Something about yet another falling-out between Lily and what's-her-name, the ex-roommate. Gotta admit my mind's been wandering, the bulk of the drive down I-95 from Bangor from whence I was fetched for this little joyride amounting to little more than Duggan's stream-of-consciousness venting on life without son Matt, whose bizarre death a month ago has left everyone reeling.

A cream-colored Lexus whizzes by in the left lane; this time even I crane for a look at the plate.

GD2BLV

David breaks from his spiel to interpret, a game he's recently taken up as part of his obsession with all things literary.

"Good to believe," he announces, and I place a mental tic on the plus side of the Duggan mood-o-meter—having weeks ago charged myself with keeping my finger on his wildly fluctuating emotional pulse.

Not that I'm complaining. David Duggan's more than simply a colleague—Writer in Residence at Dartmouth to my currently rather sketchy position at UMaine—he's also a friend of considerably long standing, which in my book means he can bend my ear anytime and for as long as necessary. Losing a kid sucks, as I well know. Not my own—parenthood having so far eluded me, thank God—but Rachel Leland's son, Ben. By far the best student I've ever had, possibly the finest the Urban Forestry Program at UMaine ever attracted. Not to mention an all-around terrific kid thanks in large part to his mother, on whom I've nurtured a spectacularly unrequited crush for years. Sadly, any chance I had with her, while admittedly slim from the start, quickly vaporized—just one of the many things I've so gloriously fucked up over the years.

EZ2LUV, I spontaneously decide. Much 2.

But back to Ben. While his death was truly tragic—carried off as he was by a particularly aggressive form of non-Hodgkins lymphoma—Matt Duggan's demise was one of pure, unmitigated stupidity. Complicated history here; suffice it to say he's been addicted to virtually every illegal substance at one time or another, in and out of rehab since his early teens. Various therapies and psychotherapists, all of it crushingly expensive and in the end utterly useless. Over the last few years the kid seemed to be slipping even further away, spending a year in jail on a drug charge—a time David still can't bring himself to talk about—and eventually dying alone in a dingy studio apartment up in Claremont when the frozen pizza box he'd stupidly parked atop the stove's pilot light caught fire, the innocuous-looking plastic tray inside releasing a toxic stew that overwhelmed his sorry ass while the rest of the closet-sized kitchen burned around him. I kid you not. To put it bluntly, Matt Duggan burned to death. That he was blotto on booze, weed, and God only knows what else, and thus had the reaction time of a concrete block, no doubt contributed to the tragedy. Twenty-two fucking years old.

David nudges me as a boxy green thing screams by. "Now *that's* good."

I pull my mind from Matt, just managing to make out the plate.

IMINMY

Huh.

"It's that Honda thing—you know, the Element." He waits for me to get it, then sighs. "As in *I'm in my element*? Christ, Hodge. Okay, hold on."

I make a wild grab at the doorframe as he downshifts, shooting me a shit-eating grin as the engine screams and we barely make the tight wind of the highway off-ramp onto 1-A south. "Cornering on this thing's the balls," he purrs.

I grunt, tugging the bill of Dad's old '55 Dodgers cap down to where it meets the cheap Maui Jims I was forced to shell out for in order to do battle against the scorching yellow ball burning its way through the windshield of David's brand-new, cherry-red Miata—a purchase I remember arguing strongly against. Forty-five-year-old men, I cautioned—a demographic into which we've both recently slid—should avoid fixating on little red sports cars lest it be interpreted as some attempt at anatomical compensation.

Still, I suppose it's relatively harmless as outlets for grief go. Expensive, yes, and no doubt dangerous as shit with the top down like this, but—and here's the thing—it gives him the lift he so desperately needs while requiring absolutely no emotional investment in return.

Thus it is I crammed my six-foot-two frame into the absurdly cheery thing, put up with the sun and Duggan's venting, not to mention his maniacal driving, for what is essentially a spontaneous Sunday afternoon drop-in on the aforementioned Lily—his current lady-love and a cute-as-a-button landscape designer who only yesterday began an annual week-long retreat with other high-octane women on a private, two-hundred-acre island. Chicks only. Why he thinks we'll actually be welcome out there, regardless of the half-hearted invitation flung his way as Lily was heading out the door, is beyond me. Then there's the fact that we have no boat.

I admit he got my interest with the bit about the women, though. A recent departure for me, I have to say—an apparent reawakening of the Old Gil, gone and I'd hoped forgotten, my libido having been beaten into submission by a series of leather-and-lace types. Suffice it to say I've been a good boy in that regard for the better part of three years now. Almost getting my nuts shot off has that effect on me.

I veer from the thought, distracting myself with the promise of Mistake Island's old-growth interior, which is legendary. High time I made it out here, anyway, I tell myself—no matter the reason. I'm a botanist, dendrology specifically, which means I study trees. I teach as well, or did until relatively recently, and the change still has me reeling. Whole other story.

We're doing at least twenty over the limit, screaming down a country road blessedly shaded by glorious red maples, when we veer wildly into the parking lot of a small, cedar-shingled market—Duggan being determined on an offering to the island babes—and thump to a stop just inches before taking out an ice machine. Perky red awning above the entrance, big urns erupting in a profusion of wildflowers. An old Mom-and-Pop convenience store in its former life, I figure, before it went gourmet.

"Want anything?" Duggan asks, unfolding his doughy, urbanized frame from behind the wheel.

Short of an I.V. of ice water? "Cold Heineken or Moosehead would be nice." A bit optimistic, to be sure, considering the swinging corrugated sign promises sixteen-ounce cans of Narragansett, no doubt a staple of the local bass-fishing crowd.

Duggan being Duggan, he does me one better, pushing through the screen door five minutes later cradling an entire six-pack of Moosehead and a cutesy little paper sack nipped at the top with an embossed gold seal, which he tosses to me as he climbs in. I peer around the seal at a chocolate bar whose name I can't begin to pronounce, a cryovac of caramel-coated popcorn, a jar of fat-infused avocado dip—the kind of stuff I can't imagine Lily will actually consume, being not only a chick of the holistic, vegan-leaning variety, but hands-down the smallest female I've ever set eyes on.

That Inuit extraction, no doubt. Petite—five feet tops would be my guess. Might weigh a hundred pounds if she were dipped in molasses.

We reach the parking lot at the boat ramp just after one—Duggan fussing with the car's top while I'm left to fork over five bucks for an afternoon's parking to an old guy who appears out of nowhere determined to lighten my wallet. Then, snagging the collar of the six-pack and grabbing my rucksack—a traveling office of notes, trail mix, and bug repellent—I join Duggan at the top of the ramp, a truly hoppin' place on a day like today. The great weather's brought out fishermen of every description, a long line of pickups towing various craft waiting their turn to back to the water and drop their load. The guy at the market told Duggan the bluefish were running, which explains it, I suppose. Bluefish make great eating, but you gotta come prepared to do battle. They're a vicious, hard-fighting species; land one and you gotta kill it soon as it hits the cockpit or it's likely to chew your leg off.

I turn to find Duggan edging along the side of the ramp, dodging boats as he makes his way toward an admirably toned woman maneuvering a wide Carolina Skiff into the water, a handful of plastic grocery bags in the stern. Nordic features, ash blond ringlets fisted into a ponytail, dressed in the kind of techie gear so popular with wanna-be athletes these days—lime-green racerback tank and tight black kayaking shorts. Only on this chick it works. Not an ounce of fat on her; the muscles tensing along her arms signaling serious upper body strength. Competitive swimmer, maybe—that or a rock climber.

She turns as we approach and Duggan jumps right in.

"You heading out to Mistake, by any chance?"

Now I'd have hung back and flirted a little first—old habits being what they are—maybe helped her with the boat to win some points; but therein lies the single biggest difference between Duggan and myself. Love him to death, I do, but the guy's got no subtlety. An old flame of his once told me he wasn't much for foreplay. Not sure who I felt sorrier for.

Nordic chick says nothing—her gaze traveling Duggan as she works the boat, then sliding my way and tracking from what's left of my second Moosehead to the looped collar of the six-pack. No fool, this one. Hell if she's gonna reveal her plans to a couple middle-aged, beer-swigging perverts accosting her on a boat ramp, at least not without first being introduced.

"Gil Hodges," I say, offering up my goofiest grin as I extend a hand. "Want some help with that?"

She ignores me, chin-nods at Duggan. "You looking for someone on the island?"

"Hoping for a ride out, actually."

More ocular appraisal. I glance down, wondering exactly what it is she finds so fascinating. My usual ensemble—faded jeans and worn hikers, my favorite Frank Zappa tee—looks okay, if you ignore the small ketchup stain from lunch. Even David, in today's natty semi-nautical attire, is nothing out of the ordinary. Chinos, polo, Docksiders sans socks.

"Problem is we've booked the island for the week," she explains. "All-female retreat—no men. No offense, it's just this thing we have."

Duggan's wearing the look of mild befuddlement I've seen him use on students, though the woman's clearly in her thirties and obviously too intelligent to be so easily thrown. Over her shoulder, a couple miles out, I spy the tops of towering pines poking through the steaming haze. Mistake, I'm assuming, which is frankly how all this is starting to feel.

"I'm a friend of Lily Kilabuk's," Duggan tells her. "She's invited me out for the day." As proof of his veracity, he holds up the twee little bag wherein that ten-dollar bar of chocolate is doubtless turning to goo.

She snorts a laugh, amused by what I'm not sure—the bag itself, perhaps, or maybe Lily's choice in men. "Well, then, by all means." She holds the skiff while we climb in, makes quick work of hoisting herself aboard, and we're off.

Some time later—after picking her way carefully through the final tricky, rock-strewn approach—our guide, who's somewhat belatedly introduced herself as Margot, ties off to a float flanked by several serious-looking kayaks. As we climb the aluminum ramp, I notice a wooden swim raft bobbing lazily in the cove to our right, a weathered oar inexplicably tacked to a half-dead spruce tree up ahead.

The trail, which takes us beneath a canopy of shaggy, tightly-packed conifers, proves blessedly cool—the air humid and heady with the scent of pine. The path itself is narrow and cumbersome to navigate, what with the heavy crosshatch of tree roots so common to islands where granite underlies the forest floor and the ground is packed with more decaying pine needles than actual soil.

A few hundred yards of this, and we're dumped into a broad, open meadow busy with the grind of cicadas—the scientist in me taking note as we go. Ground cover of Cornis canadensis, or Bunchberry, a green-leafed shrub sporting the cheery red berries of childhood nursery rhymes. Lots of wild low-bush blueberry and creeping raspberry here, too. The trees are red oak and birch for the most part, set off from which are two of the most enormous arborvitae I've ever seen, each spanning maybe thirty feet.

Nordic chick moves quickly—the bugs are ferocious out here—passing a well of the old hand-pump variety, a few outbuildings. I glance back at Duggan, who's gamely trying to keep up. Have to say, for a guy who

regularly beats me at squash he seems oddly clumsy in the out-of-doors.
The extra weight doesn't help, of course. When we first met, he could have
leapt from the pages of an L.L. Bean catalogue—muscled and fit, hair the
color of wet sand. The ten or so extra pounds he's picked up over the years
having ballooned to twenty or twenty-five since Matt's death.

We tuck back beneath the pines at the far end of the meadow, and a
hundred yards in I begin to catch glimpses of a house through the trees. An
early 20th-century hunting lodge, by the look of it—long and low, cedar-
shingled, slung atop an outcropping of rock and birch trees.

Shafts of sunlight strike through the boughs, revealing movement in
the dooryard. Glimpses of flesh. A woman, I realize, as the trees part before
me—svelte, long of leg, and gloriously naked—bent at the waist as she
tips a pan of water to rinse shampoo from her cropped dark hair, water
sluicing over her head, her neck. Her movements are slow and languid,
unselfconscious as women can only be when they believe themselves to be
unobserved.

For the briefest of moments, my heart all but stops—certain as I am
that the woman before me is Rachel, the astronomical odds against such a
thing be damned. Hair's all wrong, of course; she of my fantasies wore hers
in long, curling ropes of auburn. Still, I drink her in, the physical similari-
ties enough to kick-start the old longing again.

"Cover up, girls," our reluctant guide calls as she sets the groceries at
her feet. "Men doth approach." Amusement in the glance she flicks our
way. Let the butter melt, that look says, the milk curdle. No way I'm gonna
miss this.

The vision before us whirls, grabbing up her towel and covering herself
as best she can as she scrambles for the screen door—through which, once
opened, a furry black projectile launches itself toward us amid bursts of
staccato yapping. Lily's cocker spaniel, I realize. Never can remember the
thing's name.

A full minute goes by, time I spend trying to spit-clean my miserable
Maui Jims—replacements for the Ray-Ban Aviators that rather inexplicably
disappeared from my campus office sometime over the last few days. Or
maybe not so inexplicably. But more on that later.

Still nothing from the house. I shift my rucksack, slapping at mosquitoes while Duggan appears unperturbed by the continuing delay—
patiently kneeing the pooch away from the foolish little bag still dangling
from his hand.

A cackling laugh sounds from somewhere within, and Lily finally
pushes through the door, looking about as irritated as I'm starting to feel—
a freckled, gum-popping redhead fast on her heels. She of the laugh, no

doubt, the irreverent sound of it somehow in keeping with the tatts wrapping an otherwise bare upper arm.

"Hey, Lil, " Duggan grins, extending the bag. "Brought you a little something. Hello, Brit."

Brit. The name is familiar, as is the lopsided, challenging grin. Do I know this chick? I nearly panic at the thought she might be some ex-student-cum-lover—one of many I've left in my wake. An unfortunate specialty of mine. They've been popping up with alarming regularity lately; I ran into one in a bar in Portland a few months back, nowhere near my home territory, and she actually tried to deck me. But Brit shows none of the usual signs of recognition: disbelief tinged with the almost pathological level of rage I've grown so used to, so I relax.

Lily, on the other hand, is visibly shocked to see us. Whatever it is she might have mumbled to Duggan about a possible visit, she clearly didn't think he'd show.

"Gus," she snaps toward the dog, her gaze meeting Nordic chick's. "Chill." Cocking her head then. "What's he doing here?" Meaning me, of course.

I should tell you that Lily doesn't like me much, having mistakenly pegged me as the reason Duggan has not yet slid into marital mode. True, the two of us have been spending a lot of time together since Matt's death—okay, we've been pretty much inseparable—but I refuse to apologize for that. The guy needs me right now. Love, like sex, runs hot and cold, and I expect the emotional ups and downs he and Lily are going through—her relationship with Matt was never easy—are a bit much for him just now. Friendship is simpler, cleaner. Road trips, ballgames, bar-hopping—hey, I'm there.

Strangely enough, though, I like Lily. Her funky spiritual bent's a bit of an eye-roller, but she's sweet and for the most part sincere—two attributes I've come at long last to appreciate in a woman. And I actually have hope for the two of them. Perhaps David can accomplish the thing I seem so singularly incapable of, that being sustained monogamy. He came close with Matt's mother, as I remember, and I've often wondered if things might have turned out differently for the kid if the two of them had stayed together, or if Matt had seen more of Duggan than he did in those early years.

Before Duggan can respond, the screen door snaps open yet again, this time disgorging a stunning black woman with a beautiful smile come to check out the commotion. Petite and lean, with dark hair cut short and tight, she wears a cropped top and beige cargo pants rolled to mid-calf, suggesting long, graceful limbs. My God. How many more such lovelies can there be?

"Sorry, Adria," Lily says, clearly embarrassed. "Forgot to mention I invited David out for the day."

Ah, I think. Head chick at chick week.

"Dr. David Duggan," he announces in the stentorian tones normally reserved for book tours and ladies' club appearances. Extending his hand as she trips lightly down the short rise of stone steps from the house. "A pleasure."

"The novelist. I know your work," she says, grinning broadly as they shake. "Adria Jackman. It's great to finally meet you. I carry your books in my store—Cambridge Books outside Boston. Love to have you in for a reading sometime."

"I'd be honored."

David's a bit old-school, which is part of his charm; not to mention he's an absolute sucker for this kind of thing—probably 'cause it happens all too infrequently these days—and I feel a warm flush of gratitude toward this woman. Who cares if she really means it? David's books, mysteries mostly, are considered a little, well, light. The night I met him, his breakout novel, *Murder on Monhegan*, had just won some prize from the Mystery Writers of America, so he was flying pretty high. He was in Portland for a series of lectures and signings, and I remember spending a good chunk of the night with him taste-testing our way through top-shelf single malts at the Olde Port Tavern. A couple more books followed, including a better-than-average swashbuckler series pitting colonists against Native Americans, which proved surprisingly popular. All of this back in the late nineties, his artistic muse having for the most part eluded him since.

"This is Gil Hodges," he says, turning to me. "A botanist friend of mine specializing in trees. He's writing a book about the Maine islands."

"Biodiversity of Maine's outer islands," I correct as we shake. I, too, could trot out my credentials, but it's been my experience that women of this quality really don't give a shit. "Hope you don't mind my poking around while these two are visiting." Visiting being a euphemism, of course. Based on the tension-charged looks Lily's still shooting our way, it's a safe bet they'll spend the time either fighting or screwing. Both, probably.

"Absolutely," Adria says. "Day visitors are always welcome. One of us will ferry you back to the mainland about five, if that works." Something about the way she says this reminds me of a bumper sticker I once saw on a rusted-out pickup rumbling down I-95: *Welcome to Maine—now please go home.*

I nod. "My folks had a Carolina Skiff a lot like yours. Brings back memories. Like trying to steer a bathtub, as I remember."

Margot snorts a laugh. "Dumpster's more like it."

I shoot her a glance. A couple years back I'd have put some serious effort into flirting with this chick, wedding band or no, but I've sampled others of her hyper, controlling type with alarming results. A guy can only take so much.

Adria points to where the trail we came in on dips back into deep woods just beyond the house. "Follow this path past the Twig—the little cottage maybe a hundred yards down the hill—then bear right. It'll take you around the south side of the island and back to the dock. About a two-hour hike. The interior's a lot tougher to explore, I'm afraid, unless you're into slogging your way up mountain trails."

I thank her, hand off the collar of Moosehead she promises to keep cold, and tossing a final fruitless glance toward the screen door for a glimpse of she-who-stands-naked-in-dooryards, heft my pack and head out.

Every island has its own distinct personality, I've found, one based on the interaction of a particular combination of flora, fauna, and climate—the most fascinating having suffered only minimal human interference. And so it appears here. Maybe thirty minutes after leaving Duggan to navigate the tricky emotional minefield of our visit, the botanist in me is starting to get a feel for the place. It seems the owners are good stewards, for the most part allowing nature its head. No clearing of brush or blow-down, other than to keep the trails open; where streams need to be crossed, simple bridges have been fashioned of native materials.

Working my way southeast along a sharply-scarped granite shelf that drops a gut-clenching forty feet to a series of rocky inlets, I find a mixed forest of hardwoods and spruce—white, the Picea glauca variety. Far more interesting, though, and what's got me reaching for my notebook, is the heady, resinous scent of deep woods drifting down on me from an intersecting uphill trail, the quick glimpse of a small stand of red spruce through the dappled light. This is the stuff that gets me juiced, and I decide to strike inland despite Adria's warning, or maybe because of it. I'm funny like that.

Amazing the amount of deadfall in here. Last time I encountered this much of it was on Matinicus—a period in my life I try not to dwell on. Oddly enough, it was Rachel's son Ben who first lured me out there, promising not only his mom's stellar cooking but a phenomenal seven hundred species of flora on an island less than three miles long—including some forty-four different kinds of trees and a purported twenty-two of wild orchid, many of which Ben claimed to have catalogued himself. A botanical treasure-trove, assuming it was true. Skeptical as I was, the adventure of it intrigued me. I figured we'd drink a lot of beer, do a bit of camping and, if I was lucky, I might somehow manage to get laid. Meeting Rachel for the first time knocked me on my ass—my gleefully sophomoric and ultimately failed attempts at seducing her something I can never possibly live down. I should mention that Rachel's not simply beautiful; she's poised and graceful, and an artist, it happens, of considerable talent. The proverbial one that got away.

Fast forward a couple years. Ben had died by then, and I was embarking on what you might call a strongly encouraged sabbatical when I flew back to the island for a much-needed break from academia—not to mention my own self-destructive tendencies, or so I was told at the time—having recently ended a wildly inappropriate fling with a psychotic grad student whose initial desire for me had slowly morphed into a determined attempt to ruin my life.

Of all the murderous types I've been attracted to, and believe me there've been plenty, Annika Gunderssen scores right up there on the scary chick-o-meter. Spiked blonde hair, haunting blue eyes, and a total fucking whacko. There was absolutely nothing sane about the relationship, and after it ended, I figured the best way to avoid her was to leave town. Indefinitely. Matinicus was perfect—a place so remote, so rugged, so utterly unwelcoming to strangers it would deter even this chick. Little did I know that just as I was bolting for the island, tail tucked firmly between my legs, Annika was herself on a return flight to Iceland—a good place for her, by the way—never to return.

Of course, I told anyone who'd listen I that was heading back to the island to complete the cataloguing Ben had begun before he got sick. I almost believed it myself, had some vague idea of producing a botanical write-up of the island in all its mind-boggling biodiversity—the kind of obscure scholarly drivel so valued in academia, and with which I could redeem myself in the eyes of my peers. Sneaky thing, the libido, 'cause all the while I was angling for another chance at Rachel. You see the problem. I never finished the cataloguing work, which surprised no one, especially not me. Instead, I got dragged into a couple particularly grisly murders, was targeted by yet another bizzaro chick, one who hounds me to this day, and was stupid enough to get shot by someone I knew all along I couldn't trust—all the while living cheek by jowl with a little island girl some two hundred years dead. Yeah, yeah—laugh all you want. You weren't there.

Kicker was, I never did meet up with Rachel, which might have made most of what happened out there at least somewhat bearable. Unfortunately she was off-island the entire time, and no sign of her since, which has only increased my longing. Thus my reaction an hour ago when I thought for just an instant I'd seen her at the house. Hope springs eternal; never more so, I've found, than when there's no hope at all.

All of this is particularly ironic, because the paper I eventually did write as a result of that horrific summer—a kind of eco-socio treatise on the interdependence of all that biodiversity and its various metaphors to the decline of island life, blah, blah, blah—attracted a lot of attention and resulted in my being offered the contract to do the book on the Maine out-islands. On top of that, after news of the book deal made its way up the ancient, creaking ladder of academia, the university bigwigs started getting nervous about the possibility I might leave their fold—a prospect that would have delighted them less than a year before. So instead of being shit-canned for years of admittedly inappropriate behavior, I found myself Chair of my department which, in our particular institution, is rather vaguely defined and involves very little actual teaching. Which, strangely enough, I find I miss.

Nothing like slogging through the thick brush of a mountain trail for begging unwelcome introspection, so I'm more than relieved to reach the top of this one. Stepping into the small clearing, enticed those last hundred yards by the unmistakable smell of the sea, I envision miles of glistening, dappled water dotted with islands, a sailboat or two straining into the wind—anything to take my mind off my past misdeeds and the longing that's kick-started in my loins. But, like so much of what I take for granted these days, expectation is once again turned on its ear.

Two thoughts occur as I glance toward the sea. Shit. And shit again. Because despite the day's heretofore stellar conditions, a solid wall of fog is slowly and inexorably heading this way—reminding me of that amorphous mass of extraterrestrial protoplasm for which the old sci-fi classic *The Blob* was named. Steve McQueen in one of his dumber roles, as I remember. And that's saying a lot.

No time to backtrack along the perimeter trail; if Duggan and I are gonna get out of here, I quickly realize, it's got to be now. Sighing, I strike off down the back side of the mountain, double-timing it along a trail which instinct tells me will spit me out somewhere in that meadow.

Man, I think. Lily's just gonna love this.

NORA

She startles from her nap rigid with terror, heart hammering at the sound of men's voices in the hallway outside her door. Lily's friends, she remembers, as sleep slowly recedes—the ones who came up the trail behind Margot just after lunch, surprising her as she was washing in the yard. Ogled her, really. Being caught naked like that was something she'd have laughed off only a few years ago; the thought filling her now with the crushing anxiety that's become her constant companion.

Nora wills her heart to slow, calms herself by remembering what she most loves about this place—calling up the pre-dawn stillness, the way the house comes alive with the lightening of the sky, shifting and ticking as the heat gradually warms the old sills, the graying cedar shingles. Next come the birds, a lazy buzzing of mosquitoes against the screen. The peace she treasured back before the change mocking her now, becoming instead the void into which all she's lost has tumbled.

Wally missed her terribly last time. Nora remembers this only now, recalls the sleepy hazel eyes full of love as he woke against her the morning she was to head out here, cupping a breast in his hand as he nuzzled her neck, easing himself into her.

They'd been talking about moving to Vermont—figuring it a safer, healthier place to raise a family than their Cambridge condo—envisioning the mountains, the lakes, a yard with a swing set. They'd started trying for a baby that winter, but when they weren't pregnant by May, planned what they called their procreation-vacation—an October escape to Nantucket where their first child would surely be conceived. Amazing how certain she'd been of everything back then. This is the single biggest change she's seen in herself, and it's worse, somehow, than everything else. No wonder Wally barely reacted when she brought up this year's retreat—holding her emotional breath, praying he'd give her a reason to back out.

"It's only a week, for fuck's sake," he'd grumbled instead. "I'll be gone for most of it, anyway."

She can hear Adria's voice now, mixing with those of the men. Nora tells herself it's stupid to be afraid, but the fear is pulsing and rhythmic, like the start of the monster headache it will eventually become. It can happen anytime, anywhere. She refuses to call it panic; that's Wally's word—the attacks, as he calls them, brought on by anything even remotely threatening. It's one of the things that drives him nuts. For a while he tried to help, ease her through them. He suggested therapy—gently at first, then more urgently. She refused, couldn't tell him why. Eventually he gave up, which somehow both relieved and disappointed her. Just as she now disappoints him. His sullen response to her new job with its fifty-percent pay cut saying it all. Truth is, she'd lost the ability to focus, concentrate hard enough to get by in the old one. Routines she can handle; it's the emotional connections she can no longer manage.

The men have moved to the kitchen just beyond Nora's bedroom wall, their voices in urgent counterpoint to Adria's lilting rhythm. She feels the deep, dull throb of the headache begin, and burrows beneath her sheet, willing them all away.

BRIT

She hears voices coming back up the trail, thinks *this can't be good.*

"Shut it," Brit snaps, kneeing a yapping Gus back from the screen door. All day with the barking. Christ.

Slinging her hip against the doorjamb, she watches Adria materialize out of the fog, Dr. D and his buddy trailing her toward the kitchen.

"It's socked right in," Adria says, tugging the door open. "No way we can get them back to the mainland now." Mumbling as she pushes past, "You want to tell the others or shall I?"

"You kidding?" Brit laughs as the guys slink in—Gus all relaxed now they're inside, trotting ahead along the hall toward the greatroom where the double doors to the screened porch have been flung wide. Grabbing her water bottle, topped up with another hefty shot of Jameson, she follows—itching to razz Lil about how her stupid invitation's landed these guys in their lap for the night.

Lily glances up from where she's curled into the sofa with her knitting and does a double take, setting the thing in her lap with a thump. It's the arm of some sweater she's making for Dr. D, Brit remembers now.

"Too foggy to risk it," Adria explains as Lily jams the whole mess back into her tote. Outside by the grill, wine glasses poised, Nora and Margot go still, like they can't believe it either. "Couldn't see ten feet."

"Oh, c'mon," Margot calls. "Can't be that bad. I'll take them in if you don't want to."

"Yeah? Zero visibility out there, and with these crazy-ass currents? Remember a few years back, the Boston Whaler that lost power and got sucked out to sea? Fog was so thick, the ship that ran over it never even knew it was there. Kid driving it was never found."

"Later, then," Lily suggests. "After the fog lifts."

"Tide'll be wrong; it's marginal even now." Adria stops at the little table by the door, checks the wine bottles. "So unless one of you is up for a midnight run, and that's not me, we're looking at sometime around lunchtime tomorrow." She turns to the guys, then, going all perfect hostess on them. "Red?" she asks, "or white?"

Brit sips from the bottle, pissed at how the day's suddenly gone to hell now they're stuck with the men for the night. Seriously, throw one into a roomful of women and he'll suck the life out of it every time. Lily claims she's just bitter 'cause there's no guy in her life right now, which is total bull. She just calls it as she sees it. And how she sees it is that Lily and Dr. D will share the Twig and she'll be forced to crash on the sofa—worse yet, one of the side porches with their musty hammocks and huge spiders, other creepy-crawly shit.

She catches Lily's eye and sticks out her tongue, then turns to where Dr. D's pal stands by the screen door, Moosehead in hand, watching Nora and Margot out by the barbecue. Normally, Brit wouldn't bother with an old guy like that, but the fact Lily can't stand him makes the thought of chatting him up instantly appealing.

"Margot's night to cook," she says coming up behind him. "Super-territorial. No way you'll get anywhere near that grill, so don't even try."

He turns. Great smile—she'll give him that.

"No worries there. Afraid I missed the BBQ gene—some kind of weird mutation. Huge disappointment to my father."

She grins, takes a pull on the bottle. "I like your cap."

"'55 Dodgers," he tells her. "Great tee shirt, long as we're trading compliments. An original, too. New ones I've seen are worded all wrong."

"Yeah?" She glances down at the shirt, snagged from her ex's drawer one night way back when—black shirt, white letters: *Frankie Say Relax*. Guy's probably still wondering where it went. Bummer.

He nods. "The new ones all say *Frankie Says Relax*. Should be *Say*. Frankie was actually an eighties pop band—four Brit guys. *Relax* was their first hit single. The original shirts like yours were promos."

"No shit."

He extends a hand. "Gil Hodges. Sorry to be inconveniencing you all like this, by the way."

She shrugs. "It is what it is." She gives the guy's hand a shake. "Brit Bowman. We met at one of Dr. D's parties a while back, actually. I remember 'cause you look a lot like the actor from that old movie, *The Big-Something*. He was in *Crazy Heart*, too. Jeff what's-his-name. *The Dude*."

He nods. "Jeff Bridges. The Big Lebowski."

"Right, right."

"I get that a lot." He leans in, tips his beer toward her. "I know who you are now. You and Lily were roommates before…" He cocks his head toward the sofa, where Dr. D's arm is tucked tight around Lily.

Yeah, and Brit still doesn't get it. They've been friends for what, six years, roommates for almost four, and Lily, who could be with just about anyone she wanted—she's that cute—just ups and moves in with a guy who looks like that? She says it's LOVE, but Brit's not convinced.

"So what do you do when you're not hanging out on Mistake Island?" Gil asks.

"That's such a guy-question, isn't it? Pigeonholing people by what they do?"

"Yeah, but there's only one other guy here and I already know what *he* does."

Brit grins. "Barista. Starbucks in Hanover, couple blocks from the college. Liked it at first; met a lot of people, you know? The cutesy drink names are pretty lame, though. There are actually websites now that'll tell you what kind of clueless pseudo-intellectual you are if you plug in what you drink."

"No kidding." He points the beer can toward Nora. "So what would she drink?"

"Nora? Something safe and predictable—Grande mocha, maybe. She used to be wilder, a lot more fun." And the hair thing, a pixie cut Brit thinks it's called, when the last time Nora was here she wore it long—the kind of thick, curly stuff Brit would kill for. So what's with that?

"Now Margot, there," Brit says, looking toward the porch. "She's like totally driven. The woman can't relax. When she's not swimming, she's kayaking; when she's not kayaking, she's hiking. Runs out to Reese's Leap and back like every morning. So I'd say maybe a skinny vanilla latte."

"A what?" he laughs.

"Ninety calories of sugar-free vanilla syrup, nonfat milk, a dash of foam. Espresso, of course. That or maybe a Grande, six-pump, non-fat with extra whip chai latte." Getting into it now. "Thinks it's a diet drink because it's nonfat; forgets the whip adds back double the calories she's *saving* by drinking nonfat."

She chin-nods at Dr. D. "Half-caff, double tall, non-fat cappuccino. That one's not a guess, by the way. Comes in all the time; orders the same thing—most of them do. You, though," she says. "You seem like a no-nonsense kind of guy, not into pretense, so I'd say caffé Americano."

"Never been to a Starbucks," he tells her. "Little too cute for me." He nods toward her bottle, then. "So what's our barista drinking tonight? 'Cause that sure as hell isn't water."

She glances down. "Jameson with a little splash. Very little." About half the amount as her last one, actually. Hell, isn't Adria always telling them not to waste water?

"My kind of girl," Gil says. "If it was Laphroaig, I'd have to marry you."

She laughs. The guy's kind of a kick, even if he is old. Lily's openly glaring now, so Brit inches closer just to piss her off. "You're nothing like I thought, you know."

"Not as bad as Lily makes me out to be, you mean. So what does she say, exactly?"

"The high points? Teacher—excuse me, *professor*—never married, changes girlfriends like all the time."

"Bet she didn't tell you I've got more PhDs than Duggan does. People tend to forget that."

"So he's just a doctor, and you're like a doctor-doctor?"

"Something like that."

"She says you hang out with him way too much. So maybe you're really—you know—like a couple."

"Well, he does like to cook," Gil says, looking pensively toward the sofa. "Irons stuff a lot." Grinning at her, then. "They're kinda cute together, though, you gotta admit."

"They're both in love with him, if that's what you mean." Pisses Brit off big-time, too, the way he calls himself *Dr. Duggan* when he's just another snotty Dartmouth English professor swinging in for his morning caffeine fix—barking out his order like she's some kind of servant.

"Now Lily, she'll change it up, depending. She's a Tazo Chai tea latte with soy when she comes in alone, but if she's with Dr. D, she orders a tall soy cappuccino with nutmeg." Brit waits, but he doesn't get it. "It's all about image," she informs him. "She's not getting what *she* wants to drink; she's getting what *he* wants her to drink."

Gil takes a sip. "You don't like him."

She shrugs. "Pretentious. Arrogant. Clueless. I could go on." She pauses, sizing him up. "You knew his kid? Matt?"

"Yes," he says, wary now. "I knew Matt."

"Dr. D didn't even know he was selling drugs out of the house, that's how clueless he is. Lily was the one who found the heroin stash, made him move out. They never really got along, anyway."

She lowers her voice as he opens the screen door for Margot, who slips past them with the grilled fish, Gus on her heels. "She was the one who found him at the apartment, you know. Kitchen still burning when she walked in, Matt dead on the floor. Weird."

"It was the Teflon-coating on the cardboard that released…"

"No, I mean Lily showing up just then." She leans in. "Kind of strange, don't you think?"

"It was an accident," he says.

"Oh, yeah, I know."

The problem, Brit realizes, is that Lily can't see how wrong Dr. D is for her—even now, after all that's happened. And he can't see past her lame explanation for that night, or maybe doesn't want to. Brit just might have to tell him what was really going on before Matt died. That would finish everything for sure. She'd sworn not to, but hell. Desperate times, desperate measures—like that.

Brit counts seventeen candles burning at the center of the table, a bunch more along the long bank of windowsills—never mind it's not yet dark. Looks like some goddam medieval banquet, what with the enormous platter of grilled fish, the huge carved wooden salad bowl, the baskets of fresh bread Nora spent half the day on. One of Lily's incense sticks going somewhere, too. Patchouli maybe.

"Wally managing alright without you for the week?" Adria asks Nora as she works the corkscrew on a couple bottles of her good Zin. This as Brit snags the seat between Gil and Margot, since shooting the shit with this guy's probably the only fun she'll have all night. The little readings that Adria's announced for later—"in honor of their visiting author," la-di-da—definitely not Brit's thing. Too much like work. But she went along, did her bit, rummaging through the shelves of moldy-smelling books for "something to share with the others."

"I imagine," Nora says. "Things have changed a bit. He's in Seattle almost half the time now."

"Still writing software for He Whose Name We Dare Not Speak?"

"Worse. He's gone over to the dark side. Management. Lured by the promise of more money, less integrity."

A quick smile before Adria drops her head, takes the men's hands. The look on Dr. D's face at her unexpected touch—priceless.

"Circle prayer," she announces, and the rest of them join hands, lower heads. Usual deal. "Great food, great energy, great friends," she says—about to break the circle when Lily pipes up.

"Hail great Sedna of the deep, bountiful, and fierce sea."

Brit cocks an eye. Now this is new. Glancing around as eyes re-close and heads bounce back down again.

"She who is powerful, the bringer of food and storms, mother of sea creatures, she who is guardian of all who honor her." Lily glances up. "Sedna's an Inuit goddess," she informs them as they release hands. "She's the one who lured this gorgeous bluefish toward those fishermen off South Rocks today, whispered in the wind that they should give it to Margot when she was kayaking by. It's Sedna's gift to our table."

Brit catches the look Gil shoots Dr. D, the twitch of his lips as he fights a smile. "Lily thinks she's a shaman," she confides, leaning into him. "One with the spirits and all that. Whoooooooo," she grins, wiggling her fingers in the air.

"She tell them how to cook it, too?" Margot teases, serving herself and passing the platter to Gil. "'Cause they were pretty specific. Slather it in mayonnaise and maple syrup, toss some birch bark in with the charcoal."

"Betula papyrifera," Gil says, helping himself. "Paper birch. Bark's great for all kinds of things, including smoking food. Terrific preservative properties. Holds up indefinitely. Think birch bark canoes, stuff like that."

"Here we go," Dr. D warns. "Stop him now or you're in for twenty minutes of tree facts, starting with how bloody magnificent the things are. *It's the way they bear silent witness to history, Duggan—hundreds, even thousands of years sometimes.* Bore you to death by dessert, you're not careful. And call him Hodge, for Godsake. Hasn't been called Gil in years."

The Gil-Hodge guy grins. "Happens it's true—about trees, I mean. Plus it's a great line, you gotta admit. Women love it."

"The baseball trivia is better, frankly. More manly. Offering to take some sweet young thing back to your place to see your baseball cards? Who could resist? Your name's the kicker, of course."

"Trees aren't manly? Thick trunks? All that impressive bark?"

"Not to mention the stoic resistance to change." Margot scoops some salad—tonight's version a mix of baby spinach, walnuts, blueberries and pineapple, with that great dressing she tells everyone is fresh but Brit knows for a fact is bottled.

"Tell them about the name, Hodge." Dr. D instructs.

He nods, chews, swallows. "Gilbert Hodges, named for one of the best first basemen in the game. Eight-time All-Star; helped the Dodgers put the Yankees down in the '55 World Series. Great fish, by the way."

"My father was a baseball fan," Adria tells him. "Fanatic, really. Red Sox. Season tickets for probably twenty years."

"Box seats," Brit tells them. "Only the best for daddy-o." Returning Adria's quizzical look with an innocent batting of eyelashes, as Gus takes up growling under the table. "Cool it, you."

"Not sure," Margot's telling Gil or Hodge or whoever the hell he is in response to some question Brit's missed. "Island Women, Adria—how long? That first summer I met you, right? The year we worked the Boston Marathon?"

"Volunteers, both of us—absolutely no idea what we were doing."

"What's to know?" Brit jokes, settling into the warmth of that Jameson buzz. "Hand out some water, slap a few butts. Speaking of which—tomorrow morning, seven sharp, down on the dock. Basic, beginner yoga. Stretching, breathing, working on our collective backsides."

"No way," Lily laughs, then screws up her face at Gus's continuing growl. "Enough, already. Chill."

A groan from Adria as she tops off Hodge's wine. "I'll just be rolling over. But go on, girl; you do your thing."

"About tomorrow," he says. "What time you planning to take us in?"

"High tide's around four," Adria tells him. "Earliest we can get out is twelve-thirty, one. We'll aim for that."

"Might take off before breakfast then, if you don't mind—grab some coffee, head to the north end of the island for a look."

"By all means. Couple things about the kitchen to keep in mind, just so you know. Water for drinking and cooking comes from the five-gallon cooler bottle on the counter."

"The bucket contraption by the door." He nods. "Clever setup. Water bottle's upended in the bucket, gravity fills it, spigot controls the flow."

"Brother Drew's idea. Just don't drink anything from the pump in the sink. Draws from the cistern where the skeeters and their various diseases like to breed. So we boil that, use it for dishes."

Then, as if on cue, she slips into the same tired story about Drew. Tells it every year; can't help herself. How he renamed the old box-shaped dormitory in the meadow the Dromedary when he was like four or something because he kept getting the words mixed up. And how it's been the Dromedary ever since, never mind that's really the name of some kind of camel. The whole place nothing more than a couple walls of old bunks nobody's slept in for about a hundred years and a kitchen even more basic than the one up here in the Birches. A holdover from the previous owners, who used the place when they needed somewhere to stick the hired help—cooks and maids, people who didn't really matter. From Boston or Revere, maybe. People like Brit.

She glances around, trying to imagine for maybe the thousandth time what it would be like to be a Jackman—knowing all this is yours. A whole island—yours.

"Mistake reminds me of my grandparents' place in Canada, actually," Hodge tells them. "Spent every summer there as a kid. It was the start of my love affair with all things rustic."

"Then you're gonna love the bathroom part," Brit cracks, pulling her mind back from thoughts of all she doesn't have. "Nothing like parking your ass in the outhouse only to have it chewed off by an army of mosquitoes."

"So will Mistake make it into your book?" Adria asks him.

"Too close to the mainland for my needs, I'm afraid, though it's a great botanical environment—must be a hundred different species in ten square feet of that meadow alone. But the book's a study of the outer islands, ten or fifteen miles from shore. They play a really unique role, pit stops on a kind of seaward sky-way where migrating birds chow down, cat nap, and, shall we say, *deposit* seeds consumed in other, far-off places."

The trill of a cell phone surprises everyone, reception being so sucky here in the house.

"Oh, come on," Adria gripes. "We agreed. Not at dinner, remember?"

"Sorry...thought I turned it off." Margot's face all apologetic as she riffles through the tote at her feet.

"That'll be her husband," Brit tells Hodge as Margot rises, plugging her ear. "He calls like constantly. They're partners, sales reps for a bunch of outdoor gear companies—high-tech clothing, shoes, stuff like that. Live together, work together, fight like all the time."

"No really, live it up," Adria calls as Margot heads toward the kitchen. "No way to recharge out here, remember. Once those things are dead, they're dead." She winks at Hodge. "Seems Lily and I are the only grown-ups in the group; left our babies behind. Tried to get the others to take the pledge, but no luck. Your cell is turned off, I hope?"

"Don't have one, actually," he says, helping himself to salad. "It'd be handy for making calls, I suppose, only then I'd have to leave it on so the calls could be returned. People would assume they could reach me anytime, day or night. My worst nightmare. And I know for a fact Duggan left his in the car."

Dr. D pats himself down, confused. "Did I?"

Clueless, Brit thinks. Didn't she say he was clueless? She leans toward Hodge, who's been sneaking peeks at Nora all night. Nora the Ice Queen—Christ.

"She's married," Brit whispers. "Just so you know."

"Looks like someone, is all," he says, not meeting her gaze. "She's an artist, somebody said."

"Yeah," Brit tells him. "She used to teach at some art college—in Rhode island, I think; that's how she met Adria. The charcoal sketch over the fireplace is hers. There's another of Adria in one of the bedrooms. Won some prize. Now she works with immigrants. Something about helping them assimilate into American culture—like that's doing them any favors."

Gus is full-out barking now, hackles up as he yaps his way toward the porch, where long fingers of fog have started oozing through the screen—Brit, staring after him, getting a sudden eerie vibe, like she's being watched or something. Creepy, really.

"What's *with* him?" Adria laughs as she begins clearing—Lily and Nora hopping up to help.

"No idea." Lily glances toward the porch. "Something outside, looks like."

"Must be big, the way he's acting," Adria says, arms heavy with dishes as she heads toward the kitchen. "Could be a moose."

"Careful, Lil," Brit warns. "Whatever's out there could probably eat little Gus in two bites. Chomp, chomp. Wooly mammoth, maybe. Horns like corkscrews."

"Or a bear," Hodge suggests. "They're known to swim from island to island in search of food."

"Thanks for that; I'll sleep so much better now. And just so you know," Brit tells him, "I voted against this book-reading parlor-game shit. The board games in the other room are a lot more fun, never mind they're way old. Boggle, Clue, Battleship, I don't really care. I'd even go with the Ouija board. But no, Adria's gotta play suck-up."

"I heard that," Adria says, back from the kitchen with the brandy and glasses—pausing beside the card table where last summer's jigsaw, *Outhouses From Around the World*, is still only half done, mostly because Brit keeps removing pieces. She's still waiting for someone to catch on. "Time we upped the intellectual challenge, Brit. You can only play so much Candy Land before the brain starts to go."

Lily's up first, looks like—the book she pulls from beneath her chair, just as Gus trots back in from the porch looking all bad-ass now he's finished attacking the fog, a dog-eared copy of one of Dr. D's novels. *Murder on Monhegan*, for Godsake.

A few boring minutes later, after everyone's clapped and raved—blah, blah, blah—and he's kissed her hand like ten times, it's time for the man himself.

"One of my favorites," Adria says when she sees what he's chosen. "First edition, published in London in 1926. Bound in Moroccan leather."

"No money there," Brit cracks, then moans when she sees the title. Winnie-the-Fucking-Pooh.

She starts to drift in and out after a few minutes of Dr. D's old-time radio voice—not just because Winnie-the-Pooh and his little animal buddies irritate the crap out of her and always have, but because the man never knows when to shut the hell up.

She wakes to clapping, half-dozing again through some tree-thing Hodge dug up, and then Margot's reading—something about dinner etiquette and butlers and the hands of the domestics. It's the laughter that rouses her this time. Man. That snifter Adria passed her was definitely not a good idea.

"Domestics," Lily's saying. "Does that mean blacks?"

Adria swirls her brandy. "What do you think?"

Nora reaches to the floor, hauls up the huge Birches Guest Book—something Brit herself has written in any number of times, since no one's allowed to leave the island 'til they do.

"This was written by Adria's father," Nora tells them. "August, three years ago."

Adria:

A sip from the well is my gift to you.
There is nothing more life-giving than this water—
A treasure buried deep, eluding all, sustaining all.
When we first arrive we run for the red-handled pump;
When at last we leave, we take a final sip—
Guarding it in our hearts 'til our return in the spring.

"Dad wrote that a few months before he died," Adria says. "We thought he'd dodged the bullet, was getting better. He never told us the cancer had spread."

No one says a word. Nadda. Brit gives it a beat, stifles a yawn.

"Okay, then," she says—reaching to the floor beneath her chair. "This is from *A History of Mistake Island*, written...oh hell, I don't know; it doesn't say. It's not even technically a book, I don't think—just typed and then stapled together. And I mean typed," she tells them, holding it up.

"Actually," Margot says, peering hard at it, "looks like it might even be mimeographed. Jesus, that thing *is* old."

Reese's Treasure, Brit begins.

"Oh, Lord," Adria moans. "Not that thing again."

The citizens of Portland, Maine were among the first to show discontent with Britain prior to the start of the Revolutionary War. In September of 1774, nine towns in Cumberland county agreed to take strong opposition to all English laws that taxed them without their approval. Part of that opposition included a refusal to drink taxed imported tea, as inspired by the Boston Tea Party in April of the previous year.

In response, the British attacked Falmouth in 1775 with a naval fleet commanded by a Captain Mowatt, who ordered its eighty-five-hundred residents to evacuate the town, after which British soldiers stole from the shops, burned some two-hundred and thirty buildings, and sank the merchant fleet.

Wendell Thornton, a merchant from Bath, was so angered by the attack that he pledged what remained of his wealth and collected other monies to help fund the fledgling Continental Army. Thornton's plan was to send this treasure to Portland in a modest fishing boat with one of his merchant captains, Nelson Pulver.

Pulver was betrayed to the British, however—the traitor, one Miles Morse, given a fast sloop and promised fifty percent of the treasure if he stopped its delivery.

Brit glances up and grins, knowing she's got them—never mind Adria's rolling her eyes.

Pulver was hoping to hide among the islands of Casco Bay, but the heavily-armed sloop was too fast for the renegade vessel, and he knew it was only a matter of time before his boat was overtaken.

Onboard were several lads, the oldest a fourteen-year-old cabin boy named Reese. Thus it was, after tacking around Bumpkin Island, now known as Mistake Island, which blocked the view between the boats, Captain Pulver instructed the cabin boy to float the treasure to the island and secrete it away.

Reese managed to leap to the water before the sloop was upon them—reaching shore and dragging the chest to the woods as the British launched a longboat in pursuit. Digging quickly, the boy managed to bury the treasure, then scurry along the upper cliffs in hopes of escape as the British fired upon him. Wounded,…

"Excellent!" Dr. D swings his gaze to Adria. "Is this true?"

"Are you kidding? It was a game my father dreamed up to interest us in scavenger hunts. Roland Jackman, heavy-hitting Boston litigation attorney—eat you alive if you're not careful—but put him on the island for a couple weeks? He was like a kid—riddles, practical jokes, pirate games. We took it all very seriously, of course."

Wounded, Brit repeats, miffed at the interruption, *rather than face capture and certain torture, he made his way to a steep rock outcropping at the island's southernmost tip and threw himself to his death, breaking his body on the rocks below where it was claimed by the outgoing tide. The treasure,* she says, glancing up and pausing for dramatic effect, *was never found.*

She grins up at them. "Pretty fucking cool, huh?"

Monday

NORA

It's the sound of someone padding down the hall that finally rouses her, the jingle of Gus's collar, the thlump and lift of the hand-pump going at the kitchen sink.

Nora grabs the cell phone from the table beside the bed, boots up. She tried Wally three times last night—that last call draining most of the phone's remaining battery. He never picked up; no message now, either. She checks the time. Eight-ten. Five-ten west-coast time—what she's come to think of as "Wally time." Even their circadian rhythms are at odds now. A strange thought, then. If she turned the clock back three hours and cradled it to her heart, would Wally roll over in his sleep, reach for her?

The sound of Adria's laughter in the kitchen brings her back, a hushing for those still asleep. Nora rises, slips on shorts and a tee, her flip-flops—willing herself into cheerfulness as she heads down the hall.

"Well, she *was* pretty toasted last night." Adria holds the teapot under the spigot, gives it a turn. "Bet even *she* didn't make it down for yoga this morning. Hey, Nora. Sleep well?"

"Always," she lies, pouring herself some coffee. "Still no sun, I see. Here, let me do that." Taking the teapot, she moves to the stove, lights the burner.

"All I know is, she was gone when I came up from the Twig this morning," Lily tells them, stirring yogurt into the usual bowl of granola, bending to check the bread toasting beneath the oven's broiler.

The screen door slaps behind them, lines of sweat running Margot's chest and arms as she heads for the water.

"This Brit we're talking about?" she asks, drawing a glass from the spigot. "Still down on the dock as of about fifteen minutes ago." She pauses, downing half the water. "God, the bugs are awful this year. I'm gonna go stretch."

Trailing them to the porch with her coffee, Nora drops into one of the rockers, picks up the book she left out here last night. Light and trashy, nothing she'll have to put any real effort into. Good thing, she thinks, fingering her way to where she left off as Lily settles at one end of the hammock, drags her knitting into her lap.

"Damn," Margot says from the floor—arms stretching down one long leg. "I should have brought *my* knitting. It's perfect for out here."

"You knit?" Adria laughs, tearing the cellophane from a box of votives—replacements for the exhausted line of candles lining the ledge behind the hammock. "Sounds way too relaxed for you, girl."

"Couple more days and I'll show you relaxed." Margot sighs, laying back and closing her eyes. "God, a whole week—no husband, no kid."

"No work, no stress." Adria bends to pick at a puddle of wax fused to the window ledge, patiently prying bits of it off with her finger. That and the click of Lily's needles, the lazy buzz of an early-rising bee against the screen are the only sounds for a minute or more.

"Thought we'd take a hike this morning before I ferry the guys in," Adria finally says, resting her hip against the wall as she sips her coffee. "A lot of trees came down in that April Nor'easter; there are some tricky spots I should walk you through. You know how easy it is to get turned around in there."

Lily stills her needles long enough to glance toward the screen. "In this fog? It's getting worse, if anything. Look at it."

Nora glances up from the book she's not really reading to consider the heavy gray mass moving inexorably up the hill toward the house.

"Oh, come on," Adria laughs. "Island Women, remember? Since when are we afraid of a little fog? We'll grab a swim at South Rocks after."

"What if it doesn't clear?" Lily asks. "Two extra people for dinner—one of them David? My lasagna's not *that* big."

"It can be socked in one minute and clear the next—you know that," Adria reminds them as the kitchen door slams yet again. "We'll meet at the dock like we planned," she says, leaning back to gaze skyward through the screen in search of the sun. "Decide what to do then."

Brit pads into the room with a fistful of Oreos, looking more put out than hung over as she drops onto the end of the hammock beside Lily.

Adria grins. "Look at you, all glowin' and shit—like you've been having sex for hours. Honey, if that's what yoga does for you, I'm in."

"Bunch of lazy slobs—all of you," Brit grouses. "Thought at least

Margot would show, super-jock that she is." She pops an Oreo in her mouth, settles back, setting the hammock swinging. "Oh, yum. I'd forgotten how good these are."

"Stop jiggling," Lily scolds. "You'll make me drop a stitch."

"Brit," Margot says, propping herself on her elbows. "It's va-ca-tion. No schedules, okay? And, besides, I already went running. Those my cookies?"

"Yup."

Margot makes a grab, but Brit's faster—lipping the wafer off a second Oreo as she leans back.

"Stop it, you two," Lily grumbles. "I'm serious."

Brit gives the sweater a tug. "So where's gramps?"

"David's still sleeping," Lily says. "And don't start."

"Snoring, you mean. You know the older a man gets, the louder he snores? I read that somewhere—some study they did in Norway or something."

Lily shoots her a look. "You've never read a study in your life."

"Plus, he talks over you like all the time."

"I hate when they do that," Adria cracks.

"Christ, Lil. Really. I mean look at you—tiny bod, sweet face—you could be with somebody really hot, as you well know. Instead you're dating some guy who's like, what, fifty?"

"No! God, Brit." Lily glares at her. "You could have a little more empathy, you know. Considering."

The son who just died, Nora remembers now—finding a raw, unexpected comfort in her failure to conceive, to offer up new life to such a random and indifferent universe. The proverbial silver lining.

"You know you only stay with him 'cause you feel guilty. Just don't come crying to me when he moves on, which he will."

"I think you've got him confused with Hodge."

Adria's had it. "Enough, you two. It's over; accept it. Go for the divorce." She turns her gaze on Margot then. "Speaking of marital tension, what was all that between you and Rob at the boat ramp Saturday?"

Margot sighs. "Let's just say he wasn't in love with my coming out this time. He says I'm different when I come home."

"Stronger?" Brit suggests. "Less willing to take his shit?"

"Anyway," Margot says, ignoring her. "I couldn't bail—not after convincing this one to come back." Nudging Nora's leg with her toe.

"Too much going on last summer," Nora tells them. "The new job, Wally's promotion…" An image then: Wally walking down the jetway at the start of yet another Seattle trip, his step growing increasingly lighter the farther he gets from the distant thing their marriage has become. Another woman? Hardly a new thought.

"At least you get some time to yourself," Margot tells her. "Rob bitches if I go off somewhere without him, then barely acknowledges me when I'm around. It's like I'm invisible."

"You think *you're* invisible," Adria laughs, "try being a gay black woman running a hole-in-the-wall bookstore within spitting distance of a Barnes & Noble."

"Cambridge Books is hardly a hole in the wall."

"Six hundred square feet? Their *bathroom's* bigger than that."

"Not small," Nora offers. "Cozy."

"That right, Miss Nora?" Adria laughs. "That why you haven't come to book group in the last six months? We're off fiction for a while, just so you know; biography this month and next. The one you've got there was panned, by the way. Ending sucks."

"Gee, thanks," Nora laughs, closing the book as Margot rises in a long, overhead stretch.

"So, anyway," Margot says. "I think I might have seen Brit's guy from yesterday morning."

"Really?" Adria mocks surprise. "And here I thought she'd made him up; you know how she is."

Brit leans forward. "Got that sexy townie thing going for him, right? Saw him myself, again, actually—not half an hour ago. Watching from the trees while I was finishing up." She wiggles a cookie Nora's way. "Breakfast? No?"

"That's creepy," Lily says, pausing her needles again. "You sure?"

Nora feels it then—the prick of adrenaline, another random bout of dread threatening to descend.

"Could have been Hodge," Adria suggests, glancing over quickly as if sensing her slide. "He was going back out this morning, remember?"

Brit shakes her head, nibbling at the cookie icing. "Definitely not. Shorter, wiry build. Had a moustache, I think."

"Bet you gave him a real show, too," Margot cracks.

"You bet. Lots of long, slow stretching. Oh, baby. When I looked again, he was gone. Just my luck he's the shy type." She nods toward the collection of driftwood tacked to the far wall. "Speaking of men, that one look like a penis to you? No, really," she objects over the guffaws. "Cock your head to the right a little. No pun."

The prick of adrenaline becomes a trickle. Nora tries deep breathing, hoping to shut the cycle down before she's forced to slink off to her room. She turns to Adria, the words out before she can check their accusatory tone. "You told me we'd be alone out here."

Adria considers her. "I also remember telling you that Mistake is part of the Maine Island Trail now. We can all thank Drew for that one. Which means anyone can land a boat here and explore or picnic on the rocks, as long as they stay away from the house and leave by dark. If they're camping, I can throw them off, but I'd have to catch them at it first. Relax. Strength in numbers, remember?"

She has the sudden feeling this whole thing was a very bad idea, never mind she had her own reasons, good reasons, for coming back this year—including the growing sense things couldn't continue this way, that something had to give. The end was near, some part of her seemed to whisper, only the end of what? Her marriage? What remained of her artistic vision? Thirty-five years old and she's lost all her confidence, her nerve. Ridiculous to think she once taught anyone anything, that she made a living from such hubris. What had she thought, that getting away would somehow stop it all from unraveling? What a joke.

Margot leans down to catch her eye, holds her gaze. "Chill, okay?"

Brit turns to Margot. "So did you talk to him?"

"Who?" Margot says, pulling her gaze from Nora.

"My sexy townie, who do you think?"

"Oh, hell, Brit. I was just yanking your chain. I did see some canoe pulled up into the trees over by South Rocks, though. One of those weird, mufti-colored things. Looks like it's been there a while."

"Washed up, maybe." This from Lily, who'd no doubt see a stranger's sudden appearance among them as some kind of spiritual aversion therapy. Nora's heard it all before. Something freaks you out, you're bound to meet up with it out here. If you're lucky, it grows less threatening. Problem is, Nora no longer believes in luck, not the good kind anyway.

"By the way," Brit says. "One of you pick up the bottle of Cuervo I left at the Dromedary last night after dinner? It's gone."

"Probably left it in the outhouse or something," Adria says. "You were pretty wasted."

"No," Brit insists. "I left it on the deck of the Dromedary; I know I did. On the corner by the steps."

"Gee," Margot drawls. "Men show up and liquor starts disappearing. What a surprise."

GIL

Fog the consistency of warm gull shit greets our little group as we gather at the dock just before one. All the island nymphs except Brit and the gorgeous Nora are here to see us off, probably to make sure we actually leave this time. Gus paces the dock, growling inexplicably at the water.

"You don't think it's worth a shot?"

This wildly optimistic comment is courtesy of Nordic chick. I can barely see the end of the float, myself, never mind the sixteen feet of skiff tied alongside. Even the dog looks skeptical.

Adria cocks her head, listening. "You hear any lobster boats out there, Margot? 'Cause I sure don't, and the only thing that keeps those guys on their moorings is this kind of fog. That should tell you something."

"We've got a compass," Margot insists. "And you've driven this thing to the landing so many times you could do it in your sleep. Hell, I could."

Perhaps we should just offer to swim the three miles to shore.

"Too many rocky ledges out here," Adria tells her. "Can't risk it blind. We tear the prop off on something, we're screwed. The tide could take us anywhere. Nothing to do but wait 'til it lifts."

Duggan takes on a baffled expression—pursed lips, furrowed brow. I throw some repetitive nodding into the repertoire, though I'm secretly pleased to have a little more time to devote to the science of this place. While this morning's exploration of the island's north side with its gently rolling terrain of blueberry fields and fern groves proved interesting enough, it's the mountain ecosystem I could use more time in. Selfish of me, considering, so I do my best to look as put out as everyone else.

Thus it is we march glumly back to the house, where a mere twenty minutes later I tug on my cap, sling my pack over my shoulder and—grabbing a slicker from a half century's worth of dispirited looking raingear, windbreakers and old duffer hats pegged along the hallway off the kitchen—happily make myself scarce, fighting the urge to whistle as I leave Duggan to slug it out with Lily and Margot over the proper way to lay a fire. I don't get the big deal, frankly. Me, I lay down a few sticks, toss in some logs. Couple squirts of lighter fluid and there you go. But Duggan's particular about this kind of thing, argues esoteric shit like the best way to twist up the newspaper, which he prefers to twigs for kindling, while Margot's into the exact geometric placement of the logs. No surprise there. Lily hangs at Duggan's elbow, picking at them both while Brit sits cross-legged in one of the rockers egging everyone on. Ah, the terra incognito of female emotion. Women, I long ago discovered, are not simply more competitive than men, they're far more devious about it. Duggan doesn't stand a chance.

I decide to pick up where I left off yesterday, take another look at that stand of red spruce on the southeast side of the island. Best way to get there, I figure, is to reverse yesterday's hasty descent from the mountaintop to the meadow, so I head there now.

Hanging a right at the well, I slog through a dense, blooming twine of wild raspberry toward that dilapidated stone wall and the start of a long uphill climb—a route that literally bisects the island's two hundred acres, and a far faster way to reach the other side than the admittedly stunning perimeter walk I got a taste of yesterday. Still, the interior, with its miles of moss-covered trails, is just as glorious in its own way.

Halfway up the mountain I pause, momentarily turned around when I fail to recognize the enormous uprooted tree lying on its side—the root system easily twice as tall as I am, which makes it twelve feet plus. The disorientation is unusual for me. A bit off my game this morning; didn't sleep well's the problem. I could blame it on the lack of proper alcohol—long being used to a nightly dram or two, or three of single malt, and Brit apparently not being of the mind to share her whiskey—but more importantly, the sleeping situation sucked. As the house was full up, I found myself billeted on one of the quaint but impractical sleeping porches, my smallish bunk a rock-hard hammock bed of 1950s vintage, complete with a petrified mattress smelling strongly of mold. A situation made all the more surreal by the fact nothing but an ancient screen door separated me from the bed where the lovely Nora lay, lending the night a sense of forced intimacy I hadn't bargained on.

Shaking the feeling off, I jack the pack to my shoulder and pick up the pace—eager for that sense of almost Zen-like relaxation that comes over me when I'm all alone in the deep stillness of an old-growth forest.

Interestingly enough, someone's taken the time to do some decent trail marking in here, laying fallen tree trunks parallel to the path to guide hikers when the way is unclear; the occasional rock cairn indicating a tricky turn. Fog's not too bad in here, either—much of it being filtered out by the understory—but when I pause at the top of the mountain for a slug of water, hoping for a bit of a water view, reality reasserts itself in the same seemingly trowelled-on wall of gray that greeted us at the dock. So much for getting out of here anytime soon.

Halfway down the mountain the terrain dips, descending into a gorge-like glen almost primordial in feel—humid and dank and crisscrossed with moss-covered paths, the air sluicing between the rock formations that border the trail increasingly warm and humid as I descend. The trees in here are alive with thrushes, the call of an osprey somewhere above—the foliage so dense and lush I expect Tarzan to swing through the canopy at any moment, a sated Jane tucked against his side.

I pause to examine a rotting tree trunk hosting a kaleidoscope of mushrooms—wide, sable-rimmed stunners of orange and pink—beautifully psychedelic and poisonous as hell, when a sudden, heavy rustling in the brush somewhere to my left startles me. Deer, most likely, but try as I might, sussing anything through all this green proves impossible.

Water burbles up ahead where the path jogs right—two vertically-halved pieces of ten-foot log laid side by side in an ad-hoc bridge over a diverging brook. Crossing, I'm presented with driftwood signs tacked to a young spruce—one pointing left to a place called Jenny Point, and another urging me right toward South Rocks. All the while, the rustling continues to my left. I stop, intrigued—only whatever's out there stops too, which changes everything. Another one of us, then—Homo sapiens, I mean.

"Duggan, that you?"

Ridiculous, of course. David could no more have beaten me out here than fly, not to mention you'd never find him slogging through the puckerbrush and sumac for the pure satisfaction of cataloguing flora. The man hates bugs.

Clearly, whoever's out here is messing with my head. Nordic chick, maybe? Keeping an eye lest some brief weather window open in which she might be rid of us? More likely the outrageous, in-your-face Brit. That one definitely strikes me as stalker material. No wonder I'm so fucking twitchy around her. Christ, what is it with me and whacko women? Flock to me like flies on shit.

Ignore her and she'll go away—it's a tactic that's worked well for me in the past, and I fall back on it now despite the eerie feeling I'm being eyeballed. It's then the noise in the bushes picks up—whoever's out here dragging something off through the brush, back for more of whatever it is maybe thirty seconds later. What to do? Another day, another place, I might strike off-trail and check it out. Instead I pick up my pace, beginning the uphill slog toward the ridge where yesterday I spotted that stand of red spruce—determined, for once, to mind my own goddam business.

Ten minutes later I've managed a quick mental critique. The trees themselves seem healthy and vigorous. Some foliar symptoms of ozone exposure, which is to be expected, but no evidence of eastern spruce beetle, or the species' worst insect enemy, the spruce budworm. The bushes in here are for the most part those you'd expect to find growing at the base of these trees: the blueberry and red raspberry I've been running into all over the island, wispy blooms of Rhododendron canadense mixed with a large patch of mountain-holly and fly honeysuckle.

It's here I pick up the perimeter path from yesterday, the fog drifting in as smoky wisps hovering maybe six feet off the ground. Another sign, this one a weathered shingle carved in the shape of a finger, encouraging me toward a place called Salt Marsh Cove. All of it vaguely familiar 'til I verge from the path into a clearing—the look and feel of the spot tripping some mental trigger and, just like that, I'm gripped with a nostalgia so visceral it takes my breath. Summers at my grandparents' place on Somerset Island, north Georgian Bay. Simpler life, simpler time. Hell of a simpler world.

The anticipation of getting there would just about kill me—that interminable drive from Long Island to Canada and then on to Killarney made worse for the lack of siblings to needle; the chips truck where I'd tuck into a greasy mess of fish and fries while the adults urged the skiff's outboard to life something I still dream about. And the hitch I'd get in my chest when I caught sight of the place after so many months away? Man.

Most of the island was little more than a rugged, windswept expanse of low bush blueberry and prickly wild rose. What trees there were—red pine and cedar mostly, a few birch—were subjected to the full force of the prevailing southwesterlies, and canted permanently northeast toward a shoreline of rough, Georgian Bay rock. Prayer trees, I called them. Thus began my love affair with all things arboreal.

Like Mistake, our island had no electricity or running water, no phone or TV. On a good night, we might get minimal reception on an old, paint-spattered transistor radio—but only after nine. Had to do with sun spots, propagation—stuff like that. Then there was the unwavering routine: breakfast bell summoning me each morning from wherever it was I'd camped the night before; then Dad—still healthy and unaware of the ALS that would claim him years later—taking me off for a morning of chores. Clearing brush, slapping linseed oil on one of the cabins, taking the skiff to a fishing camp on Rock Island every few days for ice. An hour or two spent tossing a baseball around with him every evening on a stretch of pebbled beach—the thwack of ball against mitt as he drilled me on the statistics of the game. Sun setting at my back, the lazy drone of crickets in the long bank of fragrant rugosa rose bordering the sand.

Dad was obsessed with The Game—the teams, the trades, the stats. He considered baseball a metaphor for life, teaching everything you'd ever need to know about making hard decisions. About being a man. My patrimony his Dodgers cap, along with a trove of baseball cards worth more than most peoples' homes—a collection that will help fund my retirement once U-Maine finally wises up and fires my sorry ass.

Sadly for my father, I demonstrated little athletic prowess. I consider it no small irony that the same disease that claimed Lou Gehrig, one of the old man's favorite players, claimed him as well—Mom dying three months to the day after scattering his ashes. Massive coronary, broken heart—they're pretty much the same in my book.

Anyway, there's a cove on Somerset just like this one, and I mean almost literally the same vista—same long, scarped granite slabs sloping down to a narrow finger of water, same view of the opposite shore populated by tall firs. It was there, in that cove, morning chores and lunch behind me, that I immersed myself in the natural world—fishing, swimming, poring through the local field guide. The only time I remember my parents having any kind of fight, and it was a spectacular one—the genesis of which is long gone and hardly matters—I took refuge there, the silence and solitude working to calm me.

Perfect place for a late lunch, I decide; and sliding my pack off, I turn and take in the rest of the clearing.

I don't so much see her as sense her presence. The flash of something that doesn't quite fit at the base of another arborvitae like the ones in the meadow, this one perched over the rocks at the water's edge. The tree and what it hides reminding me briefly of those Hidden Picture pages we pored over as kids—objects of domesticity superimposed onto a scene of the natural world.

For there, seated amongst all this green, is the lovely Nora—a spiral-bound sketchbook open in her lap as she gazes across the water. The multiple trunks of the arborvitae having long ago formed a kind of seat, I realize, jutting out over the edge of a rock at the water's edge, the knobby roots like toes clinging for purchase.

"You talk in your sleep, you know." As openers go, this clearly sucks, but I'm a bit thrown coming on her this way—superimposed as she's been onto one my most seminal childhood memories.

She whirls, pales, the sketchbook tumbling to the mud and marshy grass beneath her.

My God, but she looks like Rachel—the same long-limbed grace, that luminous skin. Something wounded about the eyes that doesn't fit, though—that and the hair. Thick, like Rachel's, but not much longer than mine. Not a flattering look, I decide, for one who is otherwise so lovely.

"Well, you just mumble, really," I backpedal. "I spent the night tossing around on that miserable mattress out on the porch; couldn't help over-hearing." Or taking in her citrus fragrance as it wafted toward me in the wee hours. I pause. "Nora, right?" Palming my chest. "Gil Hodges; I don't think we were actually introduced last night, what with all that was going on."

In truth, she'd been intentionally avoiding my gaze, which I put down to her humiliation at my having first come on her in the dooryard au naturel. That, or Lily's been sharing her opinion of me behind my back. Now there's a pleasant thought.

"Didn't mean to startle you; but you're all but invisible in there. Great place to hide from the world, I imagine." I'm thinking younger than Rachel by maybe five years, mentally pegging her at about thirty-five. "Surprised you didn't hear me, actually; I'm hardly known for my stealth. Clumsy feet." I glance down as if to clarify their location. "Mind if I park here while I eat my lunch?"

Her glare tells me she very much does mind; still, I shoot her my low-est-watt Jeff Bridges—a goofy, lopsided grin about as threatening as tapioca pudding—and sit my ass down on a rock maybe ten feet away.

"Adria made me this kind of chicken salad thing," I tell her, rummag-ing in my pack for the sandwich. "Little fancy for me; PB&J's more my speed. It's all that protein and sugar—keeps me going." Chewing, gazing, watching her watching me. One wrong move, I think, and she's gonna bolt. Which would surely be a shame. "Nordic chick—uh, Margot—even threw in a couple Oreos." Making up for all that hostility down on the dock, I figure. "Want one?"

Still nothing. I scratch my head, take a long pull on my water bottle.

"Getting wet," I say, cocking my head to where the sketchbook lays soaking up mud in the sea grass.

She lowers her gaze with a kind of shudder—eyes flicking this way and that as she fights some emotion she clearly doesn't want me to see.

I'm not in the habit of conversing with myself—not sober anyway—and I admit to some confusion here. The woman could at least tell me to go fuck myself. That I'd understand.

"Amazing tree, the arborvitae," I say, pointing with my water bottle.

"Conifer family. Name literally means *tree of life*."

It's like somebody threw a switch. Suddenly this chick's all nervous energy, scrambling below her for the sketchbook—almost hyperventilating in her distress as she jams those pencils or charcoals or whatever the hell she uses into a canvas tote. "Homeopathic remedy, actually," I continue. "Marvelously aromatic. Foliage is rich in vitamin C, too."

Rising, still ignoring me, she slings her pack over her shoulder and steps sandaled feet from the twined roots that formed her seat—silver toe ring winking as she begins stomping her way along the trail toward the house. Not so much as a glance back over her shoulder.

"Good for all kinds of physical and psychological conditions!" I call after her—thinking inhale deeply, babe. If anyone needs her mental health tweaked, it's you.

Man, how weird was that? Still, good thing she left when she did. I'm just about out of material. Plus, I really gotta take a piss.

I'm hardly the handiest guy in the world, but even I can chop wood, lug water. So it is I find myself dragging two empty cooler jugs toward the meadow shortly before the five-thirty call to cheap wine—Lily's pooch my sole, though wildly enthusiastic, companion.

The well on Mistake is of the old-fashioned, hand-pump variety—vigorous amounts of elbow grease being its only source of power. This one, mounted on a simple wooden platform covering what's most certainly a hand-dug shaft, is a brilliant red like the one in the kitchen. Takes me a minute to figure the proper angle for filling the narrow-necked, five gallon bottles, but once I get the hang of it, propping the bottom against a cleat nailed to the edge of the platform for just this purpose, the process goes relatively quickly—the overflow being routed down a spout to a dog bowl. Ingenious as hell.

Giving my pits a whiff, I decide on a quick rinse. Someone's been kind enough to leave one of those travel-sized bottles of shampoo in the grass, so I strip to my waist, palm a squirt and lather up. The ketchup stain on my Zappa Tee, a remnant of yesterday's road food, proves more stubborn than my sweaty pits. Working hard at it for a couple minutes merely spreads the wealth from Frank's left eye to his nose, giving it the rosy glow of a serious boozer; but as Duggan's wont to say, at least that ketchup's clean. I could use a shave, too, but no one's seen fit to leave me a razor, so I'm left to carry on with the aging surfer look.

Spiffed up much as possible for the evening's activities, I load the two newly-filled jugs onto a wooden cart no doubt kept here for this very chore, and drag the thing back up the trail—the pooch streaking past me in a blur, some kind of grody plastic bottle dragged from God-only-knows-where gripped hard in his chops.

The Portobello lasagna Lily's planned for tonight's meal has filled the air with a mouthwatering amalgam of tomato sauce, garlic, and melted cheese—a dinner choice that surprises me, frankly, as her cooking tends

toward the scrubbier hinterlands of vegan cuisine. And while I'm not a Portobello kind of guy, slather even this with enough marinara and I'm there.

Leaving one of the jugs by the door, I roll the other into the kitchen,
where I'm met with the sight of Duggan incongruously clad in a frilly,
flower-printed apron—elbow-deep in salad fixings. What a world.

"Ah, just the person I need," comes his greeting. "Hand me the colander, will you? Shelf above the counter, I think."

I scan the wooden shelves climbing the wall—fifty years of mismatched
plates, bowls and mugs; the requisite boxes of cereal, crackers, stacks of
plastic Tupperware—then spy a dented aluminum colander nesting in a
large crockery bowl at the end of the second shelf. Tacked to the wall beside
it is a sheet of paper, a wanted poster of sorts—the drawing that of a mosquito on steroids, a thick red slash through its engorged abdomen. Names,
hash marks, a couple actual mosquitoes smashed onto the thing to illustrate
the point.

"Lil out harvesting tofu or something?"

Duggan shakes his head. "No tofu 'til she can get to the store."

"Damn."

"Be of good cheer. Salad's spiked with edamame."

"Swell." Nasty-tasting little green things, as I remember. Like lima
beans, only smaller, even less taste.

Laughter draws me along the narrow, windowless hall toward the living room with its massive fieldstone fireplace and walls of musty-smelling
books—clearly the hub of this rambling, mazelike place. The laughter is
Adria's as it turns out, clear and lyrical as she lights a clutch of candles grac-
ing the mantel, tossing comments over her shoulder at Nordic chick, who's
busy with a broom in a losing battle against the continual influx of pine
needles.

There seems no end to this chick's assortment of techie clothing, her
current ensemble some kind of fancy workout gear from the look of it—
cropped pink top overlaid with a lacy sweater, her stretchy gray pants a perfect match for the hair scrunchie corralling those blond ringlets. And me in
my whiffy, two-day-old tee.

Ditching the broom, she tucks a cheery red dishcloth over her arm
sommelier-like, and extends a hand toward two boxes of wine sitting atop
the makeshift bar—a low chest of drawers nestled beside French doors
flung wide to the screened porch.

"Red?" she asks. "Or white?"

I grimace. Man what I'd give for that long-gone six-pack of Moosehead
right about now. "You wouldn't have a beer, by any chance?"

A shake of those ringlets, something that's almost a smile. "Afraid not."

"In that case, does it matter?" Have to say that on the rare occasions I do drink wine, I prefer it to be of the expensive, imported variety—a meaty French Bordeaux, say, or a German Riesling—and stored as God meant it to be: in a bottle stoppered with a cork. A real one. I know, I know—a wine snob, and I don't even like the stuff much. If I wanted grape juice, I figure, I'd buy a jug of Welch's.

"Probably not," she admits. "But it's Lily's night, so Lily's wine. Secret's in drinking enough of it."

I go with the red—the meal being lasagna of a sort, after all—and chalking my gustatory crankiness up to hunger, the chicken salad and Oreos now just a distant memory, I take a sip.

Ugh. Aromas of overripe cleaning fluid, hints of burnt cardboard. Some bitter cherry in there somewhere. I force a smile through the battery acid aftertaste, figuring to position myself beside Brit when she shows up, the better to inhale the whiskey fumes emanating from her supposed water bottle.

Adria's feeling chatty tonight, not a hint of disappointment at our continuing presence as she asks about my day. No doubt forewarned about the box of red, she's wisely gone for the white, her glass perched precariously on the stone mantel while she continues the candle ritual. Sensing genuine interest in what I've learned, I dodge the now comatose pooch lying prone in the middle of the floor, and join her at the fireplace, where I relate the health of the island's red spruce, as well as my discovery of a few stands of hickory and white pine. Not a lot of that left in coastal New England, I tell her, most having been taken for ship masts in the 17th and 18th centuries.

In return, I learn the meadow's been forested twice that she knows of—once in the mid-eighteen hundreds and again in the early 20th century, which was when the Birches and the dormitory in the meadow were both built. She remembers a time, she says, when they had a clear shot from the house down to the sea—before the trees grew in close around the place—and could see all the way to Halfway Light, catch sunsets over the White Mountains.

My mention of Salt Marsh Cove brings the assurance that therein can be found the best swimming on the island, at which I launch into a sanitized version of my encounter with Her Skittishness—of whom there has so far been no sign. Off hyperventilating somewhere, is my guess.

Must be something in my tone, because Adria cocks her head, considering me. "Nora wasn't always like this." A wistful comment clearly meant for herself as much as for me. "She was fine when she was here two years ago, then she started to change. Some sort of social anxiety disorder, don't know the specifics. It's almost physically painful for her to interact with people now—strangers, mostly." Shakes her head, takes a contemplative sip. "The real Nora? The one I used to know? Energetic, vibrant, endlessly creative. An artist in the truest sense. We thought getting her back out here would help. She was so productive last time."

"Changes in latitude, changes in attitude? Far as I know, it only works in that old Jimmy Buffet song."

Another appraising look. "Don't underestimate the magic of this place," she warns. "It works on everyone—each in his own way. No one who spends any real time out here leaves the same." With this she turns to Duggan, still clad in that prissy little apron and bearing a plate of hors d'oeuvres which he extends with a mock bow.

"Whole grain cracker with a smatter of goat cheese and soupçon of roasted red pepper jelly," he announces in stentorian tones. "Compliments of My Lady, who bids me relay the serving of dinner in but half an hour's time."

I cock a brow. Nasty stuff, goat cheese—and unfortunately something with which Lily has recently become obsessed. But never one to miss the chance to make a few hard-won points with her, I gamely grab not one but two of the things, and toss them back chased with a slug of the putrid mess in my glass. The things I do for Duggan.

"Oh yum, I love these," Nordic chick says as she snags one—to which I nod my enthusiastic agreement and scarf a couple more, my eye drawn to Lily and Nora padding down the hallway toward us.

Were I the gentleman my mother raised me to be, I'd avert my gaze to spare the woman further humiliation, but something about this chick has triggered a perverse curiosity—my gaze openly following her as she pauses at the makeshift bar to draw a glass of red. Her efforts to ignore me putting color in her cheeks as she accepts a cracker from Duggan and moves to the porch—her back to us as she cocks a hip against the frame of the screen door and gazes off into the gray gloom like some bored dame from an old Bette Davis flick.

"I think it's when cold air meets warm water," Adria's saying. "Or is it the other way around?"

A beat or two later, I realize it's me she's waiting for—the two of them, Adria and Nordic chick, so intent on me it's unnerving.

"Different types of fog," I tell them, slipping effortlessly into my practiced Mr. Wizard role. "Kind we're having is the advection sort—caused when a warm humid air mass slides over a cold surface."

"Yeah, well, when's it gonna break? That's what I want to know."

We turn at the challenge in Brit's voice, a lopsided grin lighting that freckled countenance. Just the kind of wild child the Old Gil used to go for—all hormones, no inhibition—turned on by the in-your-face attitude, the sexually-tinged bravado. I'm hoping the fact I haven't the slightest desire to jump her bones indicates progress—a train of thought broken by the sight of a guy trailing in behind her. Five feet nine, maybe, shoulder-length brown hair, wiry but well-muscled. What the fuck?

"Company for dinner," Brit chirps—her amused gaze landing defiantly on Lily before sliding to Adria. "I mean the more the merrier, right?" She waits a beat—no doubt getting off on the shock value, of which there's plenty. "Everyone, this is Pete," she says, dropping into a rocking chair. "Pete, everyone."

A tight nod—the weathered face behind the cropped mustache-beard combo guarded and watchful, the tee shirt above his worn jeans exposing tatts on both arms, the inside of a wrist. Everything about him screaming townie—laborer of some kind, by the look of him. My mouth waters at the sight of a bottle of Bud dangling at his side, not to mention the one in Brit's hand. Reduced to salivating over a Budweiser—a new low.

The pooch wanders over for a sniff of the guy as Brit continues the perfunctory intros, rocking the chair to some skitzy internal beat. "Adria," she says, pointing with the bottle. "Lily, Dr. D, Margot, Hodge, and out there on the porch we have Nora."

Indeed we do, though that winsome face has lost all color—something I'm sure surprises no one, certainly not me. This as her eyes find Margot's. *What the hell's going on?*

"Welcome," Adria says, recovering quickly. 'Course she's had a lot of practice, what with all the men popping up lately. "Adria Jackman," she says, extending a hand.

"Our hostess," Brit informs him. "A.k.a. the black lesbian den mother here at the Birches. Her family owns the place, by the way."

Adria freezes—the ill-mannered comment, one that appalls even me, rendering the rest of us mute with disbelief.

"Just kidding, you guys," Brit laughs. "Lighten up. Christ."

Adria ignores her, fixes her gaze on Pete. "Brit's a lot of fun, but you want to be careful when she's had a few," she says evenly. "She tends to get carried away."

So far the guy's said nothing—an instinctive reaction we of the y-chromosome variety are known to exhibit when confronted with a group of supremely confident women. May not be any electricity out here, but there's a hell of a lot of power. Hovers in the air, like ozone before a lightning strike. Indeed, the atmosphere feels suddenly heavier, almost ominous, and something tells me it's not just the fog.

Adria cocks her head. "We've met, I think."

He shrugs, ignoring a smiling Duggan with his outstretched plate. The emasculating apron, no doubt. "Might've seen me around. Me and my brother been comin' out here since we was kids. Musta been by this place a couple hundred times."

Having spent countless years teaching the youth of this state, I immediately peg the accent as mid-coast. I'm thinking Bath, works at the shipyard, maybe.

"Pete's the guy I saw when I was down at the dock this morning," Brit informs us.

"Well, then, mystery solved," Margot quips, moving to join Nora by the screen door. "God, I feel so much better now."

Pete takes a pull on his beer, glances around. "Always wondered what it was like in here. Open two-by-four construction—done right, too."

Adria's still studying him. "You're a carpenter?"

"I done work here and there."

Ever the gracious hostess, she ushers him toward the porch with a truncated version of the shtick she gave me, laughing as she recounts the improvements and upgrades made to the place over the years, including a reconfiguration of the kitchen some five years ago to accommodate propane-fired appliances—her mother having refused to return to the island until the original wood cook stove was replaced.

Out of the blue I remember how Mom used to bitch about the wood stove on Somerset. Smoked like a bastard, as I recall. The three of us stuck in the cabin on damp, foggy evenings like this, of which there were many—checkers with Dad after dinner under the hiss of the Coleman lamp, eating Mom's blueberry cake while we fiddled with the transistor radio looking for that illusive late night reception. Norman Rockwell corny, I know.

I'm so lost in the emotive scenery of this well-traveled road it takes me a moment to realize I'm no longer alone before the hearth—Nora having quite inexplicably appeared at my side looking shaken and oh-so-vulnerable. I feel like the pimply-faced teen I once was—flustered and speechless as the two of us stand mute, breathing in the combined odors of damp ashes and scores of burning candles—what Dad used to call The Full Catholic Ceremony.

"You look so gone with the wind, Scarlet," I finally manage.

Nothing.

"You know…lost in thought?"

Still nothing, which has me more than a little confused. She clearly wants to respond but it's like her mouth won't work or something. Instead, I try a different tack, offering to refill the wine glass she's barely touched—an offer she declines with a shake of her head and a quick peek back over her shoulder—so I head to the so-called bar for more of this horrid swill. If I drink enough, I figure, I might just manage to forget the fact she's clearly using me as a prop, apparently having decided I'm marginally less threatening than the latest drop-in.

Rejoining her, I wrack my brain for something, anything, to break the ice—hoping a second attempt at conversation doesn't send her screaming off down the hall. It's then I catch sight of the charcoaled landscape Brit mentioned last night—something I'm only now getting a good look at.

"Lovely," I say, sucking-up being an important social skill now that I've been re-embraced by the university big-wigs. Only it isn't merely lovely, it's breathtaking—an exquisitely rendered view from the mountain top, the islands in the distance done in spare strokes and lots of complicated shading that lend the whole thing a lighthearted atmospheric quality. Some fleeting bout of optimism, no doubt. "Your work, I'm told."

She glances up, considering. "Another lifetime," she finally says, sneaking yet another nervous peek toward the porch.

"Duggan rambles incessantly about the fickleness of the creative muse," I tell her. "I thank God every day for my absolute lack of anything approaching talent. Life's infinitely simpler without it."

She fights a smile. If it blossomed, it'd be a great one—an observation that severely complicates my take. Instead, she folds it up, slips it back inside.

Bolder now, I consider taking a page from Brit's book—that bit about linking Starbucks drinks to personality, maybe—the enormous potential for future barhopping only now just occurring to me. Christ, what was it she suggested for Nora last night? Grande something. Latte? Mocha? What?

Sensing her tense, I glance back to see the others slowly making their way toward us from the porch. A relief, really; this is far too much work.

But it seems Nora's not finished with me. Leaning in, that warm citrus fragrance washing over me, she lays a hand to my arm—a kind of low-level panic in those chocolate orbs, a flash of that fire Adria referred to. Looking into her face, I have to remind myself she's not Rachel, or rather the vulnerable part I might have gotten to know had I even once bothered to reach out during the long months it took her son to die. At the time, I told myself I was still too raw from going through the same shit with Dad some years earlier, but that was crap. Wounded pride was all it was. Never before had a woman proven so utterly immune to my charms.

"Don't let him talk to me," Nora pleads. "Please."

This is hands-down the strangest conversation I've ever had that didn't end in someone trying to kill me. Still, I nod as if her words make complete sense. Social anxiety disorder, I remind myself. "Of course not."

"It's just," her voice descending to an almost desperate whisper, "he looks like someone."

Join the club, I think, taking her elbow and moving her to the side of the fireplace as if our conversation were of a more private sort—resolving in decidedly chivalrous fashion to champion her cause, whatever it is. If I had a cape, I'd throw it down right here and now, never mind the dearth of any puddled moisture at her feet. Some weird sort of penance for my abominable treatment of Rachel, I suppose.

It's then Brit and what's-his-name join us before the hearth—Nora turning away as I shift to face them.

"So, Pete," I say, "you from around here?"

"Bangor," Brit informs me. "Where you happen to teach. Professor of trees or something, right?"

"About covers it," I say, extending my hand for the kind of enthusiastic pumping these Neanderthal types get off on. "Gil Hodges."

He nods. "Strong grip. Karate?" Sizing me up, no doubt wondering if I've got some prior claim on Brit—God forbid.

"Tai Kwon Do," I tell him; I don't mention the black belt. I catch something out of the corner of my eye, then—a flash of clothing, the quiet snick of Nora's bedroom door. Damn.

"Guess I'll be lookin' out for you, then."

Bet your ass, I think.

"So, does that cami-looking canoe on the south side belong to you and your brother?" Margot asks, glancing over from where she's refilling wine glasses at the bar.

"Ours, yeah, but Earl's dead," Pete informs us matter-of-factly. "Couple years now. Found his body floatin' off them cliffs out there." He points his bottle in the general direction of the sea. "Drowned, they said. You mighta heard about it."

"The cliffs on this island? On Mistake?" Lily asks, accepting a glass from Margot as Duggan, having ditched the apron, joins her on the sofa. "My God, that's awful."

"Probably floated over from Flash Island," Margot suggests. "Lot of people party over there."

Flash Island, Flash Island. I remember, then—a mere speck of land compared to this place, situated a mile or so to the south.

"Head was stove in on one side like he fell from high up, landed on a rock, maybe. Forgot to mention. Nothing like that on Flash—island's all flat beach and scrub. Besides, we never hung there."

Adria cocks her head, assessing. "When was this again?"

"Two summers back," Pete says. "I wasn't around; figure he came out here to kinda reminisce, you know?"

Adria nods. "Possible he fell, I suppose. The cliffs on the south side are steep, dangerous as hell if there's any wind. Never heard anything about a body being found, though—sorry. Probably off-island at the time."

Pete shrugs. "No biggie."

"In any event," Adria announces, "house rules forbid me from turning away a hiker stranded by the fog. So we'll relax the rule against camping for the night. Happy to loan you a blanket if you want to bunk in that canoe of yours."

The hint of a grin exposes a missing incisor. "I'm all set."

"Well, we can offer you dinner at least," she tells him, suggesting the pump in the kitchen so he can wash up.

Brit's eyes follow him from the room. "Looks like Eddie Vedder, don't you think? You know...Pearl Jam?"

Lily shoots her a disbelieving look.

"What?" Brit laughs. "He's got that bad-boy thing going for him. Love that. Definitely the alternative type."

A guffaw from Margot. "Oh, he's alternative, all right."

"You'd *date* him?" Lily's clearly aghast, her voice a hoarse whisper. "I wouldn't let him wash my *car*."

"How about we let him stay at the house tonight?" Brit suggests. "Sleeping bag on the floor or something. There's one on the side porch under Hodge's hammock—used to be, anyway."

"No way," Lily says, pulling her shawl tighter. "Guy gives me the creeps."

"Is that one of your Lily-the-shaman things?" Brit snaps. "Something some uptight sister spirit whispered in your ear? Funny, you know, 'cause I don't remember being asked before you invited *these* guys out." She jabs a finger my way.

Oh, I get it now—Pete's presence here tonight is some kind of payback. Just the kind of passive-aggressive thing I'd expect from her. Still, I hold my tongue, having long ago proven myself clueless as to the subtleties of female quid pro quo.

"I agree with Lily," Margot says. "We don't know anything about this guy."

"Oh, come on."

Adria nails her with a look. "Think about it. That canoe's been here a while, which means he has, too. Question is why."

Tuesday

BRIT

"This one's called downward-facing dog," she tells him—hamstrings tightening, ass climbing high as she comes into it from plank pose. "Down-dog for short. Reverses the forces of gravity on the spine."

Pete's sitting maybe five feet away, forearms draping his knees, staring off over the water like he could care. Hasn't said much since coming down here ten minutes into her routine, but she's felt his eyes, knows he's watching.

Grande Bold, Brit decides. He'd take it black.

He cocks his head, then, like he's listening for something. But what? Fog's so thick it's like being inside a cotton ball. Can't even see the raft in the cove behind them.

"Lobster boat," he tells her. "Means it's gonna break."

"Yeah? Could've fooled me." Sucky weather, sucky week. She flashes to the image of Hodge working on the crappy old weather radio after dinner last night—the thing so covered in cooking grease he had to pry it off the shelf with a fork. He even rigged a piece of coat hanger for an antenna, but all it got them was slightly better static.

Bailing on shavasana, the final corpse pose, she rises—settling near Pete at the edge of the dock as he fingers a pack of Marlboros from his pocket, lips one out, fires it up. A sharp inhale as he flicks the match to the water, shotguns smoke from his nose.

Dangling her feet, the icy water tickling her toes—fuck, it's cold—she reaches over, snags the ciggie-butt. "Adria will have your ass, she catches you smoking." Hands it off after a long drag. " 'This place is an inferno waiting to happen.' Bet she's said that a thousand times."

Pete snorts a kind of laugh.

She lays back on the dock, feels the current pulling at her legs, longing for the feel of sun on her body. Should have gone to the lake, she decides; it's never this foggy inland.

Pete swings his gaze to her. "You all come out here together every year, one of you said. That right?"

"Bunch of summers now, yeah. Same week each year."

"The brunette on the porch with the blonde when I come in, who's she?"

"Nora? Terrified of strangers; no idea why. The blonde's Margot. Super jock. She's the one who kept glaring at you at the table."

"Don't think that woman likes me." He chuckles like it's funny.

"It's not just you, trust me. She's super-critical, has to have her fingers in everybody's shit—like with all those questions about your brother's accident last night."

His brother the retard, she remembers him telling her. Pete and Repeat, their friends called them, 'cause it took the two of them to go anywhere. Like when they'd break into the summer places along Harpswell Neck when they were kids. They only took stuff they could hide on their bodies in case they were seen, he said—silverware, money. Earl found a ring once; gave it to some girl he liked. And booze; they always drank the booze.

My tequila, she thinks.

And how late one fall, they spent a week holed up in a big place on the water that had been closed up at Labor Day. Just moved right in; had themselves a party. Ballsy, she thinks, wondering if she had it in her to pull something like that—slip back out here when everyone was gone for the season, have the Birches to herself. Who'd know? Maybe she and Pete could come back together this fall, party for a week.

She shoots a quick glance at him, tries the feeling on. Something home-made about a couple of his tatts, she notices now—that circle of barbed wire peeking from the edge of his tee, for one. But it's the wolf head trailing two eagle feathers on the inside of his wrist that really grabs her. Killer statement.

Brit peers down fondly at the wolf wrapping her own upper arm. Primo work that cost her a fortune, but what the hell.

"What's that one?" she asks nodding toward his wrist.

He shrugs, pulling in more smoke. "Tribal thing. My ancestors were Wabanaki."

Indian, huh? Now that's different. Last guy she dated was so Wonder Bread he bored the crap out of her—in bed and out. It seems all she ever sees up in Hanover these days are those Dartmouth College dweebs, and now here's this guy—pops up out of nowhere. Edgy, a little dangerous. Maybe more than a little. She likes that, likes that he freaks the others out. Maybe the week won't be a total waste after all.

"No shit. Lily's Inuit; pretends she's some kind of shaman or something. Communes with the spirits—like that. Makes me fucking crazy sometimes."

"Shaman…that's like magic shit, right?" He shakes his head. "Too much time on your hands, all of you. Too much money."

She pulls back, shoots him a look. "Where'd you get that? I work for a living, pal. Irish from Revere—that's me. Six kids. Father's a roofer; mother's a hairdresser—excuse me, aesthetician. I've been working since I was fifteen. It's Adria's family's got all the money and this fucking place." It gets her sometimes, how Adria and Drew had it so easy as kids, spending every summer out here instead of being bussed to some grody YMCA day camp with five hundred other losers.

"That explains it, then."

"Explains what?"

"Way they talk about you. How I best watch out for you when you've had a few—like that. Like their shit don't stink and you're just some low-class skank can't handle herself." His eyes travel her. "So are you?"

"Am I what?" Her voice softer now, weaker—something in his tone reminding her of the way her father used to make her feel.

He leans in. "Some low-class skank can't handle herself?"

Stung, she glances off, ready to just tell him to go screw himself and be done with it. Never mind he's right about the way Adria's always correcting her, the way she lords it over everybody. Feeling sick to death, suddenly, of all the pseudo intellectual crap, the holier-than-thou attitude. Still, he thinks he knows everything? He doesn't know shit. The things she could tell him would fucking blow his mind.

He takes a final pull, flicks the butt to the water. "Woman week, you said, so what's with the two guys?"

"Friends of Lily's," Brit mumbles. "Long story. They'll be gone soon as it clears." If it clears.

He considers this. "Can you get me back in there tonight?" he asks, cocking his head in the direction of the house.

She smiles to herself, starting to see a way she might get back at Adria, at all of them. For everything.

"Depends," she says. "You still got my Cuervo?"

GIL

I'm halfway up the incline, irritated as hell at Duggan—sprouting a tasseled piece of meadow grass from his mouth like some doughy, middle-aged Huckleberry Finn—when I finally slow to let him catch up. Limping already, and we haven't gone half a mile.

"Told you those things were lousy hikers," I grouse, chin-nodding toward his ten-year-old Docksiders. "And no socks? Your ankles will be cut to shreds in here."

He holds up a hand, gasping for air. "Don't care," he wheezes, glancing around for a place to sit before settling against the trunk of a half-dead pine tree. "Anything to avoid another morning alone with you-know-who—a woman I adore, you understand. I do." Hand patting his chest like he's about to stroke out on me. "It's just the relationship works so much better when we don't spend so much time on it."

"Most do," I tell him, shifting my pack.

"And this whole no-men-allowed thing," he carps as I get moving again. "Tad harsh, don't you think?"

"We'll be out of their hair soon enough." Though clearly not soon enough for some—Nordic chick in particular. Have to say, for a group of women who vacation together every year, they seem an odd mix. And if I ran the kind of tight ship Adria does? I'd have booted Brit's ass from this place long ago.

"So that guy last night," Duggan calls. "What's your take?"

"Freeloader?" I suggest, tossing the word over my shoulder. "Con man?" The chicks picked up on it, too; soon as the guy walked through the door the tension ratcheted to a ten. But this isn't what Duggan means and

I know it. I've seen the funky little dance his eyebrows do when he smells a novel-worthy idea, and last night was the full cha-cha.

"Don't be obtuse," he says as I maneuver around some deadfall, force myself to slow again while he minces his way past the downed limbs; it's that or lose him—a thought that's occurred more than once since we started out on this little mid-afternoon jaunt. "I mean the thing about the dead brother. It'd make a helluva story, but he seemed totally disinterested when I brought it up at dinner."

I'm really not up to this now. Another restless night spent but a stone's throw from the lovely Nora the problem, no doubt, our bizarre exchange at the fireplace leaving me antsy and unsettled and—okay, I admit it—horny as hell. Worse, I sensed she lay as sleepless as myself, the air between us charged with a mutual awareness as undeniable as it was disconcerting.

"Whole thing's kinda weird, you ask me," I tell him. "I mean if I had a brother who died out here, it's the last place I'd want to hang out."

"Oh, I don't know."

"Then you're as screwy as he is."

"Bit snappish this morning," Duggan observes.

Gee, and here I just thought I wanted to be alone. Don't get me wrong; I'm normally a pretty tolerant guy, and chumming around with Duggan can be good fun, but today he's just a drag on my need to crank out the miles, sweat off whatever's really bothering me. Uncharitable, I know. He just lost his son, after all. But I want a shower. I'd kill for a couple pours of single malt—Laphroaig, preferably. Hell, a whole bottle. This sobriety stuff sucks.

I stop, turn—that stray thought about Duggan's son triggering another.

"How come you never told me Lily was the one who found Matt?" I demand.

He stops as if struck. Somewhere in the misty overhang a thrush calls to its mate. "Where did you hear that?"

"Brit." Plucking my Dodgers cap from my head, I slap it against my pants, loosing a dusting of pine needles. "She implied there might be something off about the whole thing." A joke, of course. You might just as well accuse Tinkerbell of being an arsonist.

"Ah, Brit," he sighs, resting his back against the smooth face of one of the boulders that erupt like so many teeth along this section of trail. "She remind you of anyone?"

The question is meant to divert, of course—something he's been doing an awful lot of lately, usually when the subject of Matt comes up. More to the point, he's forbidden to bring up this particularly nasty bit of my past, which means he's doubly desperate. I know this because denial and avoidance are my only real interpersonal skills—both highly underrated as coping mechanisms, by the way—and thus easily recognizable in others. Still, Brit's comment about Lily finding Matt's body was definitely meant to inflame. Playing me, the way Annika the blue-eyed whacko used to. Which is, of course, David's point.

That was the old me, I remind myself, banished so far back in my hyppocampi he'd need a hundred-ton backhoe to dig himself out, or so I thought. Only now it seems he's resurrected himself for this little adventure, worming his way past my meager defenses to conjure Nora's face as it looked last night—vulnerable and haunted, played to a soundtrack of Adria's comments about the vibrant, sexy woman she once was.

"No comparison," I lie, starting off again. Still, Duggan is nuts on, as usual. The three of them—Annika, Brit, Nora—they're like some Greek chorus of every failed relationship I've ever had. Frightening, really.

This little detour down Memory Lane so distracts me I somehow miss a turn, the minimal path dead-ending in a dense wall of bracken so thick we'd need machetes to hack our way through. I glare around in disbelief.

"What is it?" Duggan asks, staggering into me from behind.

"Fuck me," I explain, my glower coming to rest on David himself, whose unwelcome observations helped bring us to this pass.

"This is the trail?" Incredulous, as well he might be.

Okay, so I screwed up. Big time. Indeed, any hiker worth his salt knows to keep an eye forward for any sudden jogs in the trail. Becoming hopelessly lost in hundreds of acres of deep woods can have a negative effect on longevity.

I take my frustration out by ignoring him, thrashing my way through the knot of overgrown bush before me as I head toward the distant sound of breakers—never mind the branches are thorny, the ground beneath gone suddenly marshy. There's an ocean out there somewhere, and I'm gonna get there if it kills me. Far as I'm concerned, Duggan can follow me into the swampy terrain in those wimpy Docksiders or go fuck himself. I don't much care either way.

Ten miserable minutes of rotten tree trunks and itchy, twining underbrush later, we stumble onto a perimeter path where I hang a left for no reason other than I spy one of those hand-hewn signs another fifty yards on. This one for Reese's Leap. Mentally tripping over the name Reese—I've heard it recently, but where?—I part several small firs; and picking my way through a thick wall of fragrant bayberry, push out onto a dramatic rock promontory overlooking one of the many small coves ringing the island. Serene and dramatic, it's a part of the shoreline I've not yet seen, and as good a place as any, I figure, for a break.

Still pissed, though by now more at myself than Duggan, I drop my pack and my ass to the ground, and watch as he fumbles his way toward me. I'm almost sorry for the guy, he looks so pathetic—bloody scratches covering his arms and legs, a dark smear of something across his cheek. Both of us, I realize, whiffier than week-old socks.

"Look at me," he whines, sinking to the ground some four feet away. "I'm exhausted. Filthy." He pauses, making a wild slap at a mosquito. "Beset by marauding wildlife." A groan as he slides those shoes off.

"This little tag-along was your idea, pal—remember that." I pull a couple Power Bars from my pack and toss him one, reminding myself that we'd at least managed to fend off the dog's concerted effort to accompany us, which would have made all this even more of a cluster.

I take a pull of water from my bottle, hand it off.

Easy," I warn, as he sucks the stuff down. "We're a couple miles from reinforcements, maybe more."

"Gone are the days you packed a flask for restorative moments such as this."

"Bit early in the day."

"Never hurt Hemingway."

"Not 'til his liver gave out."

"The man died from a gunshot wound, Hodge—not liver failure."

"Self-inflicted, if I'm not mistaken. Kind of my point."

The eyebrows shoot up. "Which is an unusual position for you."

Duggan worries about me, which is kinda cute, but I remain unapologetic about my drinking. Yeah, okay, I should probably cut back, and maybe some day I will, but not today or next week or even the week after that. Still, I make it a strict rule never to imbibe during the day and never, ever, while working. Which is what sets me apart from Ernie. I mean among the other, more obvious things.

We munch in silence for a bit, a half-dozen gulls riding the breeze just above us, until Duggan breaks the silence. "Let's get back to this guy Pete's brother for a minute," he says—unwilling, as usual, to let something like this go.

"Must we?"

"Man's found dead floating off an isolated island—head all smashed in. May or may not have been an accident, nobody's sure."

"The guy fell off a cliff," I remind him, even as I glance down to where surf pounds the rock face; the undulating purl of a fierce rip current just visible from this height. "Thus the crushed head."

"Couple years later, the victim's brother shows up looking for closure—the truth behind what actually happened that day."

Victim? Truth? "For Chrissake, all the guy asked was whether they'd heard about it." I stand, tug my cap on. Might as well head back; no way I'll get any real cataloguing done with him tagging along. Plus, it smells like rain.

"Ah, but it was the way he asked," Duggan persists as I backtrack to the trail. "That tinge of suspicion, like he knows more than the rest of us."

First thing he's said I agree with. Something off about this guy I can't quite put my finger on, but since chances are I'll never see him again—no doubt he boogied out of here at first light—it hardly matters. I've got more important things to worry about, like this sudden resurrection of my libidinous alter ego—back from the dead, apparently, and lobbying hard for a shot at Nora.

"I've got a feeling about this, Hodge. I haven't been this excited about an idea in a long time." Nattering on about it 'til I start to wonder if this fixation on yet another gruesome death is exactly the kind of weird response to grief that I promised myself I'd keep an eye out for. This as we pass the turn-off to South Rocks—a place I've heard the chicks often bathe au naturel when there's any real sun to be had, which unfortunately rules out the present moment. As an image this doesn't suck, and it quickly takes precedence over my rather vague concerns about Duggan, 'til I glance skyward, anyway—the sight of vultures circling lazily above us stopping me cold.

Duggan's gaze follows mine. "Something wrong?"

"Probably nothing," I say, slipping my pack off. Which may very well be true. Still. "Wait here; I'll be back in a minute."

And with that I strike off-trail—picking up, maybe twenty yards in, the kind of dull buzzing that serves as another of death's calling cards. A burst of adrenaline as instinct kicks in, a tingle along the hairline, and I slow my pace, pick my way toward whatever.

The place isn't a clearing, exactly, more like a widened section of what might once have been a path. Empty and peaceful enough at first glance, but it sounds like a fucking fly convention in here—the buzzing so loud it's unnerving. The cloying scent of congealed blood hangs thick, catching in my throat with each breath, so I keep them short and shallow as I scan the area.

Buzzing's even louder off to the left, and when I part the bushes I all but hurl—so many flies in here they're like a living, shifting thing. I lock on the patch of ground beneath a lush rhododendron and freeze—brain going blank as I try and dredge up some rational explanation for what's before me.

The headless upper torso is alive with flies, the jagged neckline crawling with so many of the things it seems to be moving. The recently butchered remains of a deer, I realize. No, too small. Heartbreakingly so. Just a fawn, then. Tossed beneath another bush I see four tiny, stilled hooves with their own crop of busy flies, the legs hacked into ragged chunks like so much cordwood. Organs, intestines, and offal everywhere. And the blood—Christ.

As I back from the bushes, the sight of those little hooves permanently seared in my brain, I stumble on something long and cylindrical. The broken shaft of an arrow, I realize, its business end missing. Lodged deep in Bambi's flank, would be my guess. Which reminds me. Where's the rest of it—the animal's flanks, I mean, not to mention the head? They weren't back there in the bushes; no way I'd have missed that treat. It's then I flash to yesterday's trek through the interior, the sound of something being dragged through the brush. Not far from here, either, come to think of it. The deer taken for its meat, then—at least that's something. Still, what kind of sadistic creep leaves the rest of it lying around like this?

There's no hiding my edginess from Duggan; the guy reads me like a book.

"What?" he demands as I duck back onto the trail, my glare a loud and clear Don't Even Ask.

"Nothing," I lie, catching the first rumble of not-so-distant thunder, the scent of rain in the air. "Dead animal. C'mon; it's gonna pour any minute."

"Looks like Paul Bunyan out there could use some wine," Margot laugh from the protected environs of the screened porch, where she and Adria have parked themselves to watch the macho idiot splitting wood in the rain. Said macho idiot being me.

I rationalized this bit of exhibitionism by telling myself someone's gotta keep these chicks in firewood, but as usual when it comes to women I'm full of shit. The only time I get this physical—other than in the sack, of course—is when something's really eating me. But after forty-five sweaty, rain-soaked minutes swinging an ax, I still haven't figured out what's got me more rattled—the carnage back there in the woods or my ludicrous fascination with Nora, who's yet to put in an appearance.

"Don't think so," Adria says as I swing the ax up and over yet again, gaining momentum through the arc until it plants itself in the satisfying thwack of splintered wood. "Not 'til he's finished, anyway. He lops a foot off out here, that's it. We bury him where he drops."

Could just be my defenses are down, I decide, eaten away by the break in my routine—all this stirring of memory the last thing I had in mind when I climbed into Duggan's car Sunday afternoon. God, has it really only been two days? Feels like a fucking year.

A smattering of applause as my last swing lodges the ax firmly in the chopping block. Casting an eye toward the fitfully spitting sky—all that's left of the retreating thunderstorm—I head to the kitchen to wash up. It's this change in the weather that will save me, I decide—that and the bottle of ten-year-old single malt I'll insist Duggan stop for on our way back to the real world.

Hot, yeasty smells hit me as I round the corner of the house—something with berries and butter, caramelized sugar—pulling a growl from my stomach as I tug at the screen door. And wouldn't you know, there she is, Nora, bent at the waist before the open oven, scrutinizing what's inside.

I tell myself to turn around even as I'm heading for the red-handle of the pump, give it a couple good pulls as I soap up, rinse. Determined, despite the jacking of my heart, to be adult about this.

"Smells incredible," I say, reaching for a dishtowel as I turn to face her. "That what I think it is?"

"Only if you think it's blueberry pie," she tells me, resting her back against the oven door. "Meadow's full of them."

Vaccinium angustifolium, goes my mental tic.

"I could live on pie," I say as she pulls a pot of steaming water from the stove and moves in my direction. "Best eaten with the fingers," I ramble stupidly as she pours it into a dishpan set in the sink. "Pie, I mean. A student of mine taught me that." Ben Leland, that first summer. Back before any of us knew how little time he had left.

Her eyes find mine in lieu of comment, her face moist and flushed— the look she sends me effectively drop-kicking my heart to my throat.

"Listen, about last night," she says, drying her hands on the dish-towel. "I was acting a little crazy, I know. I get a kind of low-level panic around people, sometimes." A pause, a quiet chuckle. "Okay, maybe not so low-level."

Amazing how normal her voice sounds just now—surprisingly deep and smooth, almost honeyed. Not a hitch or a tremble. Fucking amazing, considering. Or maybe not. Each time I think I've got this chick pegged, out pops another persona. Could be all these women are loony. A retreat for psychos. Of course; makes sense I'd end up here.

I shoot her the goofiest Jeff Bridges I can muster. "Kind and caring— that's me. Plus, I've got a soft spot for women who feed me. Listen, let me help with something—least I can do."

"Gazpacho and hot bread." She shrugs. "Not much to it."

"And the pie," I remind her.

A quick smile. "And the pie." The unfolding of a dimple sets something trembling in the air between us. First time she's truly smiled in my presence. Rachel, I remind myself. It's just that she reminds you of Rachel.

"Happy to stay and keep you company, then," I suggest, feeling a tad giddy. "Pie could need guarding, what with Duggan afoot."

Wouldn't you know, Adria glides into the kitchen just then, and just like that, the tremulous thing between us pops like a bubble.

"Oh, there you are," she announces, as if I've taken to skulking in corners. "Here," she says, holding up a shirt. "Not sure of the fit, but it's clean and dry at least. I absolutely have to wash that tee shirt of yours, no offense—that or burn it."

Her father's shirt, I assume, or maybe her brother's—a gesture that touches me, despite the fact red-checkered flannel isn't my thing. Not to mention it's July.

"It's Duggan who really needs this," I mumble, slipping the Zappa over my head—embarrassed for some reason to be disrobing in front of Nora. Christ—what am I, fifteen?

Adria shakes her head. "Oh honey, look at those muscles. Times like these I wish I were straight."

"You know," I say as I slide the shirt on, "you could probably get us ashore tonight if we got our asses in gear. Tide's right."

"You kidding?" she laughs. "After all that work you just did? No, you've more than earned your supper. Morning will be soon enough."

"Found the tequila!" The slamming of the screen door punctuates the sing-song voice, an alcohol-fueled grin on Brit's face as she sashays in wagging a half-empty bottle of Cuervo—Pete, eyes likewise reddened with booze, bringing up the rear like a bad smell.

And just like that I'm on edge again, having pretty much pegged him for the bloodbath back there in the woods. Which is inconvenient, I realize, eyeing the tequila. This as Gus trots in, passing up his water bowl for an interested snuffling of Pete's left pant leg. Eau de Bambi blood would be my guess. I weigh Bambi against the Cuervo, the Cuervo against Bambi. What the hell, I decide, lots of people hunt. Christ, it's considered unmanly around here not to—jacking a deer now and then a simple rite of passage. Baby venison's more tender, maybe, like veal. Probably go great with a shot or two of that tequila.

"That pie smells fucking awesome," Brit says—while beside me, Nora quietly turns and moves toward the hall. "Hope you guys made two, 'cause me and Pete got plans for that one."

Snagging a couple shot glasses from one of the shelves, she uncaps the Cuervo and pours, slopping a precious ounce or so on the counter in the bargain. "Whoops," she giggles, clinking glasses with Pete before throwing the liquor back. She immediately pours them another equally messy, and clearly unnecessary, round.

Perhaps, I think, I should offer to hand down a few more glasses—it's that or give in to the wildly inappropriate urge to simply slurp the spillage from the counter.

Again with the shots. Lily appears dumbstruck, exchanges a quick glance with Adria, who offers an almost imperceptible shake of the head. Let it go.

Resigned, I turn for the hall. Bad vino it is, then. The only upside to all this is that last night's box wine has been replaced by bottles of a California vineyard even I recognize, which perks me up considerably. I offer a glass of the white to Lily, whom I spy stretched out on the hammock, then pour a rather hefty one for myself.

"Seen Duggan?" I ask, handing off her glass.

"Napping," she tells me.

Right. Some delightful, post-coital snooze, no doubt—lucky fucker.

"What we need are some tunes!" Brit announces, sweeping into the room with that bottle, Pete tight on her heels. "Time to par-tay."

"Damn, girl," Adria cracks, pausing before me with a plate of cheese and crackers. "Must have left my solar-powered boom box in the car."

"Along with the solar-powered microwave," Margot calls from the bar. "And the solar-powered hair dryer."

Brit's still grinning, a tad unsteady on her feet.

"Whoa," Margot laughs. "You need to sit. Seriously."

I avoid some gnarly-looking seeded things of suspicious origin, snag a couple Ritz instead, a thin slice of cheddar. Draw down some wine against my disappointment at Nora's having once again disappeared from the scene.

"But I want to *dance,* " Brit pouts, slapping the bottle on the floor by the chair Pete's dropped into. "C'mon," she instructs, tugging at the leg of his jeans. "Dance with me."

A twitch of the lips as Margot catches Adria's eye. "So, Pete," she says, settling on the sofa. "You find someplace dry to spend the night?"

"Margot thinks I smuggled you into my room," Brit tells him—beginning a sultry, harem-like shimmy I do my best to ignore by concentrating on another long quaff of wine. "If only, right?"

"Cave the other side of the mountain," he says. "Me and Earl used to camp there as kids."

"The one near where the brook splits down in the glen?" Lily leans forward to accept a slice of cheese from Adria's proffered plate. "Found it my first year out here; always figured it was an animal den."

Adria eyes Pete. "Impossible. We'd have known if someone was camping on the island—which isn't allowed, as I think I mentioned last night."

This amuses him for some reason. "That right?"

"Hot in here," Brit says coyly, fingering the lower edge of her green tank top as if about to peel it off. "Anybody else hot?"

"Earl liked to say we got more right to this place than anyone, 'cause of our Indian blood," he says, peering around her as if she had all the allure of a cement post. "Wabanaki."

"Those living at the sunrise," Lily murmurs.

"You can't be serious," Adria laughs—this as Duggan finally joins us, wandering in from the yard looking refreshed and a little sheepish, eyes fairly dancing at the sight of Pete.

"These islands were all part of our traditional hunting grounds," he says, cocking his foot onto the coffee table—a gesture as rude as it is oddly territorial. "Sold out from under us, you might say."

"No way you'd know this, of course," Duggan jumps in, "but I wrote a trilogy of novels set in the mid-17th century about early English settlements in the area, their conflicts with Native Americans."

His swashbuckler series, I think. *Pirates of the Penobscot, Dawn Raid, Native Revenge*—stories that followed a fictitious family of early English settlers through several Indian rebellions and the grisly murder of its venerable patriarch. This last arguably his best seller.

"Yeah, I seen 'em," Pete says, clearly unimpressed. "Earl even read 'em. He was all into that stuff."

Duggan beams at this.

"Ripoffs, he called 'em—the way you changed what real people did. Earl and me, we're descended down direct from Mollioket, so we had this crap drilled into us as kids—how she was a healer, a hunter. Not some bloodthirsty squaw like you said. Sloppy, too, calling her Iroquois when she was Pequawket. Drove him nuts."

"It's fiction," I say in David's defense. "Not history. Different genre, different rules."

"I'm hardly indifferent to the cultural issues here," Duggan says hotly.

"Haven't published anything since, according to this one," Pete says cocking his head toward Brit, who continues to sway before us—arms tangled as she struggles to remove her top, the lacy little number peeking from beneath doing little to hide those decidedly perky breasts. "Kind of a long, dry spell."

Who the fuck does this guy think he is? Only thing worse than being shredded in front of a group of hot women is being shredded by a guy who doesn't look like he made it through trade school.

Adria's clearly had it with this jerk. "Just what is it you want here, Pete?" she snaps, her voice going quiet in that steely way she has.

"Lookin' for answers, is all," he says reasonably, the smile he offers not quite making his eyes. "Earl could be a hot-head; could be he pissed somebody off."

"There's no proof he was even here," comes Margot from the sofa, not bothering to look up from the magazine she's begun flipping through.

"Canoe's still right where he always pulled it up. Can't leave without a boat," he points out. "Which puts him here when he was killed."

Not died, I think. Killed.

Silence as everyone takes this in. Duggan's absolutely rapt, of course—the insult of mere moments ago forgotten in the incipient glow of a potential bestseller.

"He was an ex-con," I say, surprising myself as much as everyone else. No idea how I know this, but I do. Just fits.

Pete shrugs. "Did some time on a bullshit charge, got out maybe a month before they found his body. Told me he was comin' out here to get his head straight. Looks like he got it stove in instead."

"This is ridiculous." Adria stoops angrily, retrieving the skimpy tank top Brit's finally managed to shed. "Enough," she snaps, tossing it at her. "No one's interested."

"What's the matter, honey?" Brit coos. "Getting turned on?"

"Christ," Margot mutters, flipping a page. "You're worse than my kid."

"Well, fuck you very much," Brit says conversationally. "Like I need your approval. Fucking boring, all of you," she tells us, dropping to the floor. "With your games and your reading and all. My grandmother's more fun."

Pete chuckles lightly, runs a hand over his beard. "Upset a bunch of folks around here when you people bought this place," he tells Adria. "Locals who been here forever. *Who them niggers think they are, buyin' up the island?*" He lets that rest a beat. "Funny thing, though. You don't sound like no nigger I ever heard. That what education does for you?"

It's like all the air's been sucked from the room. Even Gus seems to deflate—parking his muzzle between his paws and wheezing a sigh, no doubt as tired of all this as the rest of us.

A slow grin from Adria, then—some streetwise Boston side emerging in a now-we're-gonna-play look. "You feel better I talked jive, mothuh-fuckuh?" Voice like ice, the mimicry dead on—right down to the sideways, in-your-face jog of the head.

I make it a rule not to trot out the martial arts stuff at this kind of chest-thumping event, but I'd consider making an exception for this dick-wad. The right kick would do a real job on that sneer he's got going just now. In fact, the only one who's even marginally enjoying any of this is Brit—surprise, surprise. Grinning, knees tucked to her chin as this fuck-head goes head-to-head with Adria.

In the middle of all this, Margot's cell phone rings. Pulling it from her pocket, she heads for the door, squinting at the display.

"Oh, for God's sake," Brit snaps. "Just tell him to fuck off, okay? Better yet, I'll do it for you." And with that, she's up. Two steps and she's in Margot's face. Grabbing the cell, she flings open the screen door and wings the thing deep into the woods—thus proving herself an ugly drunk for anyone not yet so convinced.

Margot stares, dumbstruck. "Well, that was mature," she finally manages.

"Fuck you. Fuck all of you. That's payback for taking *my* cell. Let's pick on the low-class kid from Revere, right? Nothing else to do out here, so why not?"

"What are you talking about?" Margot snaps.

"None of us took your phone, Brit," Lily says. "What possible reason could we have?"

"What possible reason? You're seriously asking me that? You?"

"Everyone just calm down." This from Adria, who looks anything but. "I'm sorry," she inexplicably says to me. "I've no idea what's gotten into her."

Brit's about to loose another verbal volley when Pete grabs her by the arm and pulls her up tight. "C'mon," he growls, turning her roughly toward the hall. "Party's over."

"Yeah." She glares, hiccups. "We're so outta here."

"Oh, and Pete?" Adria calls after them. "You're to leave to the island immediately. And if I see you here again—ever—I'll swear out a warrant for your arrest. Trespassing, poaching, criminal mischief, anything else I can think of."

No response but the slam of the kitchen door.

Margot turns an incredulous look on us all. "Someone want to tell me what just happened here?"

BRIT

"I know where we can go," she tells him, breaking from the kiss—claiming the butt for a long drag as the smoke drifts up between them. Doesn't matter she probably won't see him again after tomorrow; this is here, this is now. A good buzz on, and about to make it with possibly the only guy she's ever known with the balls to really tell it like it is.

God, the way he reamed Dr. D a new one. And being right up in Adria's face like that, not caring at all that she owns this place. It was as if he was doing, saying, all the stuff she's wanted to for like ever. Tired to death of what she doesn't have, will never have; tired of feeling inferior to the likes of Adria and Drew, that whole fucking family. And this whole Island Women thing, like there's something special about being picked to hang out with this bunch. What a joke.

He kisses her again—long, slow, lots of tongue.

"C'mon," she urges hoarsely, taking his hand—calloused, sandpaper-rough—shivering at the thought of those hands moving over her as she leads him along the path to the Dromedary. Perfect spot for what she's got in mind.

Another long kiss when they reach the place—Brit's back against the door, feeling so hot for him now she can barely stand it. She's about to reach to the top of the jamb for the key, but he beats her to it, heel-grinding his butt on the ground before unlocking the door, holding it wide for her. Of course he'd know where it is. He's probably been in all these buildings lots of times.

Inside now, she gropes for matches to fire up one of the lamps, but he puts a hand on hers. "No lights."

"Cool," she breathes.

Wednesday

GIL

I'm slow coming to in the early-morning stillness—arm slung over my eyes, something lumpy under my butt I only now realize has been digging in for some time. It seems I slept fully clothed, too—something I never do—but the damp chill beneath me makes even less sense, the fusty smell wafting from my bedclothes not quite the permeating fug of the hammock I've grown used to. I could crack my eyes and get a visual, I suppose, but that would involve prying the pasty things apart first—something that's beyond me just now.

The shamelessly chipper bird sounding off just above me and the dry whisper of field grass are what tip me off. The meadow. I spent the night in the fucking meadow.

My groan is of the just-how-big-an-asshole-did-I-make-of-myself variety, chased by the kind of creeping, morning-after dread I've come to know so well. I vaguely recall a bottle of tawny Port, unearthed by Adria from some secret stash of her father's after everyone else had gone to bed—which was earlier than usual, thanks to the pall Brit and Pete cast over the evening. Just the two of us, then—well, three, if you count the bottle. Pure liquid ambrosia, if memory serves. No doubt I went a bit overboard. But it wasn't the booze or the thought of another night crammed onto that miserable hammock that got me out here, I recall now, but the fear of what I might do about Nora's tempting proximity while I lay in such a weakened and vulnerable state. Still, I've no clue how I managed it. Could have walked, could have flown, could have been wheeled in a barrow. But however I did it, I slept like the proverbial rock.

No reason to get up now either, I figure—at least not 'til the mosquitoes find me. Another hour, I plead, rolling over, which is when I see Pete down on his haunches studying me, face not a foot from mine.

"Jesus!" I bark, adrenaline powering my scramble to clear the sleeping bag I apparently dragged out here with me. "Don't do that!"

He cocks his head, rising to meet me as I stand. Not a good idea as it turns out, this standing business, considering the explosion of pain at the top of my head. At six-two, I'm five or six inches taller than this guy—something that would normally make me feel pretty good, only nothing feels good just now. My legs are so wobbly, it's all I can do to remain vertical. I glance down at the cool breeze running over my left foot. My sore, bare, left foot.

Where the fuck is my shoe?

"Piece of advice," Pete says, glancing toward the mountain, gaze flat and unreadable as he swings it back my way. Think Clint Eastwood's slow burn, but with none of his style. "Right now we got no real beef, you and me. Keep out of this and it'll stay that way."

What *this*? There's a *this*?

"Let me guess," I say, pinching the bridge of my nose against the vise slowly tightening at the top of my head, the forks carving out the backs of my eyeballs. The things I do to myself. "This is about your brother, right? What—you were too busy lobbing the n-word at Adria to hear her say she wasn't around? That none of these chicks know anything about this?"

"They know," he assures me. "Just not sayin'."

"They—as in…"

"All of 'em, probably."

Of course. Conspiracy among the conifers. I'll have to remember to suggest this to Duggan for the title of whatever mystery or thriller he's hoping to eke out of all this. "Come on, man. You saw the looks on their faces—total fucking surprise."

"Brit said they come out here every year—same women, same week in July."

Good old Brit. "I wouldn't know." Nor do I care. Once around with this shit's more than enough for me; besides, I desperately need to keep the sun from hitting my retinas just now. Shades, I think. I pat my pockets.

"Earl was killed the week they were here. July 21st."

"July 21st what?"

"Day he died."

"You can't possibly know that," I say, carefully lowering myself to rummage in my rucksack for those miserable Maui Jims. Sliding them on makes things marginally better, but mincing my way back to my feet brings stabbing pains from the sole of the shoeless one. Man, it hurts. What the hell did I step on, anyway? Glass, rock—what?

"So, okay," I say, cranking the foot up stork-like to peer at the dried brown goo stuck to the bottom. Mud? I wonder, hopping awkwardly to stay upright. Blood? "Say you're right, and he *was* here. Doesn't mean they *knew* he was here." Gently probing the most tender places for lacerations, protruding foreign objects. "If Adria even suspected he was camping on the island, she'd have booted his ass off. You've seen the way she is about this place."

"Earl don't listen to nobody when his mind's set. Kind of his trademark."

More of that unremitting Eastwood gaze, which is frankly starting to piss me off. Out of nowhere, another piece of yesterday slips along the edge of my mind—something weird about the timing of all this. And then it hits me. If Earl died two years ago, why's this guy just turning up now?

"You were in prison when it happened." Pure hunch, of course, but it fits. Explains why he seemed so hinky from the start, that vague whiff of what I now recognize as recent and intimate acquaintance with Maine State Corrections. I do the mental math, take a stab. "You and Earl were sent up together; only he got out early. Drugs would be my bet. That or a juicy little B&E."

"Fuck them bastards. Bullshit's what it was. Lousy pot bust. My second time, so the judge bumped me a couple extra years."

"So Earl gets out, comes here to revisit the old stomping grounds, and ends up dead."

"I knew there'd be trouble, what with me not around to keep him in line. It was me always looked out for him."

"Plus, you landed him in jail. What a bro. But hey, at least you knew where he was; there's that." Screwing with him like this probably isn't smart, but I'm still kinda punchy, and I need to piss. Besides; I really, really, really don't like this guy.

Pete cocks his head. "This funny to you?"

Fucking hilarious, actually, only it's fast becoming clear that leaving Adria et al alone while a deluded nut like this is wandering the island wouldn't be smart. There's my conscience to consider, what's left of it anyway. "So you got sprung—what—a month ago? Two?"

"Sat in that shitty jail two years knowin' he'd been murdered, countin' the days 'til I got out."

"Accidents happen, pal. You've seen the cliffs out here—dangerous as hell in the wrong conditions."

"Earl never went near them cliffs. Hated heights. No, somethin' happened out here. I'm gonna know what and I'm gonna know why. I owe him that. You bein' here just complicates things."

"Yeah, well, only person leaving the island is you," I say, trying to sound all bad-ass as I fight the urge to toss my cookies. "I'm not going anywhere."

He considers. "Your decision. Things been put in motion. Don't say I didn't warn you." A smirk as he nods toward the sleeping bag. "Nice."

I glance down, following his gaze. A faded field of blue dotted with yellow and pink flowers, the darker hue of a minimally sullied ball gown and white-gloved hands—all this capped with the lemon yellow orb of Cinderella's hair, her face lit with a saccharine smile. A little girl's sleeping bag, I realize. Swell.

"So here's what you do," he says. "You and the other girls have a meetin'. You explain how things are gonna get really ugly, really fast, if I don't find out what went down."

With that he trots back into the brush like something out of *The Last of the Mohicans*—all that bouncy action enough to set my eyeballs aching. What the fuck was in that bottle, anyway?

Nothing for it but to head to the house and fill Adria in, come up with some kind of plan.

After I find that fucking shoe.

By now it's maybe seven-thirty on what's fast becoming a stunner of a morning, despite its crazy-ass start—blue, cloudless sky, and with nary a hint of the humidity that defined this place the last few days.

Rounding the side of the house, Cinderella balled up tight under my arm, I catch sight of Adria through the porch screen. Alone, thank God, and stretched out on the hammock much as she was last night. I find the possibility that she, too, might have been too looped to actually make it to bed oddly cheering.

Draping Cindi over the clothesline for a much-needed airing, I drag myself up the steps—Adria smiling lazily as the screen door snicks shut behind me.

"I thought running a small bookstore would be easy," she says, dropping a pencil onto the stack of paperwork in her lap and raising her arms in a long, languid stretch. "You have no idea the work." She notes the missing shoe, eyes grazing mine as she raises her mug. "Fresh pot on the stove."

Look as bad as I feel, then. Terrific. This despite my having paused for a quick wash of both foot and face back in the meadow. And here she's giving off the relaxed vibe of the well-rested. Could it be I drank that entire bottle myself? Now there's a pleasant thought.

"Last night was a kick," I say, dropping into a rocker. "Please tell me I didn't make a pass."

"Would have been nice for my ego," she laughs, "but no."

I settle back, feel myself settling into the kind of stillness you get only when surrounded by absolute quiet. It's then I spy my missing shoe, cocked on its side beneath the hammock. Thank God. I mean, imagine the humiliation.

"Had a visitor this morning," I tell her, saddened that my new simpatico friend and I can't simply sit here and watch this beautiful day unfold instead of puzzling over some fucking loony tune.

The mug pauses on its way to her lips. "Oh Lord, please tell me it wasn't Brit."

"Pete," I say. "Who's totally fucking whacked by the way." With that I relay the gist of our conversation, including the weird conspiracy bit, and toss in news of Bambi's gruesome demise—the initial eight I gave Pete's involvement on the probability scale having nudged northward. I mean who else could it be? "Guy's paranoid as shit. Convinced himself you know what happened to his brother. Might even think you were in on it, for all I know. Wants answers or else."

"Me!" she snorts, rising. "Hey, if I killed some guy, no way I'd be stupid enough to let him just float away. I'd bury his ass way deep so nobody ever found him—chop him up first, maybe, like he did that poor little fawn. Boy, doesn't that burn my ass."

With that she heads for the kitchen, returning with a second steaming mug and, God bless her, a bottle of aspirin without that pesky childproof cap—good thing considering the amount of brain power I've got going just now.

"He's probably bluffing, but why take the chance?" I toss back three of the things, chug some coffee. "I'm thinking Duggan and I should stick around another day or two—you know, a show of force 'til you get him gone. Guy's a psycho."

"Psycho racist," she corrects.

"Redundant, don't you think? And you so into books, too."

She grins at this, and another memory slips to the surface—the two of us at opposite ends of the hammock 'til deep in the night, long after we'd polished off that bottle. Bits of conversation coming back to me only now—how Adria's family bought into the island years ago, her father's law partner offering him a fifty-percent stake back when Adria was just a baby.

Something else, too, about how glad she was to be getting rid of Pete because she'd finally twigged to why he was so familiar. I remember stowing it away in my liquor-soaked brain for later consideration. Whatever it was, it's gone now. See, this is why I try not to drink—well, not quite so much anyway. Leaves holes in the memory you could drive a tractor-trailer through.

"Anyway, I appreciate the offer," she tells me, "but we'll manage. You've no idea how many of these assholes we've had to deal with over the years, losers who can't make a go of it on the mainland, or survivalists who decide to live off the land—our land. Besides, Mama'd never let me forget it if some man had to pull my ass out of the fire."

Can't help but smile. Take-charge women are a turn-on; don't let any guy tell you different. Too bad she's into chicks, the Old Gil nudges—a wildly inappropriate thought that takes the rest of me by surprise. We're into chicks, too, I remind him. Think of her as a kind of man-chick. Way out of our comfort zone.

"Your mother spend much time out here" I ask to distract myself from all the cross-chatter.

"Once a season, maybe. The island was Dad's thing, really, not hers. Woman has a weakness for electricity, running water. Once he died, she lost interest in the place altogether. She's into the Boston scene—symphony, museums, art shows, all that. Does lunch every Wednesday at Copley Plaza with the girls. She'd happily sell out and be done with the place if she thought Drew and I would let her get away with it."

"Your brother."

She nods. "Budding lawyer and sole remaining Jackman male. Uses the place to thumb his nose at the honky world, I figure. Gets it from my father. Everything Daddy built up over the years, everything he earned for himself and for us, was hard won. That old black-man-in-a-white-man's-world thing—not that it's changed much. Didn't take shit from anyone; taught me to get down in the dirt if I have to in order to protect what's mine."

All of this calling to mind Pete's snarled comment about local reaction to their presence among the otherwise white populace. True, or simply more of his inane bullshit? So I ask.

"Oh, he's partly right, I suppose. Our owning the place bothers some. It was marginally okay when Daddy shared ownership with a white guy. Things changed when he bought John out about ten years back. There might've been trouble but for Burt Burdock, lobsterman friend of my father's over in Cundy's Harbor—big bear of a guy with a rifle he doesn't hesitate to use. Dad was out fishing in the skiff one morning, saw Burt getting tangled in his gear, and realized he was in trouble. By the time he reached him, Burt had been pulled overboard. He dove in, managed to cut him free. Burt was half-drowned by the time my father pulled him out, but he made it. They became great friends. He looks out for the place in the off-season now.

"But what that asshole Pete doesn't know is that we're hardly outsiders here. My family's been in this part of Maine since the 1600s."

I don't know why this should surprise me, but it does, and my confusion earns me a slow smile.

"You've heard of Malaga Island." It's not a question. "Not two miles from here. Small compared to Mistake—about forty acres."

"Rings a bell," I say, leafing through my mental arboreal index. Malaga, the Abenaki word for cedar. Then I remember its other connotation, that of Maine's dirty little secret, the one most people around here would prefer to keep under wraps—if they're white, anyway.

"Until 1912, there was what was rather euphemistically called a maroon society out there," Adria tells me. "Some blacks, some whites, some Indian, some mixed—a community started in the mid-1800s by the descendants of a freed slave named Benjamin Darling. Peaceful but dirt poor, maybe fifty people at its height. They were left pretty much alone 'til a couple towns on the mainland began eyeing the island for potential tourism, some kind of resort maybe, to bring in money and jobs.

"Rumors started that half of the people on Malaga were nuts, the other half just plain lazy. It got a reputation as a waterfront slum, which was bullshit. Problem is, they had no title to the island, though the outcome would have been the same in any case. People just wanted 'em gone, is all. Couple handshakes, a little back-slapping, and the Governor approved a kind of state-sponsored eviction.

"One day that July, the local sheriff and his thugs showed up, burned the houses, even dug up the graveyard—got rid of everything that even hinted blacks might have lived there. End of problem—for them anyway.

"Some on the island caught wind of what was going on and managed to get off; some were forcibly taken to what was then the Maine School for the Feeble-Minded in Pownal, even though there was nothing at all wrong with them. And the graves they dug up—the bones of who knows how many people? Thrown together in a few unmarked mass graves at that so-called school."

She looks off, her face a mask of regret. "My great grandmother, Liza Johnson, lost what was left of her family that day. Nine years old. Her mother had died the previous winter, was buried in that graveyard with her people—her father and brother taken down to Pownal. Both were dead within the year. Liza ran to the woods when the sheriff arrived, or she'd have been taken, too. A neighbor who was making his own way to a boat on the south side of the island just happened to find her. He took her in, ended up raising her. Her son, William Johnson Jackman, was my grandfather."

"I don't know what to say..."

She raises a hand to silence me. "She never got over it—well, how could she, you know? Drilled it into my grandfather 'til he was as trauma-tized as she was. He made sure we never forgot it, either—how easy it is to have everything you thought was yours taken away. When Drew and I were kids, Daddy and Mama used to take us to Pownal every summer to stare at that mass grave, tell us that story all over again. So when he got the chance to buy this island outright? Hell, yeah, he went for it. He saw it as a way to redeem the family honor. He'd have bought Malaga itself back, but the state wasn't selling. So Mistake it was, and this time the family would have an island no one could ever take away."

"Your dad's pal, this guy Burt, is he someone you can call in an emergency?"

"If I need to, which I don't. Not to mention we're a bit light on phones just now, in case you haven't heard. Margot's is lying out there under a bush somewhere, Nora's is dead, Brit's is missing—or more likely lost, knowing her—and Lily and I don't have ours. Well, technically."

"Technically?"

She shoots me a conspiratorial grin. "Just between you and me, I keep one in my sock drawer for emergencies. Solar-charged. Be stupid not to have one." She grins. "Don't tell the others. It'd ruin my image."

"Then let's call Burt; Duggan and I can hang out 'til he gets here. Pete's more deluded than dangerous, I think; still, a bunch of pretty women all alone in the woods? You make an easy target for someone with an ax to grind. Having a couple guys around as window dressing can't hurt."

She drills me with a look. "You're not listening, Hodge. I'll handle this my own way. Man claims this place is more his than mine? That Indian shit?" She shakes her head. "Ain't happenin'."

Never one to relinquish the whip when there's a dead horse to be flogged, I open my mouth for a final try, but Adria's clearly made up her mind.

"Enough. Go find your buddy and let's get you two on your way. See if the rest of us can salvage at least part of this week."

So much for simpatico.

I t's just after nine when I toss back another triplet of aspirin and—cap tugged low against the sun—slip on my shades, heft my pack, and make my way toward the dock behind the others. The sight of David and Lily—who are loathe to be parted now it's down to it—is bittersweet indeed, tripping my thoughts toward Nora, or maybe Rachel. Who the hell knows anymore.

The chicks are going on about some picnic they're planning for later in the day as my thoughts turn toward work and the deluge of Fall term minutia no doubt piling up in my campus mailbox. Something to throw myself into, thank God. Put the last few days behind me, chalk up all the longing and regret to the kind of hoodoo-voodoo shit my numerous unresolved issues unleash on me from time to time. Soon as I hit the mainland, though, I plan to visit Burt and that rifle of his, Adria's thoughts on the matter be damned—my parting salvo in the saga of Pete and Earl. I figure the guy can't be that hard to find.

"Where the hell are Nora and Brit?" Margot asks as we make the dock. "We said nine, right?"

"Nora's sleeping in," Adria says, climbing into the skiff as I casually scan the tree line for any sign of Pete's sneering countenance. "Brit never came home last night, far as I know."

Seating herself before the motor, she braces her feet on the floor of the boat and gives the starter cord an initial tug. Nothing. Gives it a couple more pulls, checks the gas, tries again. Chokes it. Keeps all this up 'til she's pretty well winded.

"How about I give it a go?" I offer.

"Doesn't like to start if it's been sitting a few days," she says, making room for me on the seat.

I put some elbow grease into a couple stiff pulls. Nothing.

"Try choking it again," Adria instructs, which I do, then give it another try. And again. Nada. Not so much as a spark. I pull off the engine cover.

My experience with outboards is admittedly paltry, limited as it is to the one on the Somerset Island skiff—a temperamental beast that burned through fuel faster than I go through scotch. It was a bitch to start, and almost impossible to bring to life if it rained. The first time I took it out alone—an ice run to Rock Island when I was twelve—I spent half an hour trying to restart it when it stalled in the middle of the bay. Sat there 'til a fisherman cruised by offering assistance. Turned over on the first pull.

I bring this up because, useless as I've proven myself to be when it comes to such things, even I can tell when a spark plug's missing. Leaves a hole.

"Spark plug's gone," I tell her. "See?"

"Gone?" she asks, peering into the motor. "How can it be gone?" She flicks a suspicious glance my way.

"Me? You can't be serious."

"There's a kit with extras and a socket wrench," she says, clearly unconvinced. "Blue plastic box with a flip lid stuck to the underside of the seat."

Reaching down, I feel around 'til I locate the metal bracket and release clip where said plastic box would normally snap in—only it, too, is gone.

"Not anymore," I say.

A brief inspection of the boat reveals that the oars are also missing, as is the handheld VHF radio. Adria sits back, momentarily flummoxed, stiffening as she glances to the opposite side of the float. "The kayaks," she whispers, nodding toward the spot where the three of them were last tethered together. No sign of them now.

A trickle of unease as I glance again toward the treeline where that clever fucker is no doubt watching. Crazy *and* clever—not good.

"There a problem?" Duggan asks, unwrapping himself from Lily. He grows still, his gaze joining mine as he catches my mood. Together we peer toward the woods, where everything appears deceptively serene.

We should get to the house, I'm thinking. Locate the others.

Like now.

My eyes find Adria's. "Time to dig out that cell phone, boss."

NORA

Confused, she stops to get her bearings, knowing she should have reached the switchback by now. Slipping the pack from her shoulder, she uncaps the water bottle and takes a long pull—her gaze traveling a shaft of sunlight striking deep from the leafy canopy above. Hard to tell the time— eleven, maybe?

Closing her eyes, Nora inhales the dank, earthy quiet and feels a bit better—the stillness soothing, the dread of being out here slowly losing its grip. It took every ounce of willpower she had to leave the house this morning—waiting 'til the others started for the dock to avoid the furtive looks, Adria's gentle probing. That first mile was an eternity of the sudden and unexpected: flashes of things that weren't really there, the silence—heavy and expectant—feeding her anxiety. Ridiculous, irrational fears. Getting past them is all that matters now. Never mind there could be strangers wandering the island; there almost had to be for this to work. David and Hodge would be gone by now, anyway. She tries not to think about Pete or the predatory gaze he fixed on her that first night—focusing instead on yesterday's heart-to-heart with Margot, their long overdue clearing of the air. And Margot was right; Nora knows this now. Forcing herself out of her comfort zone, making herself come out here alone, may well be the only way to get her confidence back.

So she'd risen this morning with something that felt almost like hope, or what she remembered of it, anyway—wondering if the thing that really brought her back to the island this summer wasn't Margot's relentless browbeating, but the memory of how good things had been between Wally and herself those first few years together. And how desperately she wanted it all back. Afraid that if she didn't make herself do it—if she chickened out—she'd lose him for good.

Another long pull of water and she tucks the bottle away, hefts her pack. She hoofs it another hundred yards, hoping something will look familiar—stops, turns, glances back down the trail. No, this definitely isn't right. She should be heading uphill at this point; instead she's dipping deeper into the glen toward a field of ferns she's not seen before. Still, she remembers coming through here with the others, at least she thinks she does—Adria griping about all the blow-down from the spring storms, pointing out the trickiest turns, newly marked with the deadfall. Only there's no sign of the tree trunks she remembers seeing.

"Shit," she hisses, pissed at herself for missing the turn God only knows how far back. Turning, resigned to retracing her steps, she rears back, startled.

There, before her on the trail, stands Pete.

He considers, then snaps his fingers like he's just placed her. "Nora, right?"

His tone is casual, but there's nothing warm in that gaze. And what's that he's carrying—a crossbow? Jesus.

"Wanted to talk to you the other night, but you disappeared on me."

She takes in the dirty jeans and tee shirt, the hunting knife sheathed at his waist, and almost loses it to a sudden flare of panic.

"Hey, relax," he chuckles, palms out as if pushing off her fear. "You know who I am, right?"

She manages a weak nod.

"You look lost." He sighs, glancing around. "Confusing place with all them trees down; no clear trail. Bothers me when things aren't clear, you know?"

"You shouldn't even be here."

"And I'll be gone soon as I get some answers."

"I can't help you. I don't know anything about your brother." She backs up a few steps, glancing left, then right, for some means of escape.

"Well now, see, I think you do. The look you gave that blonde the night I first come to the house? Like you seen a ghost."

She can hardly get her breath, her heart is pounding so. Full-blown anxiety attack.

Pete offers his profile. "Look a lot alike, don't we? Earl and me. Had a beard when you saw him, too, I'll bet." He leans toward her then as if to confide. "He found out, right? That it? That's why you killed him?"

She stares at him, dumbfounded. "I have to go," she says, moving to pass him.

Grinning, he steps across the path, blocking her.

GIL

"Well, finally!" I call, as if I'd been looking for her for hours—masking my relief with one of Duggan's repertoire of amiably befuddled grins.

Nora whirls as I come at them through the waist-high ferns—pack clutched protectively to her chest, those doe-eyes wide with fear or stress. Probably both. Standing before her, the worn leather strap of a small but serious-looking crossbow slung across his chest, is Pete. Christ, who does this guy think he is—William Tell?

Thank God I heard their voices, too, otherwise I'd have stuck to the trail in my panic to find her—the note she left about going hiking freaking us all out considering how bughouse this guy's turning out to be.

"Found some mushrooms for that sauce of yours," I chirp, pointing to the small canvas bag tucked at my waist. Nothing in there but a few trail-marking tools, of course; still, no way this asshole could know that.

I continue high-stepping toward them. "True morels, too, which is fucking amazing. Speaking of which, these things dry out pretty fast; we should probably head back."

"Take a hike," Pete growls. "We got business."

"No shit?" I remove my sunglasses, hook them into the neck of my shirt. "More questions about the dead brother, would be my guess. I've got a new theory about that, by the way. It was the shrooms made me think of it—hundreds of varieties out here, a lot of them so poisonous they'd drop you in your tracks before you knew what hit you."

Pete shifts, and I catch the glint of a honkin' knife clipped to his belt. Bambi's blood still on it, too, I'll bet.

"I gotta say it again?" he growls. "Get lost."

"Funny thing about mushrooms," I say breezily, though that old fight-or-flight thing's kicking in—the adrenaline shooting through me breathing new life into my killer hangover. "They're nature's main recyclers, decomposing dead vegetation to feed new growth, but you gotta know what you're looking for. You know what they say. *If it ain't hollow, don't swallow.*" I grin like some frat boy tossing out a gross one-liner to his beered-up buddies. "Which brings me to my theory. Before the poison kills you, see, it makes you really thirsty. So, say Earl runs out of potato chips or whatever and scarfs down a handful of these things. What's he gonna do but head for the freshwater pools dotting the cliffs, right? Only by now the poison's started kicking in and he blacks out, falls, and—well." Sounds reasonable enough, I figure. Almost fools me.

Confusion's fast replacing fear as Nora's primary emotion.

"You were supposed to leave," she says, clearly oblivious to my little maneuver with the shrooms. Still, it got me up here beside these two, which was the point.

"Sorry to disappoint. Seems something's wrong with the boat." I eye Pete. "You wouldn't have a spare spark plug on you by any chance? VHF radio, maybe? No?"

There follows the usual male sniff and piss program—Pete figuring how best to get rid of me while I'm sizing him up for a good kick to the nuts, should it come to that. Just might land one anyway, I'm that irritated right now. Shithead had to know I'd come looking for him once we realized what he'd done, but it seems he's got other things on his mind. The guy might be a lunatic, but he's a lunatic with a cause.

"You're lying," he snarls at Nora. "You were here; you saw him. All I want's the truth; then I'm gone—simple as that."

Nora's trying for strong, but she's trembling with the effort, her face pinched and pale. I try to ignore the little flip my heart does at this, putting it away as something to be examined later.

"You wouldn't know the truth if it crawled up your ass," I snap, and snagging Nora's arm, peel her away through the ferns, leaving Pete to stare in our wake—his glare a hot beam drilling my shoulder blades.

"Have you seen Brit?" I ask once we're out of earshot.

"No. And let go of me," she demands, almost tripping over a snarl of roots as she shakes me off.

I grab her more roughly this time, glancing behind us for signs of Pete as I pull her uphill through the brush. Fuck the path; this is faster. "Okay, then, what are her favorite spots—hiking, swimming—like that?"

"What's this about?" She ducks to avoid a thorny branch. "This isn't even a trail, you know."

"Trails are for wimps. Keep moving; we need to get back to the house."

"Why?" she demands. "What's happened? And stop dragging me around. You're hurting me."

Fine. Good, actually. I feel like hurting something right about now. "Dumb-ass back there? Guy's majorly, fucking whacked—I mean in case you hadn't noticed."

With that, and for the second time today, I relay what went down during our early morning tête-à-tête, tacking on the little matter of the sabotaged boat—all the while watching the woods for any sign that Pete's following us. The fact I don't see him means nothing, of course; this nut could be anywhere.

"What?" I ask as she screws those lovely features into some complicated stew of emotions—none of them good. "Tell me."

"It's nothing," she snaps, looking off.

We've made the summit by this time—the glorious view I saw that first afternoon suddenly back in place—and I swing her around to face me. "No, see, that checking-out thing you pull when you feel freaked? You don't get to do that now. This guy's serious; he's devious. Add crazy to the mix and we've got ourselves a real problem. If you know anything about this mess, I need to know now."

Her eyes are blazing, stress rolling off her in waves as she shakes herself free a final time. "I hardly needed rescuing back there, just so you know. Everything would've been fine if you hadn't come barreling in."

"Right," I laugh. "You're telling me you weren't scared? Anymore than usual, I mean."

She opens her mouth to make some crack and I'm shocked to find I'm about to kiss her—a feeling so seismic I couldn't stop it if I tried. If I felt fifteen around her yesterday, today I must be twelve, 'cause my mouth's gone stone-dry, my heart leapfrogging in my throat.

What's worse, she gets it—eyes widening slightly as she twigs to my distress.

It's then the shouting reaches us, the keening—short, hysterical bursts followed by wails of utter heartbreak.

The shouting continues, peppered with sobs, as I tear into the meadow—Nora close on my heels. I pick out one of the carts lying on its side by a shed set maybe thirty feet off the trail beneath a tight copse of pines—two water jugs akimbo in the grass beside it—and I pump hard in that direction. Flying around the building's corner, I all but run into Lily by the open door, sobbing helplessly into her hands. I'm thinking maybe something's happened to the dog 'til I spot the pooch trotting down the path from the house behind Margot, who's in a panicked run toward whatever's got Lily so beside herself.

I'm bent at the waist, sucking in mouthfuls of sun-scorched air and bugs, when a shaken, gray-faced Adria exits the doorway—all but collapsing against its frame.

"What is it?" I croak.

The eyes she turns on me are hollow with shock. "Brit." It's all she can manage, and even that's barely a breath.

Whatever this is, it ain't good. My heart rate, already off the charts, jacks even higher as I glance from the door to Adria and back again—only vaguely aware that Margot and Nora have joined our sorry little group. I really, really don't want to go in there, but the four of them have that look women get if a guy's standing around when a nasty job presents itself.

It's decidedly dim as I step inside—the air heavy with machine oil and the same moldy smell that seems to permeate everything out here. My eyes are still adjusting when I spot Brit on her back atop a long work table, looking like she's just hopped up there for a nap, arms and legs straight at her sides, face turned to the ceiling. Only I know dead people when I see them, and there's no question she's joined their number.

Fuck me, I think. It's Matinicus all over again.

I give it a beat, then another, waiting for the thunderbolt of memory to recede, land me back solidly in the here-and-now. I manage a slow exhale of a breath I didn't realize I was holding as my gaze travels the room—ten by fifteen, maybe—and filled with the kinds of things you'd expect: a small riding lawn mower, a couple gas cans, all manner of shears and rakes and shovels hanging along the walls. A line of propane cylinders in the corner. I give it all a quick once-over before stepping to the table—Adria and Margot taking up positions on either side of me.

There's little odor of decay—not yet anyway—and no obvious sign as to how or why Brit died.

"Who found her?" I ask.

Adria shifts beside me. "I did. I came out for more propane."

"Jesus," Margot breathes, gazing down at Brit, whose eyes are open, her gaze empty—the skin beneath last night's shorts and tank top gone the bluish-purple of recent death. This close to the table there's a slight pissy smell from when her bladder let go, but neither Margot nor Adria seem to notice. No blood, thank Christ, so she wasn't beaten to death or shot, or— as in the case of one Matinican—rather gruesomely crushed by a car—all clearly unnatural deaths in anyone's book. But this?

"Alcohol poisoning?" I wonder aloud.

Adria considers. "She might have kept drinking after she and Pete left last night."

Margot snorts. "You think?"

"She's off cocaine, right, Lil?" Adria asks, glancing over her shoulder to where Nora and Lily stand mute in the doorway, arms linked in mutual support.

"Far as I know." Lily's voice is thick with tears. "Smokes a little pot once in a while, is all." She edges forward, reaching out a tentative hand before thinking better of it. "My God, Brit," she breathes. "What have you done?"

I suppose it's conceivable Brit drank herself into oblivion—certainly fits that wild child persona—but it doesn't feel right somehow. Besides, yoga diva or no, it's hard to imagine she could manage to crawl onto a table set as high off the ground as this if she were that shitfaced. The floor is far more manageable at such times. Believe me, I know.

I suggest we leave her where she is 'til we can get someone out here to deal with all this. The shed, being shut up and little-used, is relatively cool, and will keep the wildlife at bay while we figure a way to get her body off the island. No need to mention what this place is gonna smell like by this time tomorrow.

"Can't we at least cover her with something?" Lily whispers.

Seems reasonable, so I rummage a bit, eventually unearthing a faded blue tarp from a wooden crate, which I shake free of about ten years' worth of spider webs, mouse turds, and dust. It's when I'm reaching across Brit to cover her, that I first see the marks—the bruising on her throat unmistakable this close up.

"Little problem," I say, pointing to Brit's neck. "Bruises, see? Strangled would be my guess." Post-mortem bruising—a concept I've learned far more than I care to know about—is a pretty good indicator of time of death, and Brit's tells me she was killed sometime late last night. Dawn, maybe, but not much later. Then set here on the table, to taunt us perhaps.

"Strangled?" Lily's voice is hushed, disbelieving. "But who..."

"Everyone here sleep at the house last night?" I ask. "I mean other than..." Tipping my head toward the table.

Adria whirls. "You think *we* had something to do with this?"

If only. Dealing with a pint-sized chick I could sling over a shoulder without so much as breaking stride would pose far fewer challenges than the alternative of a stone-cold ex-con carrying around a grudge the size of Texas.

"I was thinking more about anything you might have seen," I say. "Or anyone. It would have been late."

Margot pulls her gaze from Brit to glare at me. "*Or anyone?* Are you kidding? It was that slimy new boyfriend of hers—has to be."

"Dark energy there," Lily tells us. "I felt it right away."

Adria shakes her head. "But why? He seemed to like her. It doesn't make any sense."

True. Seems a stretch even for this slimeball. Jacking a deer is one thing; murdering a woman quite another. Though what was it he said to me in the meadow? Something about having already set things in motion?

"This is all about the brother," I tell them. No question.

"So he kills Brit?" Margot hisses. "That's insane."

Guy's probably right outside, too, I think, getting off on our reaction. A sudden bloom of panic as I realize there's one person who's not yet made an appearance at our little party.

"Where's Duggan?" I snap toward the doorway where Nora, deathly pale, jumps at the sound of my voice. Clearly there's been no stumbling over dead bodies in this chick's resume.

"Said he was going for a swim," Lily says. "Salt Marsh Cove."

"Right," I say, picturing him contentedly slack-jawed and oh-so-vulnerable as he suns himself on one of the long flat rocks at the water's edge. His abysmal condition aside, the man's simply unequipped psychologically to defend himself against any kind of physical assault—his omnipresent pocket Shakespeare the only weapon he could conceivably whip out if attacked.

"Okay," I say, glancing toward Brit a final time as I shoo them toward the door. "Everyone back to the house. Stay together, locked in, 'til we figure this thing out. I'm going for Duggan."

"Yeah, well, plenty of locks," Adria says as I pull the door shut behind us. "Problem is keys. The one to the main house was lost years ago."

Of course it was. It's then I remember Adria striding purposely in that direction after we'd found the scuttled boat to dig out that emergency cell phone of hers—this as I was heading off on my own panicked search for Nora and Brit. Brit—Christ.

"You reach your buddy, Burt?" I ask. "Time to call in the police or Coasties, too—whoever the hell has jurisdiction on these islands." Get them out here with those reassuring Beretta M9s or Sig Sauers, I'm thinking—whatever it is they're strapped with these days.

She shakes her head. "Phone's missing. And, no, I didn't lose it. Like I told you, I keep it hidden, pull it out once in a while to up the solar charge."

Just like Brit's cell. Not good.

The two of us have dropped behind as if by mutual consent—my gaze scanning the trees for any sign of Pete as Lily and Margot dip beneath the pines, arms linked in mutual comfort; Nora, a few paces behind, hugging herself against the realization of this ugly new reality.

"I can't believe this is happening." Adria's trying like hell to keep it together, but I can hear the tears in her voice. "Shit."

"Who else knew where it was?"

"No one even knows I have it." She shoots me a quick, apologetic glance. "That's not completely true. I had to get Burt out here to work on the outboard two summers ago. It was a few days before Island Women started." A pause. "Brit came a couple days early to help out. She might have been with me when I went for the phone; I can't remember."

I have a hard time with the idea of coincidence, and more than one at a time pretty much negates the concept altogether for me. Brit knew where the phone was. Brit was hanging with Pete. The phone's gone.

Doesn't take a genius.

I t's sometime after ten when I drag my weary ass to the porch, having designated myself defender of hearth and home. The candles have burned low in the inky darkness, so it takes me a minute to notice Nora curled into a corner of the hammock—knees tucked to her chin as she stares out toward the stark outlines of the unknown.

"It's not safe out here," I remind her in rather snappish fashion—being, as I am, at the tail end of a day-long adrenaline jag that's left me antsy and pissed off. Not to mention I'm still pretty steamed about what happened back there on the mountain—her less-than-forthcoming attitude, maybe, or that aborted kiss, who the hell knows—so I could give a rat's ass what she thinks.

"And yet here you are," she says, not looking my way.

"I'm on watch," I remind her, dropping into an armchair.

She swings her head and eyes first me, then the ancient rifle I've propped against the wall beside me.

"You think he's coming, then." Her gaze is steady, deceptively cool, but relaxed this woman is not. Beneath the loose cotton pants and baggy tee, the sweater draped casually over her shoulders, she's rigid with tension. "You'll shoot him if it comes to that?"

I nod, which seems enough for her. "Good," she says, swinging her gaze back toward the screen.

"But unfortunately not with this thing. Probably been around since the Indian wars—kind of a musket, I think. Doubt it'd even fire. More of a deterrent, really, in case he decides to surprise us in the night."

It was Adria who dug up the gun. I was in the kitchen polishing off the dinner dishes when she found me, looking for answers I didn't have.

"Thanks for making supper," she said, settling against the counter as I shook a plate free of water, slid it into the dish rack. "And for keeping everyone together the way you did—bucking us up like that. I doubt any of us could have managed it tonight."

109

I needn't have bothered. The chicks had haunted the kitchen looking shell-shocked while Duggan and I went through the motions—throwing omelets together, broiling bread for toast, and generally flitting about as if eating were the answer to all our problems. Never have I sat through a meal as grim. Lily, eyes swollen almost shut from crying, nestled her head deep in Duggan's shoulder while he and I hammered out the semblance of a plan we hoped would keep us all safe through the night—everyone else sitting silent, their faces stunned with grief. We had no idea why Brit was murdered, I reminded them, and until we knew exactly what was going on, we'd stay hunkered down here at the house. Lily and Duggan's little cottage was officially off limits, I announced, as were the porches—sleeping or otherwise. Outhouse, too. We'd use the chamber pots 'til further notice, with either Duggan or I handling the disposal.

No one had the energy to argue.

In the end, Margot gave her room up to Lily and David, announcing she'd bunk with Adria. I'd alternate between dozing in one of the chairs and checking the porch, I told them, in case Pete was skulking around outside—waking David sometime after midnight to relieve me. The real planning would come in the morning, when everyone was fresh—as if any of us would actually get any sleep. And that's how we left it.

Adria grabbed a dishtowel, snagged a dripping plate—careful to keep her eyes from mine. "We're in deep shit, aren't we?"

"We are that." I rinsed the final dish, slid it into the rack. "We've got to be smarter, more careful, 'til we find some way to get out of here. Lily's little shindig this evening, for instance—singing to the heavens and all that…"

"Singing the ajaajaas."

"Whatever." An Inuit service for Brit that Lily was adamant be held outside the tool shed—something about greeting Anguta, gatherer of the dead, as he arrived to carry Brit to the underground. It was a stunningly stupid idea I vetoed hands down. Too out in the open. The gods would just have to join us on the porch, I announced, where we'd have at least some semblance of cover. "Way I see it, Pete sabotaged the boat, then waited 'til we left for the dock before sneaking in and grabbing your cell. Probably took Brit's earlier."

She shook her head. "No way he could have known where it was."

"Hell, Adria, the guy probably goes through this place all the time; gets his kicks filching whatever's lying around, pawing through your undies. But my money's on Brit as snitch. Point's moot anyway. The boat's all but useless, the last phone is gone and no one leaves the island 'til this nutjob gets what he wants." I sighed, turned to face her. "You know anything more about what happened two years ago, now would be the time to tell me."

"There's nothing. You have to believe me. He's just wrong. You've got to find a way to convince him, negotiate something."

I snorted a laugh. "I'd say negotiations are over, wouldn't you? Besides, he wants information we don't have, which leaves us zip to bargain with." I considered her. "Job right now is to tighten this place up best we can." Moving to the door, I crouched to check out what proved to be a pretty heavy-duty sliding bolt setup. All the metal parts were there—the screwed-in bits, anyway. Just one problem.

"Throw bolt's gone," I told her.

"Years ago."

Swell.

A search of the utility drawer yielded nothing that wouldn't snap immediately should Pete decide to bust the door in. The hickory-handled paring knife I spied in the dish drainer probably stood the best chance—hickory being the preferred wood for baseball bats early on, it's that strong.

I slid the knife in place, glanced around for inspiration. What we needed now was some sort of ad-hoc alarm system, something so massive that if toppled would be sure to wake the house. My gaze fell on the four heavy wooden chairs ringing the kitchen table. Now those suckers would make some noise.

I dragged two of them over, cocked one beneath the door handle, slammed the other up against it. "Grab the other two?" I asked her.

Rope. I needed rope. Lash these two against the door, wedge the others between them and the fridge. That would at least slow him down 'til I got my ass back in here. And then what? Beat him to death with my personality?

"You have any weapons?"

"Good Lord, no," she laughed. "Carving knife, maybe."

Yeah, well, I've seen those knives. "You sure? Something your father kept around to fend off the bears, maybe?"

It's then I spied the tangle of clothesline—part of a hodge-podge of flyswatters, batteries, and bug dope piled on top of the fridge.

"He used to keep an old rifle above the fireplace when I was a kid, but I haven't seen it in years."

I'm no expert in the knot-tying department, but I managed to secure the chairs using what Dad used to call the Shadoofer knot—a string of shitty little grannies tied one atop the other 'til it's virtually impossible to untangle the mess.

I nodded toward my spider web-meets-Lincoln Logs construction. "Not pretty, I know, but he'll make a helluva racket if he tries to get in this way. Only other way's through the porch. And that's where I'll be." I shoot her a sideways glance. "How about we go look for that rifle?"

I'm stewing about all this when Nora's voice jolts me back to the present. "You really believe all that stuff you and David were talking about the other night? About trees experiencing everything that happens around them? Silent witness, you said."

I was hoping for something more along the lines of *Gee, Hodge—thanks for pulling my ass out of the fire back there in the woods.* Some hint of regret in those eyes at not going for that kiss on the mountain, maybe. But no.

"Who's to say?" This as I peer over the arm of the chair, skimming the floor for the source of a whiffy odor that seems to come and go. Can't be food, I reason; the dog's mined this place a thousand times over. Wet socks or a dead mouse maybe. "Some species live thousands of years," I tell her. "Literally. There's a cluster of Norway spruce in the mountains of western Sweden that are over nine thousand years old. Hard to imagine all they've seen."

"You think they absorb feelings, then. Emotions." Her look an odd mix of hope and derision.

I get this kind of crap all the time—condescension, disbelief that a man of science could put any stock in this kind of nonsense, the bluster almost always an attempt to hide a secret desire to believe in such transcendent mysteries. Doesn't usually bother me, but tonight? Coming from her? Well.

The moon, just now rising above the trees, sinks a sudden bright shaft deep into the room, illuminating Nora's long, creamy-looking toes, bare now but for that silver toe ring—a small stab of desire stirring the resentment that's been building since that aborted kiss. Around us, the house has grown deeply silent, heavy with the pall of fitful sleep.

"I'm sure Lily would tell you they do," I say, feeling her eyes on me as I rise to pinch out the few remaining candles. Moonlight's bad enough, I figure; no reason to make it any easier for this asshole than we have to. Plus, it's a lot harder to fall asleep standing up. "Or Adria with her shtick about how the island changes everyone. Some mystical thing where the past rises up to nip you in the ass. Strongest memories, deepest desires, all somehow tied to the peaceful vibe of the place. Guess it's gone now."

Nora's chuckle is bitter, her right foot starting a nervous tap, tap, tap against the sill of the long screen window—that toe ring winking in the moonlight.

"Where I grew up, peaceful is just another word for comatose." She shoots me a quick, assessing glance, probably wondering how much to reveal. "Florida. Little town on the St. John River." She swings her gaze back toward the yard. "Four beauty parlors, five churches, miles of Spanish moss that would fall from the trees, roll across the road in drifts, like sea foam."

"Air plant," I tell her, squeezing the bridge of my nose against another wave of fatigue. "Related to the pineapple, believe it or not." Been years since I felt this tired—the shock, I figure. Hard to believe it was only this morning I woke to Pete's ugly mug hanging over me in the meadow.

"I had a friend who lived on a pineapple farm," she tells the screen. "Lot of them in that part of Florida."

"I fell in love in Florida once. Lasted a day and a half, as I remember."

"That long?"

"Sort of set the tone."

A dismissive shake of the head. "So you've never been married. Why aren't I surprised?"

"My parents spent almost forty years together, rarely a night apart. Tough act to follow, so why try, you know? And yeah, I keep my world simple, mostly because I don't have the juice to go the distance. I'm more of a relationship sprinter. Lots of early enthusiasm, then the interest just peters out."

"You obviously don't understand women."

I want to. I try. I've had glimpses. "I'm a shallow prick," I agree. "Ask any…" My reply cut off by the snap of a branch from somewhere close by. A furtive rustling just beyond the tree line brings another.

Padding back to the chair, I take up my useless pseudo-rifle and slip toward the screen door in a half-crouch, angling myself along the narrow bit of wall between frame and window. This thing'll make a honkin' club, should Pete be stupid enough to try and rush the place; I could probably break both his legs in one swing, assuming I can get close enough. Otherwise I've got zero chance against this guy; I know this. I mean I get into it when I absolutely have to, which is where the Tai Kwon Do comes in, but only in bad movies do the martial arts outfox the kind of weaponry this guy totes around. Christ, he could have fucking poison darts, for all I know.

Nora's eyes meet mine in a wide-eyed plea. Mixed in with the naked fear, the unexpected vulnerability, is some kind of complicated question I'm struggling to get a handle on when an enormous porcupine straight out of a Disney flick waddles out of the dense foliage into the clearing—turning his snout briefly toward the moon before heading around the side of the house in search of the rest of the woodland cast.

Slumping against that minimal stretch of wall, I will my heart back to something approaching its normal rhythm and try making light. "You were saying?"

"You were, actually. Something about being a shallow prick." And just like that, Defensive Nora's back, replacing Nakedly Vulnerable Nora in the personality lineup. Damn shame, too.

"A shallow prick who's never been married," I correct. Christ, what *is* that smell?

Giving my right pit a furtive sniff, I about pass out at the eau de fear and boozy sweat. Didn't the Zappa get a wash just yesterday? I run a hand over three days' worth of stubble, try and remember the last time I spritzed at the well, and realize I don't give a shit.

"We were happy once," Nora murmurs wistfully into the silence. "Seems like a lifetime ago."

Huh? Oh, yeah—the husband, the stale marriage.

"Another case of love gone bad," I quip, my mind tumbling toward Rachel and all that might have been, leaving me choked with a longing so sudden, so intense, it literally takes my breath.

"Love's got nothing to do with it," Nora snaps. "*Wally's* got nothing to do with it."

Man, I hate it when they give me the guy's name. Up 'til then he doesn't really exist for me, making possible all manner of delightful, albeit inappropriate fantasies. No doubt I should leave all this alone, but the dark uglies are on me now, so I let fly.

"We're gonna change the subject," I tell her—the sudden urge to goad like an itch I can't quite reach. "Something more immediate, like whatever the hell was going on between you and that psychopath back there in the woods. Talk about a deer in the headlights."

"He took me by surprise, is all. Scared me." Her gaze flicks my way. "You've heard him; he thinks we're all lying."

"Are you? All lying?"

"Now you sound like him," she snaps, pulling her sweater tighter. "And no, I didn't kill anyone. But then I'm sure Brit told him the same thing."

"How well did you know her? Brit?"

She turns away, good and steamed now she's the one being grilled. Fine with me. Nothing like company when you're in this kind of first-rate snit.

"Adria thinks Pete's the one who lifted this hidden cell phone she had," I tell her. "Probably after Brit told him where it was." Bit of a stretch, but what the hell? "Which has me wondering what else she might have told him and why. Thus my question. How well did you know Brit?"

Nothing.

"Was she pissed at all of you for some reason? Enough that she'd do something this two-faced to get back at you?"

"*If* she knew about the phone, and *if* she told him, it wouldn't have had anything to do with us. Look, Brit's relationships were spontaneous to the point of recklessness—well, obviously. But she wouldn't do anything to put the rest of us in danger, not on purpose. She was probably just trying to impress him. It was all about the moment with her."

"All right," I concede, "so could she have known something about what happened two years ago and not know she knew? Something innocuous enough on its surface, say, and she let it slip?"

"How the hell should I know?"

"She could have told him all kinds of things, for that matter—willingly or unwillingly," I say, running with it. "And once he realized he'd gotten everything he could out of her, he made sure she couldn't tip any of you off."

I think for a minute, struggling to hang on to what's left of my mental focus. Has to be more to it than this. It takes real rage to strangle a woman, literally squeeze the life from her. Rage and determination. Plus, the way he laid her out like that was just plain weird, creepy-weird, like a take-off on some kids' fairytale—absurd and darkly comedic. Sleeping Beauty or Cinderella—one of those. Which trips me back to the sleeping bag from the meadow, Pete's look of utter disdain as he took it in. The lunacy of the whole thing twisting my face into a kind of ill-tempered smirk.

Nora eyes me sharply. "His killing her like that is somehow funny to you?"

I run a hand over my face as an unintended snicker escapes. Because this whole thing is, really—funny as shit, you ask me. I mean here I am, stranded on an island with a bunch of women who never wanted me here in the first place, bent on defending them against some armed-to-the-teeth ex-con I didn't know from Adam just three days ago—with nothing more than a broken rifle and a bad case of body odor. Fucking hilarious.

I fight another laugh that unfortunately has nowhere to go but out my nose. Then snort another. The more I try and hold it in, the worse it gets. And then I just lose it. I get to laughing so hard I don't make a sound, mostly 'cause I can't catch my breath. It's all I can do to throw myself back against the cushion, helpless against the tears streaming down my face.

Nora's on her feet by this time. I hold up a hand as she strides angrily past—outraged, no doubt, by my freakish behavior. And rightly so. Stop, I want to plead—wait, but I'm laughing so hard I can't get the words out. Even in the moonlight I can see the red of her face, the tears welling in her eyes. Fuck.

Suddenly I'm alone in the moonlight, any possibility of getting to know the real Nora fast receding from my flimsy grasp. Yet another in a long line of missed chances. The realization sobers me fast, and I get a quick, rather grim glimpse of my future self in the psychic mirror: lonely, more than a little arrogant, desperate for connection. The truth of it comes like a slap. I don't want to be that man—not now, not ever.

I'm up like a shot, then, all weariness forgotten as I trail her down the hall—nothing on my mind but reclaiming that one chance for connection, if it even exists.

"Nora, wait." I reach out, grab an arm, swing her to face me. "I'm sorry. Listen…"

Suddenly my fingers find her hair, my lips those tears. She wafts faintly of the citrus aroma that's hers alone; the kiss she returns with an almost violent passion when our lips finally meet tastes faintly of the eggs I made for supper.

This means nothing, I tell myself as we back our way toward her bedroom door, push our way into the darkness. Means nothing to her and thus even less to you, I lie as I yank her tee shirt over her head, peel off her dark tank top. Small tight breasts, no bra, her nipples dark and rigid, salty sweet.

Her body's firm, almost taut—all angles and sinew. She's quiet, no soft groans of pleasure escaping as I explore this new terrain. Confusing, all this reticence, after that kiss.

I draw back, try and read her face in the dark. "You don't want this?"

She doesn't speak, but instead rises up to kiss me hard, almost angrily, before pulling me down onto her.

Thursday

I'm pounding up this long run of granite steps—the kind you'd find outside a big city courthouse or museum, maybe—my eyes on a group of kids, five or six years old, milling at the top. It's then I spot him—a small, naked black boy even younger than the others—and sporting my missing Ray Bans, the little fucker. He's parked his skinny ass maybe ten steps from the top, and sits staring into a brown paper bag balanced on his knees. Crying softly, too, I see, as is the woman who's suddenly appeared at his side. A dead ringer for Annika, arguably the craziest of my whacko ex-lovers, though I'm strangely unfazed by this.

Next thing I know, I've taken her place beside him, peering down into that bag. At first I think the wet-looking smudge at the bottom is a squashed blueberry, 'til I realize it's actually a miniscule puppy shot through the heart with a bitty arrow. The kid is inconsolable.

I gaze at his face—Adria's in miniature, I realize—as he explains how it's all his fault 'cause there are two gay guys in the next room. The tail end of his comment all but drowned out by the heavy thunk of something metal that someone's just dropped at our feet.

Which is what jolts me awake.

My frantic fight toward consciousness blooms with increasing awareness, the sudden certainty that Pete's hanging over me with that crossbow of his—the pain from the arrow he's just shot into my foot not yet having reached my brain. I cock an eye, glance down. No holes, no blood; just that worthless rifle having slid from lap to floor.

It's maybe seven o'clock, based on the way the sun's crawling up the tree line—the sky impossibly blue, the air so piney fresh I could almost convince myself yesterday never happened. Almost. But there's a dead chick growing ripe in the tool shed, and the guy who put her there is still out wandering the woods, no doubt getting ready for another day of grisly fun.

Shaking off the dregs of my dream—a bizzarro one even by my standards—and drawn by the aroma of coffee, the murmur of conversation, I unwind myself from the chair feeling stiff but oddly happy, and, yeah, a little sheepish. Some guard I turned out to be, slipping away from my post for a few sweet hours with Nora before dropping off deliciously spent. Wanting nothing more as I pad barefoot toward the kitchen, my gaze skimming her closed bedroom door, than to dive back between those sheets, steal a few more minutes of joy before the start of what is certain to be another truly sucky day.

Rounding the corner, I find Adria, Lily, and Nordic chick deep into something—Gus at their feet lapping noisily from his bowl.

"About time," Margot snaps at me. "So what's your plan? You do have one, right? I mean other than…" Gesturing dismissively toward my burglar-foiling set up—the Rube Goldberg-like rope system that last night snugged door to chairs to fridge having gone slack overnight.

"Thought I'd have coffee, some breakfast. You guys eaten?" Sounding all casual as I snag a spoon, pull a cereal bowl from the shelf.

"We can't just sit here," she informs me. "This could drag on for days, with that asshole waiting out there to pick us off one by one."

I'm too caffeine-deprived to deal with this kind of assault—those hours in Nora's bed having reduced my usual mental acuity to mere puddled sludge—so I fall back on the ignore-her-and-she'll-go-away strategy I've spent a lifetime fine-tuning. Instead I turn to Lily.

"Duggan up?" I ask as Adria pours me a cup of coffee, hands it off.

"Getting dressed." Lily's eyes aren't quite as swollen this morning, but her face is just as troubled. "Thanks for not waking him last night. We talked 'til probably two. He's reeling, though he'd never say so. It's just too soon after Matt."

I nod. My thought exactly. Two bizarre deaths back to back is more than anyone should have to handle. Giving him last night to hash things over with Lily was the least I could do.

"Come on, Hodge," Margot pushes, determined to verbalize us out of this mess. "Six against one. I say we lure him into the open, beat him to a bloody pulp."

"Just stumble on him in two hundred acres of deep woods, huh?" I eye the shelves for cereal, pull down a half-gone box of Wheaties. Breakfast of champions. We better fucking hope so. "And say we somehow manage to find him, he's the one with all the weapons, remember? Makes more sense to force him to come to us; gives us some semblance of control, at least."

"Hodge is right," Adria says as I pad to the fridge for milk, fight the flaccid rope contraption only to find there's none left. "Last thing we want is to lose somebody else to all this."

"My guess?" I say, surreptitiously eyeballing the hallway for any sign of

Nora. "He's giving us time to think things over, wants us good and scared when he shows up to grill us about the brother again."

"The house changes hands on Saturday, right?" Lily says, brightening. "When the boats aren't there for the new renters, they'll call Burt and he'll come out and check. We just have to make it 'til then."

"Only no one's rented the house next week," Adria says, pushing off from the counter. "Or the week after. Rustic vacations are out, it seems; luxury in. Things like electricity, running water, toilets. Imagine."

I like Adria; I do. She's got a gritty dignity about her, what Dad used to call a spine of steel. Someone you can count on in a pinch.

"Well, there's got be another way off the island," Margot says. "We're smart women; we can figure this out."

"You could try swimming," I tell her—topping off first my mug, then Adria's, "but I doubt even you could make it three miles. And from what I've heard, drowning as your body shuts down from hypothermia's not a particularly fun way to go." A bit cavalier, I know, but you try leaving a warm bed and exceptionally willing body to cradle a cold rifle in a lumpy chair and see how chipper you feel.

"What about the canoe?" she tries. "The one I saw in the cove just east of South Rocks. It was pulled up into the tree line…"

"Gone," I tell her around a mouthful of dry cereal. "Checked when I was out there yesterday. Guy's thought of everything—the boats, the VHF; he probably took Brit's cell, too. We need to start thinking like him, find angles he hasn't thought of yet."

Then I remember. If nothing else, it'll give them something to focus on. "Your phone is still out there somewhere, right? I know you've already looked, but…"

Nothing makes people happier when things are spinning out of control than being given a job—anything to keep from thinking about whatever else is going on; and just like that, coffee cups slap to the counter, bodies move past me toward the hall.

"And stay together!" I yell.

I'm standing in the kitchen, dumping my backpack onto the counter in search of the can of bug spray I threw in there not ten minutes ago, when I sense someone behind me. Nora, I think giddily as I turn, only to find Margot instead—back resting against the edge of the door jamb.

"No luck on the phone?" I ask, heart still knocking as I turn my attention back to the counter. Get a grip, for God's sake.

"You knew we wouldn't find it," she says. "You were just trying to take our minds off everything for a while. Which was nice of you, I suppose, but useless."

"That obvious, huh?"

She shifts against the doorway, clearly uncomfortable with what she's about to do. "I found this on Nora's dresser just now," she says, stabbing a torn piece of paper towel toward me.

Two thoughts: Nora and More Bad News. I take it from her, scan it once. Twice.

"*Have to do this myself,*" I read aloud. "*Back soon. Don't worry. N.*" I nail her with a look. "What the fuck, Margot?"

"I think she's gone to Reese's Leap."

"After what happened to Brit? Are you kidding me?"

"She used to teach art, you know," Margot says, apropos to absolutely nothing. "Rhode Island School of Design. She was great, too—incredibly talented. But she's developed these fears; strange people and unfamiliar situations terrify her now. She doesn't draw anymore, her marriage is crumbling..." She shakes her head. "Then again, whose isn't?"

"She told you I found Pete grilling her yesterday? Of course she did. So why risk going back out there? It makes no sense." My eyes drop again to the note, as if the words might have somehow rearranged themselves in the last five seconds. "And what's this thing she has to do by herself?"

"Work through her fears. It's like post-traumatic stress or something—I don't know."

I glare in utter disbelief. "Post-traumatic stress. From some kind of social anxiety disorder."

"Anyway, she thought going out there alone might help her get past it."

"Get past it," I say, mocking her. "She decides to do this today, with all that's going on?"

"Apparently," Margot snaps. "Look, I read the same note you did, okay? You know as much as I do." Sounding angry herself now—angry and scared.

I shake my head, muttering as I jam everything back into my pack, zip it shut. "Anyone see her this morning?"

"No."

More terrific news. No idea how long she's been gone, then. Could be minutes, could be hours—either way, plenty of time to get nabbed or worse.

I jam my cap on, turning as I reach the door. "Why Reese's Leap?" I demand.

"Because she hates it there. It's this big cliff that juts out over the water; gives her the willies."

"Yeah, well, if Pete finds her, anxiety's gonna be the least of her worries." I swing the pack over my shoulder, tell her to tie up the door again as best she can, and head out.

"Just find her, okay?"

T wo ways to reach this place, according to the chicks—the path from the meadow that crawls up and over the mountain, and the other, more circuitous perimeter trail that takes you past Salt Marsh Cove and South Rocks, beyond which lie the treacherous granite cliffs and the turnoff to Reese's Leap.

I opt for the trail along the water—Gus trotting before me in the role I've reluctantly granted him as personal doggie alarm—figuring it's the route Nora would have taken. Hoping it's the route she's taken. Pete tends to keep to the interior, I've noticed—better hunting; easier to hide.

Just for the hell of it, we check out the arborvitae where I ran across her on my initial island explore, my mind placing her there again—all jangled nerves and fear—images that combine with those of last night's lovemaking to form an endless loop in my head.

I'm torturing myself with all this as the path leads me higher and I skirt the top of the cliffs, eyes scanning the uphill climb toward the interior when the pooch suddenly erupts in an ear-piercing burst of yapping some twenty feet ahead. That little body gone taut as he strains over the precipice toward the craggy shoreline below—someone down there, it seems. Nora, if I'm lucky; Pete if I'm not.

Craning my neck, I catch sight of something on an outcropping some forty feet away—what looks like a pant leg, a bloom of sand-colored hair lifted in the breeze. I stare stupidly, unable to process. No, I tell myself. Can't be, though the thrum of visceral alarm running through me begs to differ. I take off in a half-run, half-crawl along the cliff edge, desperate for a tenable way down. For there below me, crumpled on the rock at an odd, sickening angle, lies the body of my best friend. My gut rolls.

"Duggan!"

No response. Has he fallen? The man's lack of coordination is legendary, after all. "Duggan—you okay?" Ridiculous question, of course, as he's so obviously not.

I'm barely aware of picking my way toward him across the scarped rock face—glancing up every few feet to scrutinize him, hoping for some movement and seeing none. Wrenched ankle, I pray; broken arm, maybe—something we can just strap up and immobilize 'til I can get him the hell out of here.

"Hold on, David," I say from maybe ten feet away. "I'm just about there." His left foot moves slightly, or maybe it's just the breeze playing at his pant leg—not sure. "Stay still," I instruct, heart hammering in my chest while thirty feet below us, angry surf pounds rock. "Don't move."

"Of course I have to move, you idiot," Duggan snaps, jerking his head my way. A long scratch on his cheek oozes blood. " How the hell else am I going to get out of here?"

I could shout with joy, I'm that relieved. Peevishness in Duggan indicates impatience with a situation, disgust with having somehow been caught off guard—nothing more serious than that. I should give him hell for being out here, but he looks so pathetic I relent. Then he shifts, revealing the arrow that's skewered his right calf just below the knee. The whole thing so ludicrously out of place, it's got to be some kind of joke, except for the wet circle of blood spreading on his chinos and Gus's determined attempts to get his nose into the mess.

"Look at this!" All outrage as Gus circles, whining. "That idiot Neanderthal shot me! *Me!*"

I quickly cover the few feet between us—Duggan shifting carefully to a sitting position as I crouch beside him, fumble for my water. "Did you fall?" I ask, trying to keep my eyes from all the blood. "Hit your head?" I'm thinking brain injury, concussion at the very least. He seems alert enough, but still. "Count backward from a hundred; can you do that for me?"

"Are you insane?" he bellows, pushing Gus away. "Will you get this animal off me? My God," he groans, "but this hurts." A shaking hand raised to massage his brow leaves a streak of blood.

Now that I know he's relatively okay, the anger's kicking in. I hand off the water bottle, pointing in disgust to the sockless Docksiders. "What the hell were you thinking, climbing around out here in those? In fact, why are you out here at all? You're supposed to be back at the house with the others."

"And what kind of man would that make me?" he barks. "What kind of friend? You didn't bother to wake me last night to relieve you, you'll remember; I had to do something."

"Okay," I say, my gaze nervously skimming the dense wall of foliage above us. "You're right."

"I was walking just there," he says, somewhat mollified—trying to turn his body and wincing, waving behind us with the water bottle instead. "Had this brilliant idea I could flag down a lobster boat. Next thing I know..." He shakes his head, scarfs some water.

I consider my options. I could leave him where he is, go and fetch the others—which is probably what Pete's hoping I'll do. Hell, he could be up there drawing a bead on us even now. Better to get Duggan out of here while I've got the chance, head down the rock face toward the surf and out of the line of fire. Lucky for us, the receding tide's revealed a narrow strip of beach running west along this section of the island toward a gentle rise of woods. Even Duggan should be able to climb out there, hobbled as he is.

"We need to get you out of here," I tell him. Problem, I realize, is the shaft of that arrow. No way we can drag that thing through the brush without causing even more damage to his leg. "I have to break this off," I say, nodding toward it. "Both sides. We'll take a look back at the house, decide whether or not to take it out. Okay with you?"

His response is a mere flip of the hand—dismissing this as simply one more indignity.

"You believe not one but three boats went by while I was lying here in extremis?" He winces as I break first one side of the shaft and then the other—causing fresh blood to ooze from the wound as I fight the urge to toss my cookies. "One of them wasn't twenty feet from shore. Man looked right at me, never even called over to see if I was alright. I could have been dead for all he knew."

"You hurt anywhere else?"

"Just sore, stiff. Twisted my ankle on the way down, I think."

"Can you stand?"

"I'll have to, wouldn't you say? Besides," he says as I help him up, "if Thurber can take an arrow in the eye and still make a literary career, such as it was, I can certainly walk as far as the house."

"James Thurber? How can you not like James Thurber?"

"Oh, I know; I know," he says, leaning on me as we start picking our way down. "Everyone drools over Thurber. But please. All those silly fables, *The Life of Walter Middy*—you call that literature?"

"As opposed to what?" I laugh, almost giddy with relief. Guy's shaky, a little pale, but otherwise fine if he's back to sniping at other writers. "*Murder on Monhegan*?"

"Is that what this is about?" he sputters, drawing himself up. "Some grudge against my work? My supposed cultural insensitivity? Good God."

He's got a point. Duggan is clearly no threat to Pete; and unlike Brit, he wasn't even out here two years ago. So why go after him like this?

"I was going to portray him sympathetically in the book, too. You know, grieving man down on his luck returns to the scene of his brother's mysterious death—that kind of thing. Well, no more. Wait 'til you see what I do with him now."

He turns to face me, then, somber and with a touch of fear in those eyes. "He could have killed me, Hodge."

Good point. This is a guy who doesn't leave loose ends, evidence Brit. So why, I wonder, didn't he finish the job?

"Just pull the damn thing out!" Duggan barks from where he's laid out on the sofa—bored and grumpy as any bloodied Hollywood extra forced to wait hours between takes.

Lily steps back—having just finished scissoring open his pant leg—and together we peer over Margot's shoulder at the skewered calf, the swollen flesh oozing a pinkish fluid.

"Not that much blood," Margot says, Duggan squirming as she palpates the wound. "Could be a good thing or a bad thing." The only one here with even a modicum of medical training—a Red Cross thing she took a few years back as part of some wilderness program, apparently—her take is to simply yank the thing.

"What if it's sliced through an artery or something?" I counter. "The shaft could be plugging the hole."

"We'll have to chance it," she says, swinging her gaze to me. "The wound has to be cleaned. It gets infected, we're in real trouble."

"Nora should be back by now." This out of nowhere from a clearly overwhelmed Adria, alone against the wall as she watches us. First thing she's said since we brought Duggan in. Fear does strange things to people, as I well know, and in the last few minutes I've seen this woman—one of the strongest I've ever met—reduced to a shocky mess. "Even if she hiked the whole island, she'd be back by now. We've got to find her."

Margot's uneasy gaze locks on mine.

"So," I say, "leave it and it becomes infected, or yank it and risk his bleeding to death."

She stands. "About sums it up."

"For God sake, just get on with it!" Duggan bellows.

Lily hops up, plants a kiss on his cheek. "I'll get the medical kit."

"Dragging him back here through the woods was insanely stupid, by the way," Margot hisses, going all sotto voce on me now we're face to face.

"Could've flown him here," I snap, "but he's got this thing about heights."

"You should've wrapped it with something, at least—a shirt, anything. We'll be lucky if his bloodstream isn't full of bacteria already." She glances down, lays a hand to Duggan's forehead. "At least there's no fever."

Both of us are glaring now, ready to get into it. That's the other thing about fear. Makes people testy.

"Did you hear me?" Adria snaps. "I said we have to find her."

"We will, Adria. Chill." Lily, back now with the emergency kit, crouches beside Duggan, snaps it open. Gauze wrap, adhesive tape, Betadine solution. All appearing relatively new, thank God.

Margot squats beside her. "I'm going to pull this out now," she tells Duggan, his face paling at the words. She nods tightly at me. "You need to hold his leg down, so it doesn't move. It absolutely cannot move. Ready?"

"Christ!" he barks as she yanks it out in one go. "My God, woman!"

"Oh, stop whining," she mutters, holding the gory thing up in triumph as Lily swabs at the wound with a shaking hand. "You're lucky the arrow was wooden. My brother's a hunter, has a serious thing for crossbows. The fancy new ones use these metal arrows with razor tips that shred their way through flesh. But this guy's either too poor for that or he's a purist. Thank God for small miracles."

Duggan sends a pleading look Lily's way. "A sip of water, my love? Something stronger, perhaps?"

"I'll go," Adria says, pushing off from the wall.

I wait 'til they finish dressing the wound and Duggan's sipping happily at a pony of some tawny hooch or other before trailing Margot to the kitchen. Time for some answers.

"Nora knows what happened to Earl, doesn't she," I snap. It's not a question. "Did she kill him?"

"Of course not!" Margot glares hotly, slapping the emergency kit on the counter. "You might as well accuse Adria or Lily. Me for that matter."

"So why was Pete grilling her yesterday?"

"Just fishing, probably—same as he'd do with any of us. Why does it matter?"

"Oh, gee, I don't know…because of what happened to Brit, maybe? The possibility he's planning to take Nora, too, if he hasn't already?"

She crosses her arms, stares me down. "You don't know that."

"I don't know jack shit, Margot; that's the problem. Only thing I know for sure is he could've finished Duggan off out there but didn't. You gotta ask yourself why, I mean considering he didn't hesitate to kill Brit. Struck me funny at the time, and now I'm thinking he got distracted by someone he found much more interesting. Someone who just about passed out the night he showed up here with Brit."

"They look a lot alike, Pete and his brother. It freaked her out, is all. There were others out here, too, that summer—just so you know. Shelley, for one. And she hasn't been back since."

"Shelley," I growl. "Who the hell is she?"

NORA

She comes to in a rush, eyes wide with panic, no idea just how long she's been out. Face in the dirt, the arm pinned beneath her aching for release. Still, she refuses to move, hoping silence will keep him at bay. He's close—somewhere just above her. She can feel him.

"I know you can hear me."

Nora recoils at the sound of that singsong voice, the smell of him—ignoring the sticky feel of spider webs on her cheek and arms as she tries to scramble backward, her hands and feet not working right. Tied, some part of her realizes.

He shadows her moves, won't let up. Grabbing her hair, he yanks her head back hard 'til she's forced to look at him. Face to face, something evil in his crazy grin. "Go ahead and scream. Ain't nobody gonna hear you—not in this place."

Vague, fleeting thoughts of the others. There's something about Brit, but she can't remember—the thought distant, hazy, like the feel of his finger along her cheek.

"You bit me, bitch!" Yanking her head up again, smashing it twice into the dirt, dazing her. She rolls to her back, gazes up—two of him swimming in her vision now.

"Hey!" So loud the cords of muscle stand out on his neck. "You listenin' to me?"

She waits for him to slap her again; something crawling across her forehead as she tries to focus, forcing the words. "I didn't kill you," she says thickly. "Please. I need water."

He ignores her, just as he did last time, the time before that. "I know

133

you saw him, talked to him. See, I can understand his maybe pissing some-body off; I know how he was."

They'd gotten to this part before, and she'd drawn a blank—his hitting her like that knocking all the words from her mind.

"Falling from the cliffs is easy, like Adria said," she blurts wildly, shak-ing uncontrollably as she tries again to scramble away. "He wasn't careful. We should all be careful." Her eyes lock on the hunting knife at his waist, not a foot from her face, and she gags on her fear.

"…came back looking…"

"Don't," she moans, eyes still on the knife. Her thirst forgotten, now; the dirt and spiders nothing. There's just the fear, taking her over, pulling her down.

"…nigger's old man."

A shudder, and she gives in to the darkness—exhausted, terrified, receding to nothing.

GIL

What I really need to do is sit down and suss all this out, figure the connections, but as usual I'm shit out of time. I've got to find Nora before Pete does, assuming he hasn't already, so I double-time it up the path toward the cliffs, fighting a new sense of urgency. I think of Brit; I think of Duggan— shot for no reason other than the old wrong place, wrong time—and I pick up my pace even more.

I'm concentrating so hard on the path before me, I almost miss the flat wooden hand tacked to a spruce—the words *Reese's Leap* painted on the absurdly long, pointing finger. A feeling of déjà vu, then. Have I been here before, or is it just the name that resonates? Calling softly so as not to startle Nora should she indeed be out here, I push my way through the fragrant bayberry bushes ringing the point.

No Nora.

Hands on hips, I gaze toward the blue of a crystal clear sky. Where to now? Continue along the perimeter, head inland—what? The question's answered for me when I turn again to the path, heart drop-kicked to my throat when I catch sight of the vultures through a break in the overhang— back in force, it seems, and circling a couple hundred yards uphill from my position.

Please God, not Nora.

I break into a run, moving frantically along the uphill trail, trying to keep them in view, taking first this path, then another. It's not 'til I feel the damp seeping into my shoes that I realize I'm slogging through a marshy stretch—the path having disappeared somewhere behind me.

What the fuck? Unlike the morning Duggan and I got turned around,

I've been careful to follow the deadfall laid to mark the forks and tricky turns. I'm doing a slow three-sixty, puzzling this out, when I spot him maybe fifteen feet to my left, the strap of that goddam crossbow slung across his naked chest.

I return his glare, upping it a notch. "You screwed with the trails."

A slow grin reveals that missing incisor. "I been screwin' with a lot more than that, if you get my drift." All relaxed as he cranks a boot onto a rotting tree stump, gazes toward the vultures circling lazily in the canopy. "Lotta time to kill, you know, waitin' for you to show the hell up."

This shithead better be messing with me. If he's so much as breathed hard in Nora's direction, I'll ram that goddam bow up his ass.

"Had to get your arrow out of Duggan first. He's fine by the way; asked me to tell you to go fuck yourself."

"Not why you're out here, though, is it?"

He's fishing; no way he can know how desperate I am to find Nora, how frantic everyone's getting at the house. I sneak another glance toward the ever-circling birds, tell myself she's managed to elude him, is even now making her way back to the others.

"See, I know you got a thing for her," he says, as if reading my mind. "'Course from what I saw last night, that's an understatement. Best show I seen in a long time."

Nora's room, I realize. The window. Gauzy curtains billowing in the breeze.

I have to remind myself to breathe.

"Little skinny for my taste," he tells me. "Hell of a fighter, though—gotta give her that."

I try and ignore the thrum of panic racing through me, focus on the ecstatic little voice whispering Nora's still alive. Doesn't work. The realization he's got her stashed her somewhere with all that implies creeps over me like a hot rash, that taunting look cranking my anger and frustration to a murderous rage.

I consider the mass of cold steel slung across his chest. If I were going to take him, now would be the time. No way he could get an arrow off before I was on him. The knife tucked at his waist is slightly more problematic, but a decent kick could knock it from his hand—break his arm if I was lucky. Another to the solar plexus, and he'd be toast. I feel myself tensing, readying—all that Tai Kwon Do pure muscle memory now—but it's the thought of Nora bound and gagged somewhere that stops me. I like to think I've learned at least something over the years. Ignore the knee-jerk reaction; stop to consider what you know. And, more importantly, what you don't. In this case I've no clue where Nora is, which makes dropping this guy right here and now, satisfying as that might be, a poor choice. I could break half the bones in his body and he still wouldn't tell me where she is, he's that hard-core. Or nuts. Or both. Plus, he dies and I could spend the next ten years searching for her in two-hundred acres of foliage-encrusted hidey-holes.

I take a breath, steady myself. "You're wasting your time with her. No way she killed your brother." I didn't really need Margot to tell me this back at the house; I've had sex with female killers before—unbeknownst to me at the time, thank God—and no way is the woman I made love to last night among their number.

"Yeah, well, little problem with that," he says, his gaze holding mine. "She says she did."

My heart does a double tap, threatens to stop altogether. "You're lying."

A lame response he clearly expected. He nods, squints again toward the ever-circling birds. "She wasn't the only one in on it, though; no way one chick could overpower a bulldog like Earl. All of 'em working together, now that I can see." He taps his head lightly. "And I know why."

Certainly liquor hasn't so rotted my brain that the idea of collusion hasn't occurred; these chicks are nothing if not resourceful. Working together, a few of them could easily overpower one smelly emotional retard; still, there's the small matter of motive.

"You know why," I repeat.

Another nod. "So this is what you're gonna do. You go back there, talk to the nigger. She's the key. Tell her I know she's lying."

What the fuck? "We still talking about your brother, here?"

"It's all connected, pal. You go back, explain the situation. You want to see your girlfriend again—the living, breathing version, I mean—you make sure I get what I want."

"What you want," I again repeat.

"We're done here," he says, cranking his foot from the stump. "Now you're gonna turn around; head back out same way you came in."

"The fuck we are. First I see Nora, make sure she's all right. Not leaving 'til I do."

He inches the crossbow toward my gut, eyes flat and expressionless. "Could be you're not leaving at all, then." He shrugs. "All the same to me."

"Whoa." Raising my hands, scrambling for some kind of Plan B—like backtracking, then overpowering him once he's led me to her. Sounds good, only it'd never work. This guy might be as silent as a fucking ninja, but the way I move through the woods? Shit, he'd twig to me in no time, be lying in wait—that bow cocked and aimed at my nuts—before I ever saw him.

"Bring me what I want, and she gets out of this okay," he says, backing away. "Tomorrow morning. Ten o'clock. Don't fuck it up."

"He's got Nora," I blurt—beyond furious as I charge into the dining room. Someone's been holding out on me, maybe a lot of someones.

"No," Lily says, stiffening.

Adria seems to physically deflate. "You're sure?"

"Of course I'm sure," I spit.

The table holds the leavings of a late lunch—a few pieces of cold chicken, some sliced fruit. The sight makes my stomach growl, but there's no way I could slide anything past the rage and confusion I've got going just now.

"It gets worse," I say. "She told Pete she killed his brother." Watching the shock take hold, the disbelief—reading their faces for even the briefest flash of deception.

"But she didn't," Margot groans, as if we've been arguing this for hours. "She couldn't.

It's just not in her."

"Of course she didn't," I snap.

"What's happened? What's going on in there?" Duggan bellows from the sofa.

"It makes no sense," Adria says. "Why would she lie? She had to know what he'd do to her…"

"This is all my fault." Margot looks stricken. "I was the one who pushed her to come back this summer." Her eyes lock on mine. "We came up with this plan. She'd spend some time alone in the woods each day, a little longer each time. Try and get over her fear—like I told you.

"Yesterday was her first walk through the interior; today was supposed to be the big challenge—Reese's Leap."

"Only yesterday didn't go so well," I snap. "Pete found her, started grilling her about some run-in with Earl—which is where I came in. So why risk going back out there this morning?"

I wait for Margot to get it; doesn't take long.

"Jesus," she breathes. "She wanted him to find her."

I nod, having puzzled over this much of the way back. It's the only thing that makes any sense. "Question is why."

"How would *we* know?" Adria blurts. "She doesn't always think straight; you've seen how she is. Maybe she thought she could talk some sense into him, or somehow save the rest of us from something. There's no telling with her."

"Why is he so sure it's one of us, anyway?" Margot grouses. "I mean what possible reason could we have?"

"The brother might have had someone with him when he got here," Lily suggests. "Another guy from the jail. They could have fought, and the other guy pushed him or something."

"Or," Adria says, covering her face with her hands. "He just fell. Period. We all know how dangerous those cliffs are."

"I may be wounded, but I'm not deaf!" Duggan bellows again. "What's going on?"

Lily pushes from the table. "I'll go."

"What reason did Nora give him?" Margot asks. "You don't kill someone without a reason. He'd know she was lying."

"He's got his own whacko theory—has to do with something he claims Adria's lying about," I say, leveling my gaze at her. "Everyone else covering for you, including Nora. All of it somehow connected to the dead brother."

"Me!" Adria barks. "That's absurd."

"Not to this guy," I laugh bitterly.

"What did he say, exactly?"

"Talk to the nigger. She's the key. Tell her I know she's lying. Like that. Whatever it is, I'm supposed to bring your answer to him tomorrow morning. I think we can all guess what happens if it's not the one he wants." I give it a beat. "We're on the same side, you know," I remind her. "Might've helped if I'd had some idea what I was walking into out there."

Adria stands, begins gathering dishes. "No idea what he's talking about, unless he's on about that idiotic treasure again. Fool thinks it's real," she says, heading off down the hall.

Treasure? "Hold on," I say, Margot and I trailing her to the kitchen. "You talked to him? When?"

"Couple days ago, maybe?" Staring toward the window as she concentrates. "Tuesday," she finally says, laying the plates in the dishpan. "It was Tuesday. I was on the dock, bailing out the boat. I turned around, and he wasn't ten feet away. Spooked me. Said he knew about the treasure, and that I was going to tell him where to find it. Idiot."

"That's what this is really about?" Margot blurts from behind me. "Fucking *money*?"

"I blew him off," Adria tells us. "Probably not the smartest thing to do, but I mean really. Nobody takes that story seriously. All that nonsense about colonists being chased by British soldiers? The cabin boy swimming ashore with a chest of gold? I mean think about it…how could anybody even do that?"

All this sounds vaguely familiar; then I remember: the pseudo island history one of the chicks read our first night here. Brit, I realize.

"I told him the truth, that it was just something my father made up when we were kids. My father the drama queen," she says, shaking her head. "Only thing he missed was putting a knife between the kid's teeth."

"And you never thought to mention this?" I demand. "Didn't think it might be part of what's going on here?"

"You mean that Pete would kill Brit because of some twenty-year-old fairy tale?" she shoots back. "Frankly no, I didn't. Why would I? And what with David being shot and now Nora, it hardly seemed important."

"You're telling me there *is* no treasure."

"Not unless it's the magic of this place—beauty, tranquility, peace. That's what my father really meant. The treasure story was just a way to get us out there to experience it. That, and put one over on us. Dad was big on jokes. The more elaborate, the better."

I nod. "And Pete didn't believe you."

"No." A shake of the head, her chuckle bitter. "No, he did not."

I watch as she works the red handle of the sink pump, trying to fill the kettle with water for the dishes and getting little more than short blasts of dirty air.

"Why would he think it's real?" Margot asks. "It's not even plausible."

Adria snorts a laugh. "Wishful thinking? I mean look at him. Anything to avoid actual work."

"Doesn't matter," I say. "He's convinced himself it's real. Way I see it, we've got two choices. Insist on the truth—something he'll never believe anyway, and which gives him zero incentive to keep Nora alive—or agree to hand it over."

"But. It. Doesn't. Exist." Adria's patience is clearly gone—both with me and the pump, which continues to give forth nothing but foul-smelling air.

Margot gets it, though. "So stalling, basically."

"And what do you think is going happen to Nora when he realizes you're lying?" Adria snaps. Giving up on the pump, she turns to fill the kettle from the cooler, places it on the stove.

"Nothing. I'll have cut her loose by then. Look, it's all we've got. Otherwise, he pushes her for what little she knows, kills her, and just starts again with someone else."

This sobers all of us, especially me, since I'm the one on the action end of all this.

"Well, we've got another problem," Adria informs us. "A more immediate one, if that's even possible. He's disabled the pump down at the well, broke the pumping mechanism off with something. We found it when we snuck down to refill the jugs a while ago. And yes, I know you told us to stay put and let you and David handle things outside, but you were out looking for Nora, and David's hardly up to it. Food we can manage without—for a while, anyway. Not water."

"How much do we have left?" I ask.

She cocks her head to where the inverted cooler jug is about a quarter gone. "That's it—four gallons, maybe."

"We can boil what comes out of the sink pump, though. Correct?"

"The dog can drink it; we can't. Washing only. Doesn't seem to be working right, though." She bends to peer at it. "Clogged or something."

"Same thing this morning, too," Lily says, struggling into the kitchen under the weight of the limping Duggan. "Sorry. He wouldn't stay put."

"I'll not be treated like some child," he says, glowering down at her.

"Then stop acting like one," Margot shoots back. "You should not be on that leg. Sit."

I leave them to their sniping, announcing a moratorium on any washing 'til I've fixed the pump. Giving the thing a go, I get nothing but another moist burp of swamp air. Something in the line? I stoop to check the clear tubing beneath the sink that delivers water from the cistern to the pump. Looks dry. Clogged check valve at the cistern end, probably. I head outside.

Cisterns act as simple water collection systems, this one little more than a covered wooden box—six by six by eight maybe, and slumping against the building to the left of the kitchen door—where rainwater from the roof is shunted. When I lift the cover, I'm met with a smell you wouldn't believe, the source of which makes me stumble back in revulsion as a horde of flies and mosquitoes rise from the stagnant mess.

"What is it?" David asks from where he's propped himself against the edge of the open screen door.

Sightless eyes gone milky in a severed head, the whole of it still painfully recognizable as it bobs in a putrefying puddle. I don't even want to think about what's clogging the lines.

I drop the lid, shoot him a disgusted look. "I think I just found Bambi's head."

Margot can't stop pacing. "We've been washing in that fucking water," she says, rubbing her arms as if cold, though it's got to be eighty-five out. "Our hair, our bodies."

"Not anymore," I tell them from beneath the sink where I've just detached the feeder tube from the pump—not that any of these chicks would ever consider using the thing again.

"He's playing with us." Adria, arms crossed, stands against the wall, her gaze locked on the ceiling. "Trying to get us to panic."

Lily looks about to jump out of her skin. "Well, he's doing a good job. God knows how long that thing's been in there."

"Couple days—no more," I say as I stand, leaving it at that. No need to go into the gruesome details of Bambi's butchered remains, the fact they were relatively fresh when I found them. "Doubt you'll get sick, if that's what's worrying you. You haven't been drinking it, after all. I agree with Adria. He's messing with our heads."

"Are you kidding?" Margot's laugh has taken on an edge. "How would *he* know we aren't drinking it?"

Good point.

"We're totally vulnerable here," Lily says quietly. "He could be watching us now…"

"She's right, Hodge." Duggan's voice is strained, his color that of wet cement as he lowers himself into a chair. "We should cover the windows. *Dawn Raid*, remember?"

One of the novels in his swashbuckler series. The story of a family of settlers holed up in some cabin fending off an attack by the local Indian tribe 'til somebody-or-other could show up with reinforcements. Shutter-ing the windows allowed them some semblance of safety, while keeping the war party guessing as to what they were planning, how much weaponry they actually had.

"I agree," I say. "We're far too exposed." Mentally kicking myself for not thinking of this before that shithead pulled last night's little Peeping Tom routine. "So we cover the windows. Pillows, quilts, blankets—shit, clothes even, I don't care. Anything this guy can't see through. Leave a strip at the top for light, but keep it narrow."

"None of this solves our water problem," Margot points out. "By this time tomorrow there'll be nothing left to drink."

My gaze moves to the pump again and just like that, realization hits. "They're the same color," I blurt. "This pump and the one at the well, I mean. Same size, too, or close to it. Any chance they're the same model?"

Adria stares at me dully. "I have no idea."

"If so, we could scuttle this one, use the parts for the one at the well."

Margot gapes. "After what's been coming out of it? No way."

"We'll boil the parts using what's left in the cooler bottle. We fix the well, we've got water."

"What good will that do?" Lily grouses. "He'll just break it again."

"Not if you throw a tarp over the whole thing. He'll just think we've covered it 'til we can get it fixed. But first we need to get those parts back here, figure out if they're a match."

"Wait. *You*, as in the three of *us*?" Margot laughs. "You've got to be kidding."

"It's too dangerous," Lily says, shaking her head. "I mean he could be anywhere."

"I meet him tomorrow at ten," I tell them. "Even he can't be in two places at once."

Adria nods, considering. "Might work."

"I'll take this thing apart before I head out in the morning," I tell her, chin-nodding toward the pump. "Can you manage okay on the other end?"

"Oh, please. I've been fixing shit out here since I was ten years old; must've had that pump apart a dozen times. There's an old piece of canvas in the Dromedary we can use to cover the well after."

Gus, muzzle parked on the floor between his paws, flicks his gaze from Adria to me and back again, as if to say "You people are so screwed." Out of nowhere, I remember the poor mutt out on Matinicus who was rather grue-somely nail-gunned to a barn door by someone with considerably less of an ax to grind than this asshole. A thought that takes me tra-la-la-ing down a thorny mental path toward that bit of female fallout I think I mentioned from my time out there—one who tends to pop back into my life at the worst possible moment, after which things tend to go missing, those fuck-ing Ray-Bans included. My gut tells me it's way past time for one of those visits, and patience not being one of her virtues, she'll no doubt grow dis-pleased when I'm not around for her to torment—displeased being perhaps too mild a term. Still, I can only deal with one psychopath at a time, and it appears I'm stuck with this one.

Friday

The wee hours find me baby-sitting Duggan—cap pulled low, butt parked on a hard-ass chair, and robbed of all possibility of sleep while I torment myself over the long night Nora's being forced to spend with that demented fuckhead, his leering commentary on our tender few hours together forever poisoning them for me. And if she really has thrown herself under the bus to save the others, what does that say about all that happened between us that night? A kind of my-life's-over-anyway-so-who-gives-a-shit kind of give-over? Fucking depressing thought.

I creep from the chair sometime before dawn, antsy to get on with this. Stretching to work out a night's worth of kinks, I bury a long yawn lest I wake the sleeping Duggan. Needn't have bothered.

"You snore like a bastard, you know that?" His voice, hoarse and raw, is laced with phlegm.

"The fuck I do," I say, stepping to the door and pulling a duct-taped corner of Cindi's tattered sleeping bag from a pane of window, letting in a triangle of slowly brightening sky. "Goddam chainsaw, pal, that's you."

I pour him some water, move to the sofa—noting the feverish sheen to his face, the leg which looks swollen and a bit off-color. I tell myself it's the low light, knowing better.

"Cut that out," he says, batting my hand away as I attempt a feel of his damp forehead. "I'm fine." Emphasizing the fact with a few raspy coughs.

"Be a good boy or I'll fetch the rectal thermometer. Here," I tell him. "Drink this."

He cranks himself onto an elbow, empties the glass greedily. Doesn't hear the soft, surreptitious creak of the kitchen door, the quiet rustle of movement from the far end of the hallway. Three long strides later, I've slipped to the wall, flattened my back against a bookcase—ready to launch myself at whoever's heading our way.

"You're awake." Adria, trailing the scent of pine needles and morning dew, makes a beeline for Duggan. Claiming the edge of his sofa, she leans in—her hand, as opposed to mine I can't help noting, permitted a test of that brow. "How are you feeling?"

"Never better," he croaks. "Though I could use another glass of that port, if you've a mind."

Enough of this. "Tell me you weren't just out there," I growl, stepping from the shadows.

If I've surprised her, she doesn't let on.

"Couldn't sleep," she says, concentrating on David's face. "He's got a fever. Not high, but it's there." Swinging her gaze to me, then. "I decided to check out the well before we tramped out there in the morning; seemed better than lying awake all night worrying about it. News isn't good. Same company, different model. Bigger, heavier duty. The parts will never fit."

I push off the disappointment, my frustration cranking toward over-load at the danger she put herself in. All this spunky self-reliance is really starting to piss me off.

"You should've taken someone with you; if nothing else, told us so we could bolt the door behind you. Your little stunt put us all at risk. Jesus, what part of this don't you get?"

"What part of this don't *you* get? Nora won't stand a chance when this guy realizes you're playing him. Whatever happens to her will be on you; you ready for that?"

"I'll deal with that when the time comes, if it comes. Right now your job is to avoid getting grabbed, since it seems you're the one he's fixated on. That means no more sneaking off to check on things. I'm serious."

"Yeah, well, the man's got to sleep sometime." She rises stiffly. "I'm gonna put some coffee on."

Nine-thirty finds me hot-footing it along to the appointed meet when, swinging through yet another turnoff toward the interior, it strikes me I've no clue where this handoff of nonexistent information is supposed to take place. I've either forgotten, or Pete never said, having already hatched his own twisted plan—a hunch borne out when I realize yesterday's reconfiguration of the trail has changed yet again. Fucker thinks he can disorient me, has no idea that my obsession with all things arboreal has more than once pulled my ass from just this kind of fire. I know, for instance, that thanks to the vagaries of wind, weather, and seed distribution, the copse of red spruce to my right is most likely part of the larger stand I noticed my first day out here—the trees hop-scotching up the mountain from the shoreline in a roughly ten-degree arc, then dipping toward the marsh of yesterday's fun and games before finally petering out here, in this deceptively bucolic, fern-filled glen.

"Nigger tell you where it is?"

I do a fast one-eighty at the sound of that voice. Not on the trail, so where the fuck is he?

"Just so I understand," I say, scanning the foliage, "all that whining about how you owe it to your brother to find his killer—that was just bullshit, right?" I watch as he unfolds from a crouch beneath one of the enormous ferns crowding the path. "I mean it all sounds noble as hell, but then you're hardly the noble type. It's been about this so-called treasure all along."

"Enough crap," he says, stepping onto the trail. "She tell you or not?"

No sign of that honkin' bow this morning, so he must be pretty confident I'll deliver; got that knife still sheathed at his waist, though, on the off chance I don't. Guy's no dummy. Which is when I realize that the half-baked plan I came out here with can't possibly work. This entailed convincing Pete that Adria would cooperate, but only after I'd seen Nora and assured her that she's okay. Which means he'd have to take me to her, at which point

I'd somehow disarm him, beat him to a bloody pulp—which would be the high point of my year, I don't mind telling you—and secure him for the cops. Couple problems with this that have only just now become clear. First is the abrupt turn-around on Adria's part. Think about it. If the gold really existed, and she didn't run out here and literally throw the stuff at the guy's feet after finding Brit like that, why would she suddenly change her tune now? And then there's my own rather transparent attempt to get within arm's length of Nora. Christ, the entire plan is so lame, he'd see through it in a heartbeat.

"No. Well, sort of," I punt, working up a good smirk to hide my panic. "The gold doesn't exist, according to her. Never did. The *treasure*, such as it is, is just the beauty and tranquility of this place. Says her father made the whole thing up years ago as a kind of game. Family joke, like that."

Pete snorts a laugh. "And you believe her."

"Hell no," I lie. "But what I don't get is how you found out about it." Stall, I tell myself, feel the guy out for just where the fuck I need to take this. Can't hurt he knows I have a thing for Nora, and thus a vested interest in bringing all this to a quick, happy conclusion.

"Look," I say, tugging my cap down against a fine mist that's making its way through the canopy. "We both want the same thing here. But I'm gonna need something tangible to convince Adria we know she's lying." Thus allying myself, however marginally, with his nutso take on reality—something that adds a decidedly sleazy feel to an already sucky day. Yet something else to hate him for.

He cocks his head, considering—the dried blood of a long, ugly scratch marking his left cheek. Nora's doing, I can only hope. Down, maybe, but definitely not out.

"Heard about it years ago," he finally says. "Brit confirmed it."

"The woman laid out in the shed with your fingerprints all over her throat? That Brit?"

"Loved to fuck, that one. Liked to talk after, too."

"That's it?" I laugh. "You're basing all this on a little pillow talk?"

Again he considers. Takes his time with it, too. "It was the old man first told me," he finally says. "Five years back, maybe."

"Adria's father?" I croak, making no effort to hide my disbelief. "You're telling me you were friends with Adria's father. The lawyer."

Helluva poker face on this guy, except when he's pissed and his eyes go all flat—like now. Ditto when he gets that jaw pumping. Good. Excellent, actually. Anger blocks judgment, frees the tongue.

"I was one of the guys he brought in to redo that kitchen." Lets that sink in. "Nigger bitch wasn't around much; ignored us when she was. Not even a blip on her radar."

"They never remember the help."

"Old man kept me on a few days after we finished—odd jobs, shit like that. Big talker, liked having another guy around to knock a few back with at the end of the day. That last afternoon he got into it pretty hard. *You know any other black man owns his own island?* he fucking asked me. *One with an honest-to-God buried treasure?*"

This just gets weirder and weirder. "The man just came out and told you this—you, a perfect stranger." Then I remember Adria's story about Malaga Island, how her father's owning his own island was a way to redeem the family honor in some way. Maybe thumbing his nose at the locals was another part of the payback.

"Shitfaced, like I said. Gold bars—enough to retire on. Me and Earl been looking for 'em since."

"So Earl gets out of jail first and comes back…"

"Told him to wait, the dumb fuck, but that's Earl for you. Figured to impress me, maybe—that or keep it all for himself."

"Only he ends up dead."

Pete nods. "They killed him cause he found it—guaranteed."

Could it be this guy's not as smart as I thought? No way this conversation, assuming it actually ever took place, was anything more than just a rich black man's yanking some low-life townie's chain.

"So you're saying Earl somehow managed to find buried gold in two hundred acres of woods. All by his little backward self." I trot out Lily's theory—anything to muddy the waters. "You ever think he might have had a buddy along, some guy you didn't know about? A little booze, a little weed, a lot of bragging and—bang—somebody gets his ass booted off the cliff."

A flip of the hand, like he could give a crap. It's then I realize. This isn't about the brother at all; his death was mere inconvenience. Or maybe not. Greed springs eternal.

"Go back," Pete says, "tell her what the old man said. You'll want to convince her this time, you want a chance to fuck your girlfriend again. Ten tomorrow. Bring a shovel; you got some digging to do."

"You don't get it," I say, desperate to keep Nora from being forced to spend yet another night with this sleazeball. "I know Adria. She won't go for it unless I've got proof Nora's all right. Take me to her. Thirty seconds, that's all. then I'm gone."

He nods, snaps his fingers like he forgot something. "Proof of life—yeah, almost forgot."

Not sure I heard him right; the rain's coming down hard now, the trail I came along turning muddy and slick. There's a rumble of thunder in the distance.

"I'm a fair guy," he says, pulling something from his jacket pocket, "so I let her choose. Ear? Finger? *Anything but a finger,* she says all calm-like. She's an artist, she tells me; needs 'em all." With this he tosses something that looks like a balled-up paper towel at me.

I've got a sixth sense about stuff like this, and the sudden pound of adrenaline's sent it into overdrive. Instinctively recoiling, I miss the catch and have to stoop to retrieve the thing from the fast-growing puddle at my feet. When I glance up again, Pete's slipped away—dripping fern fronds dancing in his wake.

Alone in the wet, fingers trembling, I stare in horror as the damp toweling swells in a crimson bloom.

Late Friday Night

It's an act of pure desperation—nothing else could get me out here just shy of midnight scrambling up the back side of the mountain in the pouring rain, buoyed by hope and almost crazy with anticipation. Because the tide has turned; I can feel it.

I know where he's keeping her now.

After this morning's disturbing tête-à-tête, I stomped my way back through the woods, determined to keep Pete's parting gift in my mental rearview 'til I made the house. There I found Lily and Margot hushed and whispering over a groggy Duggan—the normalcy of the scene, relatively speaking of course, more than surreal after the bizarre turn everything had taken.

"Fever's worse," Margot said, swinging her gaze to me—taking in my rain-soaked clothes, my shocky, wild-eyed demeanor as I lurched my way into the room. "You look awful."

No shit. "Where's Adria?"

"In the dining room," Lily said, eyeing me. "Getting sandwiches. Your shirt pocket's bleeding, you know."

Food. Another disconnect, though on some level I recognized the growl of my stomach in response. Classical conditioning, like Pavlov's dogs. What I really needed was a stiff drink. Fuck this sobriety shit. If Brit still had some booze lying around, I promised myself, I'd nose it out later. Other things to do at the moment.

Turning for the dining room, I came face-to-face with the queen of secrets herself—plate of sandwiches in hand—enough of something ugly in my gaze to stop her in her tracks.

"Nora?" Her voice hushed, fearful. Man, she's good.

I grabbed her by the elbow, pulled her back into the dining room, out of earshot. "Why didn't you tell me Pete worked for your father?" The question ate at me all the way back from the woods, along with its even more worrisome corollary: what the fuck else is she holding back?

Her eyes searched mine. "He was one of the guys hired to redo the kitchen. I told you that." Cocking her head toward my chest, then. "What's with the shirt?"

"No," I corrected. "You did not tell me that." Swinging my gaze as Margot appeared in the doorway. "Get out," I barked. "This is between us."

"Screw you," she said, leaning back against the door jamb, crossing her arms. "I'm not leaving." She shot a look toward the other room. "And keep your voice down; David's agitated enough as it is."

"God," Adria laughed, sliding the plate of sandwiches to the table, "you really don't remember, do you? It was the night you and I knocked off that entire bottle of outrageously expensive Port—well, you mostly. Don't know why I'm surprised; you could barely walk."

Ah. I remembered the Port, of course, but little of the attending conversation. I did recall having the feeling that next morning that I'd been surprised by something she'd told me, but the specifics themselves? Long gone.

"Took me a while to make the connection," she said, "but that first night Pete showed up here with Brit? The way he talked about the construction of this place? He was testing me, I think, to see if I remembered him. And I didn't, not 'til the next day."

"Your father's the one who told him about the gold, Adria. Brit confirmed it."

"Brit?" she scoffed. "Do you hear yourself? She'd known for years the whole thing was a crock; plus, she'd read the story out to us that first night you were here. Probably still fresh in her mind, wanted to use it to impress the guy."

"But your father…"

"Might have said something? Sure. He wasn't above sticking it to whitey when he got the chance. For years, anyone new to the island got the same treatment—heard all about the so-called treasure, from all of us. It was a family joke. And my father was the worst. That's after Drew and I finally figured out it wasn't real, of course, which took years."

"Touching. Any other little family secrets you're planning to spring on me, I'd rather you do it now."

"You knew about this already," she snapped. "Not my fault you were too wasted to remember."

"Bullshit."

"Look," she sighed, "I'm tired of having to prove the obvious. Okay, the names? That cabin boy, Reese, for one, as in the Reese's Leap thing?"

"The Reese's Leap thing." Lost again—two words I should probably just have tattooed on my forehead and be done with it.

"You know…the kid who supposedly swam ashore with the gold, then leapt off a cliff to keep from being captured? When he was really little, every time Dad said the words Reese's Leap, Drew thought he was saying *Reese asleep*—that's how long ago this crap started. Anyway, my uncle's name was Reese. My mother's maiden name was Pulver—same as that so-called British sailor trying to capture the treasure. Took me forever to catch on. Dad had a good laugh when I finally called him on it. He only wondered what took me so long."

Huh. I had to admit this made a lot more sense than Pete's wild-ass scenario with all its twisted permutations. I mean, why would Daddy Jackman reveal the existence of the family fortune to this bird, in his cups or no? Some secrets even liquor can't loose. Well, for most people.

I still had a laundry list of questions, not to mention a bombshell of my own to drop, but a bark of something from Duggan drew us to the doorway—Lily, still kneeling beside him, looking as helpless as I felt. The sight of his damp hair, that face gone slack in a fevered semi-sleep, squeezing something in my chest. This is the guy who once tried to convince me that the word *fuck* was really an acronym for *Fornicating Under Consent of the King*. We argued about it one night over beer at Three Dollar Dewey's, a favorite watering hole of the more adventurous young lovelies on the Portland waterfront. It was the bartender, a petite little thing not unlike Lily herself, who finally informed us that acronyms were all but unheard of prior to the twentieth century, that *fuck* is actually a very old word with Germanic roots that's always meant exactly what it does today. She was a grad student in linguistics at the University of Southern Maine, as it turns out, so I guess she'd know.

"He's in trouble," Margot said quietly. "The leg's definitely infected." Then eyeing me, "I'd have told you when you first came in, but you were too busy being a shithead."

"Okay," I said, knowing it really wasn't—nothing about this was. "What do we do?"

"He needs a real doctor, real medicine—a lot more than just this useless cream which we're about out of anyway."

"Yeah, well, it's all we've got," Adria groused. "I can try and find some more."

"Lily's already checked the Twig. And it's not good enough. When the infection gets into his system—and that's when, not if—he'll go into shock."

I couldn't leave it alone, of course, though I was pretty sure I knew the answer already. "Then what?"

She looked me square in the eye. "Then he dies."

Ten minutes of fruitless argument later, Adria claiming I'd never find the stuff on my own, we struck out together in grim silence for the Dromedary—armed, if you can call it that, with a kitchen knife worn dull by thirty years of sawing through slab bacon. There, it was hoped, we'd uncover some stash of medical supplies—years out of date and no doubt yellowed with age. Waste of time, if you ask me; still anything was better than sitting around watching Duggan get worse by the minute. Besides, it was time for show-and-tell.

She stopped dead maybe forty feet from the house, peered up at me from beneath her rain hood. "There's something else, isn't there?"

Oh, is there ever. I glanced to my breast pocket, its gruesome contents finally having stopped oozing blood, then quickly away as my queasiness returned.

"Not here," I said, continuing along the trail 'til we reached the place— eyes scanning the woods while she fished a key from over the door and unlocked it.

"Okay, enough," she said once we'd made it inside. "This is *my* island; these women are *my* responsibility. Tell me now—whatever it is."

I gave the room a cursory glance, took a whiff of that Eau de Dust and Dead Rodent so common to island dwellings of a certain age. Cobwebs and mouse turds everywhere, the desiccated bird lying belly up in the otherwise empty fireplace giving it that added touch.

No way to prepare her—you know, considering—so I simply reached to my pocket and pulled out the bloody paper towel, feeling suddenly and rather oddly territorial. Not to mention kind of shitty. I was about to rock this chick's world, and not in a good way. She'd been wearing the drained, hollow-eyed look of the emotionally sucker-punched since sometime yesterday, as if just one more piece of bad news might drive her over the edge. But hey, join the club.

"Don't freak, okay?" I said, unwrapping the pulpy mess.

Then there it was, pathetically small and absurdly out of place resting in the palm of my hand. A toe—the second from Nora's right foot to be exact, the silver toe ring still lodged at its first joint. This last a kind of gag, I assumed—some twisted way of proving it belonged to her.

A small cry as Adria's hand flew to her mouth, eyes tearing as she jerked her gaze up to meet mine before bolting around the corner to an adjacent room. Sighing, I followed in time to see her hurl spectacularly into an old enameled sink in what was once a kitchen of sorts—a surprised spider scrambling madly up its steeply vertical side in an attempt to avoid the spewage.

Pulling a wad of paper toweling from the roll above Adria's head, I carefully rewrapped the toe—flinching when, for one truly hallucinatory moment, I thought the thing moved—then returned it to my pocket for lack of a better plan.

Adria was still busy at the sink, so I struck off in search of medical supplies—hitting the mother load when I spied a makeshift shelf on the opposite wall loaded with Band-Aids, gauze, and other First Aid crap, then stuffed my jeans with whatever I could carry, including bandages and another half-tube of that useless antibiotic ointment.

"Motherfucker." Tearing a wad of towels from the roll, she leaned back against the wall, swiped angrily at a fresh burst of tears. "What kind of a monster does this?"

"The whatever-it-takes-to-get-what-he-wants kind."

"So what's next?"

I shrugged. "I've got 'til ten tomorrow morning to come up with my next brilliant plan."

"Well, I've got one, " she said, pushing off from the wall. "Trade me for Nora."

"Yeah? Listen, Pete gets his hands on you, it's all over. No reason to leave any of us alive once he realizes this whole treasure thing is a hoax. Keeping you safe buys us some time, at least." I held up the tube of ointment—only three years out of date, too. "We should get back."

I stood around trying to look busy while she cleaned the sink as best she could with paper towels, then stuffed them in a loose plastic bag and tossed the whole mess into a corner of the room. Worked for me.

"Listen," she said as she was locking up. "No need to tell the others about...you know." Shooting a quick, pained glance at my shirt as she pocketed the key.

"Our little secret."

"I mean freaked out wouldn't even begin to describe it. They're on the edge as it is."

"Agreed."

She went all quiet and unreadable as we started back, which was fine with me. Keeping both eyes peeled for murdering shitbags and their attendant weaponry takes focus. And I needed an uninterrupted minute or two to scrounge for something hard and sharp of my own—screwdriver, metal file, fucking ball-peen hammer, I didn't care.

"Over here," I said as we reached the tool shed. "Wait outside. Scream if you hear anything."

The overwhelming odor of decay you'd expect from a body two days gone was strangely absent this side of the door, but inside would be a different matter. Reaching to my pocket for the greasy jar of Vicks I'd just pilfered from the Dromedary, I smeared some of the menthol glop beneath my nose and pushed the door open. Sixty seconds, I told myself, no more.

I gagged a couple times before finally shooting a cursory look toward the thing that used to be Brit, surprised by how slowly decomposition was progressing. Being shut up in a small, dark building smothered by pines has its upside, it appears. Bit like a cave.

A cave. Of course.

Pete's used the caves out here for years, said so himself—he and that shithead brother of his. And why not? They're dry and relatively secure, not to mention private—the perfect place for the keeping of hostages, the extraction of information at a painful, leisurely pace. How much time, I found myself wondering, did it take to hack off an innocent woman's toe? The casual brutality of the act taking me back to the grisly spectacle of Bambi's butchered hooves.

Sometimes one plus one equal more than two; they make four, or maybe even six. Like Nora's toe, Bambi's bloodied body parts, the way all this then triggered the memory of my first day on the trails—of picking my way through the boulder-strewn glen when I thought I heard someone tracking me, the sound of something being dragged through the brush. Bambi's meat, maybe, being moved from the kill site to wherever Pete was holed up?

What was it one of the chicks said a couple nights back about some cave down in the glen near where the brook splits? I've been past there any number of times myself. Also happens to be pretty fucking close to the last place I saw Pete.

It all fit.

Which is how I come to be out here clawing my way upwards along a trail turned Slip 'n Slide, with nothing to guide me but a penlight clenched in my teeth. One of those headlamps I've seen the chicks strap to their foreheads would've been nice, but I can't risk being seen. No matter. I've hoofed this path so many times, I could find my way blindfolded. Every bit of me antsy to get on with this, having spent a long afternoon and evening knowing the plan I'd concocted could only be pulled off in the dead of night, and then only if I proved far luckier than I had any right to expect. No longer caring if my thing for Nora is somehow twisted up with Rachel and Ben, with what I did and didn't do back then. No way she's gonna be taken out by some squirrel-chomping survivalist—not while I draw breath.

The terrain dips precipitously on the back side of the mountain—tough to navigate in the best of conditions, and treacherous as hell on a night like this—the path slick with mud and loose skree as it descends toward the glen. Sure enough, I slip and go down hard on my knee, my bark of pain more chirp than bellow lest I drop the penlight. It's in the middle of all this fun that the metal file I pinched from the tool shed slips from my belt, my puny light following the glint of metal as it washes away into the night.

Never fucking fails.

I glance around for another way down, deciding to leave the trail and parallel the fling of red spruce running the bluff above the glen. Let Pete spend hours altering the trails; I could give a shit. No one ever checks the back door, and up here is as back as it gets—the foliage more dense, the noise of the rain hitting the canopy nothing short of cacophonous. If memory serves, the bluff's cliff-like drop-off is somewhere to my right; finding that thing in the dark would end my search for Nora permanently, so I stick to the tree line, slowly picking my way toward flat ground and that long chain of boulders bracing the hillside. If my hunch is right, and that's a helluva big *if*, that's where the cave will be.

Maybe a hundred yards along, I find myself in one of the small, broad-ferned meadows, grown soggy as a rice paddy on this night. The low chortle of running water somewhere ahead confuses me 'til I realize it's the brook—close by, too, if I can hear it like this over the sound of the rain. Crouching, I crab my way vaguely right, figuring to follow it 'til I reach the log bridge. Easy enough to backtrack to the boulders from there.

Suddenly, an enormous black slab of rock rears up before me. I stare in disbelief, struggle to get my bearings. Have I gone too far? Not far enough? Is this even the right place?

Christ, I think; get a grip. Misjudged the angle, you dimwit. Veered too far right and came on the whole mess somewhere along its length. But where? Pocketing the penlight, I glance left, right. Nothing but darkness and wet. Crap shoot at best, I figure, so I head right—carefully sweeping the face of each enormous boulder with my hands, feeling for any opening large enough for a person to squeeze through. The going is torturously slow. Ten minutes, maybe, 'til I reach the end. Nothing.

I double back, frustrated and pissed—shaking off the image of Nora lying lifeless on some skuzzy dirt floor, Pete standing over her snicking an arrow with my name on it into that crossbow. That or chambering a round into some piece of crap semi-automatic he's kept under wraps 'til now.

I'm feeling up what must be my fortieth wet rock when I stumble over something and tumble sideways, the blinding pain of ramming my shoulder into unforgiving granite nothing compared to my driving need to find and finish this guy. Crouching, I grope blindly for whatever it was that tripped me up. Plastic, about two feet square. A crate with holes, I realize—the kind used for lugging milk cartons. Only this one's full of rope.

Heart pounding with a trippy fusion of hope and exhilaration—never mind I no longer have a weapon to use on this guy—I flatten myself against the wall and feel for the entry, ready to launch myself soon as I see him.

My fingers find it first and I grow still, my eyes finally picking out the narrow slice in the rock—a foot-and-a-half wide, maybe, and very, very dark within.

Game on, asshole.

Saturday, Sometime Before Dawn

I t's dark as shit, a heavy mist all that's left of last night's deluge when I finally limp up to the kitchen door—cold, soaked through, and thoroughly depressed.

Funny, I think on some level I knew before I even slipped inside that cave that it would be empty; the place was just too still. No Pete rushed me, no Nora called out in warning. The weak beam of my penlight picked out a pile of musty-smelling clothes, rust-rimmed cans of baked beans and peaches tumbled together in a broken cardboard box ringed with spider webs. I stepped to where a small calendar was pegged to the wall—two years out of date, tacked open to July, the days crudely struck off to the 21st. A prickle of recognition at this, some disturbing association too vague to call up—the date staying with me as I ran my light over the cave's uneven floor looking for anything that would prove Nora had been there. I found it in the corner, stooping to touch the small dark circle and quarter-sized droplets peppering the ground—their sticky feel jump-starting another adrenaline surge. It's then the thing about the date kicked in. Pete insisted his brother had died on July 21st. Earl's calendar, then—had to be. His food, his clothes, his fucking hidey-hole.

Ego and adrenaline a weird combination make, the duo keeping me jazzed while I combed the area for another hour or so, despite the throb of my mashed knee, that aching shoulder—unwilling to give up on the idea of bringing Nora home. Fucking bust, the whole thing.

I nudge the screen door open, pound twice on the door—the code, if you will, for entry. I wait a minute or two, pound again. Finally, a groggy Lily unbolts the thing, then turns and pads off without a word. Fine with me; I've no interest in trying to explain the failure of the hopeless errand I'd sent myself on.

By this time I'm punchy with exhaustion, nothing on my mind other than picking my way through the kitchen toward someplace I can get horizontal. Fuck that hard-ass chair in the living room, from whose dimmed maw Lily's demented dog now lay in low growl mode. Warmth, I'm thinking. Blankets, quilts. Pillows would be nice.

Nora's bedroom door stands ajar in silent accusation, and I stop dead just beyond the threshold—something squeezing in my chest when I spy her hairbrush on the dresser. But it's the pale blue tee tossed casually to the bed that decides me. This is where I'll sleep 'til I bring her home—and bring her home, I will—hell with what anyone thinks. The thought of drifting off steeped in her scent is so intoxicating I almost drop right then and there; it's only my reluctance to leave half a mountain's worth of mud between her sheets that drives me to the sink—as if my fear of incurring her wrath makes her eventual return inevitable.

I draw maybe a cup of water from our fast-dwindling supply, spill it into the shallow dishpan in the sink. I consider, then splash some to my face, almost wishing the pump still worked so I could have a decent wash—never mind the gruesome mess at the other end. I've crawled through so many festering pools of bacteria in the last few hours, I might well be doomed anyway.

A little soap, a quick angry scrub of my face, and I grab up a semi-clean dishtowel to pat myself dry—glancing vaguely toward the window, covered now with a wide hunk of cardboard torn from a case of wine emblazoned with the word *Boomerang*. An Aussie vineyard, if memory serves.

My weary gaze fixes on the useless red pump, and for some bizzaro reason I find myself teasing out something I read about it. No, that's not right—something that was read to me. But that's wrong, too. It wasn't about *this* pump, I realize, but the other one—the one at the well. *Boomerang*, I think dully, as in things that return to bite you in the ass.

Tossing the towel to the counter, I head for the living room—where, penlight clenched in my teeth, I peruse that long wall of books until I find the so-called island history. No, I think, paging quickly through it, what I want is that dedication to Adria from her father. More rummaging 'til I come across the guest book Nora read from that first night. Maybe ten minutes later, there it is:

Adria:
A sip from the well is my gift to you.
There is nothing more life-giving than this water—
a treasure buried deep, eluding all, sustaining all.
When we first arrive we run for the red-handled pump...

A treasure buried deep, eluding all. Red-handled pump.
Fuckin' A.

"No treasure, huh?" I roar, tossing the thing onto her bed. "Then what the hell is this?"

She's instantly awake, despite the hour—eyes going wide as she catches sight of the slimy gold bar dirtying the blanket beside her.

"Where did you find that?" Trying for innocent as she scrambles to sit.

"Save it," I snarl, wanting nothing more than to ring this chick's neck. Knowing I'd never have found the stuff at all if the family Jackman had planted these things any further down the inside wall of that well—a spot Adria visited slightly more than twenty-four hours ago, I remind myself. Couldn't sleep, she said. Checking on the pump parts, she said. Bullshit. She was out there making sure her secret was still safe, that Pete hadn't managed to stumble on the gold when he smashed the thing up.

It had still been dark when I slogged back through the meadow after re-reading Papa-San's cutesy little poem to his daughter, powered by a potent combo of rage and disbelief. Leaving nothing to chance, I put two nails through the wood of both the kitchen and porch screen doors into the heavier frames beneath—tap-tap, tap-tap—securing them. No one comes, no one goes 'til I figured out just what was going on.

By the time I'd hauled what was left of the pump assembly and its wooden platform from the top of the well shaft—the whole mess smashed with a sledgehammer by the look of it—the pre-dawn sky had lightened enough that I could see more than a yard.

The wells out on Matinicus are very much like this one: old hand-dug shafts set flush to the ground—deep and gaping and dangerous as hell. This one had some heavy, rough stones worked into its sides, at least—no doubt to give the upper walls some structural integrity. Something to clutch at as you tumble helplessly God knows how far to its unforgiving bottom.

I craned my neck around the remaining bits of apparatus while trying not to focus too hard on what might be down there. Last time I stared into one of these things, the gory mess that greeted me taught a grim lesson about the kind of crazy-ass shit one person was willing to do to another.

Nothing. So much for my assumption that the superstructure, such as it was, had been resting on a honkin' pile of glittering gold bars. Seems making life easy for me wasn't foremost on Daddy Jackman's mind when he squirreled this stuff away.

Sprawled on my stomach in the wet grass, I crabbed as close to the edge as I dared, extending an arm down the interior wall to find nothing but slimy, uneven rock face. I scooted maybe a quarter way around the perimeter and tried again. Same thing. On my third try, I thought to feel my way up the wall from my original reach, and maybe a foot from the top the craggy, pitted stones instead became elongated, smoother, denser to the touch.

Three-hundred and sixty degrees of solid gold bars.

Adria, you goddam bitch.

Took a while, but I finally managed to pry one of those suckers out—no easy task with everything so slippery—then I rocked back on my haunches and hefted it a few times. Five pounds, give or take; small and oblong, like a brick. I scrubbed some of the slime off it in the grass and voila…the unmistakable glint of money.

"You have to understand," Adria says, all defiance now she's fully awake. "The gold's been part of Mistake for hundreds of years; it belongs to the island. No one can profit from it; that was my father's number one rule. And number two? No one takes what's ours. Ever again."

Is this chick for real? "So you're telling me you and your brother have no personal interest in the gold—that it?"

"Only in making sure it stays where it is. Letting that asshole—letting anyone—claim it for themselves would be a desecration."

"Yeah, well, I don't buy it. Nobody passes up millions of dollars, especially millions of dollars the IRS knows nothing about—not in this day and age."

Margot appears in the doorway, stifling a yawn. "What the hell, you guys? You know it's only five-thirty?" Eyes widening as she takes in the glinting bar on the bed. "That looks like…"

"That's because it is," I say, my eyes boring into Adria. "Enough starry-eyed bullshit. Tell me about Pete and your father. The real story this time."

"You'd have to know Dad to get it," she says, her gaze wary. "Back home, he was this conservative, circumspect Boston lawyer, but out here on the island he dropped his guard completely, was everyone's buddy. The year we redid the kitchen, he bought beer for the guys working on the place, chummed it up with them after they quit each day.

"Pete finessed him is what it came down to. He'd hang around, pull out another cold six pack or two after the others had gone home, and the two of them would go off for a while. Dad was pretty tanked the day he told him about the gold. He knew right away it was a mistake, but figured he was probably safe. He got the impression Pete thought he was full of shit, anyway.

"A couple summers after that, Pete and his brother started sniffing around again, pressing Dad about it. He made us promise to call Burt if we ever saw them hanging around."

Margot's gaze is still with the gold. "So the whole history thing Brit read to us is true."

"Let me guess," I snarl. "Your uncle's name isn't really Reese."

She shakes her head. "Malcolm."

"And Pulver…"

"Not my mother's maiden name, either, no."

Christ, talk about being finessed.

"Fuck, Adria," Margot breathes—hands on hips, pacing the four feet between bed and wall.

"Let's back up to the part about Earl," I say. "He twigged to the gold that summer two years ago, right? Somehow figured out where it was?"

"I told you," Adria says. "I never saw him. I had no idea he was even on the island."

"But *you* knew he was here," I say, swinging my gaze to Margot.

"This is bullshit!" she explodes, pointing to the bed. "I knew nothing about any of this."

"None of them did," Adria tells me wearily. "That's the truth."

Right. The truth. Lots of versions of that going around just now.

Just then a barefoot, sleepy-eyed Lily cruises past the doorway heading toward the kitchen, Gus in tow, draping a shawl over her shoulders as she shoots a sideways peek at our unhappy little group. If she notices the gold, she says nothing.

"Nice work, guys," she grumbles. "You woke David." A yawn as she pads off down the hall. "Don't suppose there's anything left to eat…"

Margot leans into the hallway. "We're down to dry cereal, crackers, a few hard-boiled eggs. Might be some soup left. And I found some bottled water in one of the back closets, so we can at least have some coffee."

"Look, you have to understand," Adria pleads. "This was a sacred thing to my father. He was dying. He made me swear…"

"Enough!" I bark. "We're shit out of time here, Adria, not to mention options. No way Nora's gonna die out there if I can stop it. So fuck you with all your holier-than-thou bullshit."

"What are you going to do?" she demands, defiant even now.

"Give this asshole what he wants. Period. Pray to God he lets Nora go."

Adria's eyes narrow to slits. "That's not your call," she snaps. "I'll remind you that you're a guest here, nothing more."

"You can remind me all you want after I find Nora."

A stifled cry from the kitchen, then, the quick padding of feet.

Oh shit, I think. Nora's toe.

A shaken Lily appears in the doorway moments later, extending the capped margarine tub I'd stashed at the back of the fridge wherein sits—you guessed it. Holding the thing at arm's length as if it were radioactive. "Margot..."

"What," she says, instinctively stepping back.

"Little gift from Pete," I inform her. "To prove he has Nora."

"Take it," Lily says quietly—her face ashen, a bit of shawl raised to cover her nose—but Margot doesn't move. "Just...please, somebody take this thing." When nobody responds, she drops it at the foot of Adria's bed, steps to the hallway. "I'm not coming back in there," she warns. "Just so you know."

I throw her a weary glance, only now thinking to ask. "How's Duggan holding up?"

"Fever's worse," she says, her gaze drawn toward the living room. "And he's started rambling—something about seals dropping their fins on the steps."

Navy Seals, I think. His brother was one. Not good.

"That's it, then," I say, snatching the gold from the bed, hefting it once as I head to the door—the glimmer of a plan only now taking shape.

Adria stiffens with indignation. "You've no right to do this!" she insists. "You don't even know if she's still alive."

"Yeah, well, I'll take that chance. My ass and Nora's on the line, not yours. Well, and Duggan's, of course. We don't get him off the island soon, he'll die. So I'm meeting Pete at ten as planned. And I'm taking him this."

Still, she needn't worry. I've no intention of letting him get his hands on any more of the gold than necessary. Nothing to do with that promise she made to her father; I simply refuse to let this asshole win.

Pete's a no show for the ten o'clock meet, hardly a surprise considering the way things are going. Hauling around my heavy-ass payload—one of Nora's pillowcases stuffed with a half dozen dirty bricks from beneath the porch and that single gold bar as teaser—a waste of what little time and energy I've got left.

I'm hefting the pillowcase the last five yards or so to the kitchen door when a bit of torn paper fluttering beneath the edge of a shingle draws my gaze.

I snag the paper, letting the pillowcase slip to the ground.

You come looking for me in the night again, you ain't gonna like what you find next morning. Tomorrow same time. Place she calls Reese's Leap.

Bloody hell. Not only did this shithead know I was out there last night, he caught on early enough to grab Nora and make a run for it. But how? That unerring sixth sense of his, no doubt; guy's been ahead of me every step of the way.

I pound on the door the requisite two times, which elicits some growling from Gus before Margot cracks it open, drawing up short when she sees my face.

"What's happened?" she blurts, eyes dropping to the filthy sack at my feet.

I jam the note into my pocket. "Nothing," I grumble, hefting the pillowcase as I push past. "Pete was a no-show."

It's then I notice Lily, standing by the sink looking pale and haunted as she tries to take this in. "But what does that mean?"

"Just more of his fucking games." I glance around for someplace to stash the pillowcase. "Moved the meeting to tomorrow." Back of the fridge, I'm thinking. Out of sight, out of mind.

Lily's gaze drifts, then comes back to me as I heave the thing in one go—thirty pounds of brick and gold bar hitting the floor in a thundering crash. She barely reacts.

"The water's gone. And I can't get Adria to talk at all. She just stares off into space."

"So now we can't do anything until tomorrow?" Margot snaps, glaring as if this latest fuck-up is mine and mine alone. If she only knew. "I mean that's what you're telling us, right?"

"About sums it up." I can't just sit here, though. Weary as I am, I'm too hepped-up to sleep. God only knows how many more layers there are to all this, and time, like the water, has about run out. I glance to Lily, the only chick I haven't quizzed at length, I now realize. Well, no time like the present.

"Lily," I say.

Nothing.

"Yo, Lil." Louder this time. "Get your shoes; we're going for water." I point at Gus, nudge him back from the doorway with my foot. "He stays."

The gaze that meets mine is dull, almost shocky, and edged with despair. Well-nigh catatonic, to be honest, which on this particular day seems to work in my favor. Too worn down by everything to resist, she moves to the door without comment and slips on the sneakers she keeps just inside— hand reaching absently for the rawhide pouch dangling from a nail.

"Barricade the door behind us," I tell Margot as I wrestle two empty cooler jugs toward a waiting cart.

She shoots me a withering look. "Really? You think?" Slamming the door on us as we turn and head down the path.

Lily and I have never been easy together—a situation that's hardly improved over the last week—so neither of us say much as we alternately push and pull the cart through the broad, open fields defining the north side of the island.

It's maybe a half-mile to the small natural spring I stumbled on during my only other trek out here—back before life hooked left into the bizarre— and while yet another hike isn't exactly what I need just now, the day has blossomed into one of those rare, singularly stellar summer afternoons that linger in the mind for weeks. Ironic, when you think about it.

The spring surfaces in a pool maybe twenty feet wide surrounded by a mass of fragrant bayberry, beyond which rafts of daisies bob in a light breeze. I drag the first of the bottles to its edge—hold it under 'til the neck begins sucking in the cool, untainted water as Lily heads to the opposite bank.

"We didn't have to come this far, you know," she grouses, gingerly picking her way through the vegetation as I do a slow three-sixty of the tree line looking for stray psychopaths out walking their crossbows. "Plenty of streams closer to the house."

"We're safer this side of the island." For now, anyway. Swinging my gaze back, I see her tuck a handful of leafy, yellow-flowered spikes into that rawhide pouch. St. Johns Wort, I realize.

"Thought they debunked that myth. The anti-depressant benefits, I mean."

"Depends on who you talk to." Her tone defiant, a little resentful. A bit more like herself now she's had some fresh air—the house having taken on the stale, sweaty funk of a post-game NFL locker room. "Has good anti-bacterial and anti-inflammatory properties. There's comfrey here, too— makes an excellent poultice. And David likes the tea."

"So you really are some kind of shaman, like Brit said."

She flicks a hard gaze my way. "You obviously didn't know her very well."

"I didn't know her at all."

"Yeah, well, she'd say anything to get a rise out of someone. She dug up some article once that claimed naturopathic medicines and treatments were used by shamans to fly through the air in search of the soul or something; that's when the whole thing started."

A skill that would have surely come in handy last night.

"Herbal medicine's part of my heritage; it's eons old in tribal culture. Shamanism is totally different. A true shaman wouldn't focus on just healing David's wound, but why it became infected to begin with."

"Shot by an arrow," I remind her. "Sterility's not really part of the program."

"And a shaman would tell you that infection is caused by an imbalance of the spirit—what some call the subtle body—which lives in and around the physical body. Stress, lack of rest, recent emotional trauma, they all play a part."

Only one kind of recent emotional trauma in Duggan's life that I know of. "So—what—you're saying if Matt didn't die, Duggan's wound wouldn't have become infected?"

"Physical health's the result of a complicated feedback system between mind, body, and spirit," she informs me. "Matt's death, David's weight and stress about his writing, Brit's murder—it all works to lower resistance—allow infection to take hold."

Lily had been Brit's closest friend, I remind myself, only according to Duggan the friendship had begun to cool. It only now occurs to me to wonder why, and whether Matt's death might have played any part.

First bottle's full, and I wrestle it upright, cap it—Lily joining me in hefting it back to the cart, rolling the second one to the spring. Together we watch as water is again drawn in.

"You were the one who found him—Matt, I mean. Must have been tough." This is new territory for us, and I'm careful to keep my gaze on the bottle, my expression neutral. "Sorry, Brit again. Duggan would never have said."

She shrugs. "Doesn't matter anymore. Brit could be petty and funny and vindictive all at the same time, and still you liked her; you couldn't help it. She was wrong about a lot of stuff, but she was right about my not liking Matt. She used to rag me about it; thought David and I were being too hard on him."

A pause as she fiddles with her bag—a stall tactic, I figure, 'til she decides what else to reveal. "After he got out of jail, he started hiding his dope at the house. Our house. Cocaine, heroin, whatever. I used to find little packets of it everywhere—the garage, the linen closet, the freezer. Like he didn't have his own place."

I shrug. "Being paranoid comes with the territory. That way, if he got busted and the cops searched his apartment, he wouldn't lose the whole stash."

"I guess. Anyway, I planned to have it out with him, tell him next time I found any of his shit I'd call the police. Without David's knowing, of course. He'd never have let me."

"That's why you went to his apartment that night?"

"Not exactly." Another awkward pause. There's something else she wants me to know, I realize, but isn't sure how to tell me. "I was in town that night for another reason," she finally says. "I was meeting a friend—a man."

I glance over sharply, but she doesn't meet my gaze. "He lives in Claremont, like Matt. We'd meet like once a week, just to talk. He wanted more, but I..." She gives it a beat. "Things had been tense between us for a while—David and me, I mean; we'd been arguing a lot. About Matt, of course. It felt great to be able to vent. Dan's a good listener. And no, I didn't sleep with him."

All this is news to me. Duggan's as loyal as they come, so I shouldn't be surprised he'd keep his troubles with Lily under his hat. Still, my head must be pretty far up my ass if I noticed nothing.

"Anyway, the night Matt died, I was really ticked off, upset about the effect all his lies were having on David, the way he'd started playing us against each other. Dan told me I had to find some way to mend fences with Matt—that or probably lose Duggan. Blood is thicker than water, and all that. Surprised me he'd say that, considering how he said he felt about me."

I busy myself rolling the bottle uselessly about as it fills, resentment blooming inside me. Why the hell is she telling me all this, and why now? Getting it off her chest in case none of us makes it off the island alive? Is that what this fuckhead's reduced us to?

"I knew he was right about Matt—about David, too—so when we left the bar that night, I headed over there to try and make a start toward, I don't know exactly, something better than the way it was. But when I walked in and found him—like that—part of me was glad. All I could think was that the whole thing was over. Finally. Terrible, I know."

"Are you still seeing this guy?" My tone perhaps not as gentle as it should be.

She looks at me deeply for the first time. "Not since that night. Look, I know it was selfish, but I was under a lot of stress and I figured he didn't know David; David had no idea who he was, so what harm could it do?

What I didn't know was that Dan also knew Brit from Starbucks, and he'd told her about me—that he'd met this woman he really liked and so on—totally unaware we'd been roommates. I mean what are the odds?"

"And being who she was…"

"Yeah, right. That was a totally weird conversation. She called me maybe a week after Matt died, and let me have it. At first I thought she was pissed about Dan, but that wasn't it at all. Turns out Matt was her connection; that's what really ticked her off; she'd have to find somewhere else to get her pot. I think in some weird way she blamed me for the whole mess.

"I never told David, of course. Made Brit swear she wouldn't either. And he has no idea she was getting drugs from Matt, or that he was selling from the house. I'd like to keep it that way."

Implying, of course, that I'm now sworn to secrecy as well. I could argue the point, I suppose, but instead I nod, giving it a beat, then another. Selfish bastard that I am, I see a chance to stretch this rare, easy intimacy to the real reason I brought her out here. I want her take on Adria, what makes the woman tick, so I ask Lily if she trusts her, believes this crazy story about not wanting the gold for herself.

"You kidding? Adria's the most honest person I know. If she says the gold belongs to the island, she believes it completely. Besides, if she really wanted it for herself she could have taken it a long time ago, don't you think?"

The truth of this slams into me, turning my entire theory on its head. So what if Adria was checking on the gold the night she snuck off to the meadow? What matters is that here, on an island with a population density close to that of the North Pole, knowledge equals opportunity. No getting around it. She could have dug the gold up any time she wanted to—every single bar of it—but the only one missing from the wall of that well was the one I tossed on her bed this morning.

Christ, don't I feel like a schmuck.

"He's going to kill us all, isn't he?" Lily asks quietly, staring off into the distance.

I follow her gaze, the water jug forgotten between us, praying this isn't some half-realized Inuit prophesy. "He's gonna try."

And soon, is my bet. He's been watching this place long enough to know its rhythms, the days on which people come and go, and he's sure as shit got a plan to end it all before anyone else shows up. I figure we've got a day or two, tops, before he just throws in the towel and pulls a Rambo—dragging Adria off to that cave where he'll simply beat the information out of her. After that, he digs up the gold and breaks out the canoe. Unless, of course, he held on to those spark plugs, and why wouldn't he? Pop them back in the motor and he's got a real boat. Cut the work load considerably.

And like that, I've got it—the germ of an idea that just might get us out of here alive, most of us, anyway. Amazed it hasn't come to me sooner. Who the hell needs a motor, when all we ever really needed was something that floats? I'll just load everyone in the skiff, set them adrift. Tide will be right early tomorrow morning, low and coming. If I time it right, the current will suck them straight to the mainland and out of Pete's reach. Me? Well, let's just say it's time to end this thing, once and for all.

We cap the second bottle, roll it back to the cart, load it. A final question occurs—one I struggle how to phrase as Lily catches her breath. Gone is the pallor of just an hour ago, the dull unresponsive gaze.

"That first night at dinner," I venture, "Brit was filling me in about your group, how Adria's connected to each of you. Only she never mentioned herself, how she knew Adria. Or how you did, for that matter."

"Brit brought me in."

"Brought you in?"

She nods. "We were roommates back then. Once you're an Island Woman, you're free to bring in someone else you think is like-minded. With the group's approval, of course. So Brit brought me in. That was, what, four years ago now."

"And Brit? Who brought her in?"

She glances up, surprised. "I thought you knew. Brit dated Adria's brother Drew for a long time—couple years, anyway. They were quite an item, as David would say. He broke it off suddenly a few years back. Really tore her up."

Sunday

Lily and Margot have no trouble with my plan—would have left last night if they could have, so eager are they to be beyond Pete's reach. Convincing Adria, even in her withdrawn, listless state, was another matter. Nora's safety, mine, the possibility Pete might actually get his hands on the rest of the gold—take your pick. But I was stone-cold unmoved, insisted I could only do what needed doing if I knew they were all safely away.

Getting Duggan to the dock proves our biggest hurdle. Lily's attentions notwithstanding, he's simply too sick, too out of it to go anywhere under his own power. Good thing, actually; no way he'd leave me to deal with the Pete problem alone if he was in his right mind. So we douse him with liberal amounts of Daddy Jackman's last and very good bottle of brandy, duck-walk him out the door—split pant-leg flapping in the breeze—and tumble him into the largest of the carts, arms and legs dangling loosely over the sides.

It's hot and muggy already, never mind it's not yet seven—temps well above eighty as we barrel-ass through the meadow, the chicks pulling while I push for all I'm worth, Duggan spouting bits of Shakespeare along the way.

"Time shall unfold what plaited cunning hides!" he crows, pointing vaguely toward the sky—Lily and Margot shushing him while I simply hunker down and push harder, nervously scanning the trees for signs of Pete, whose shadowy presence slipped along the edges of last night's fractured dreams as if searching my subconscious for our next move.

I'm so into this pushing business, it takes me a moment to realize the chicks have come to a dead stop not ten feet from the top of the ramp. Drawing myself up, I follow the group gaze to the float below us where the skiff should be bobbing gently on its lines. Only it's not. Which is a major fucking problem.

"Shit," Lily offers.

Parking Duggan, who's switched to something that sounds suspiciously like Chaucer, we scramble down the ramp to where the pooch is pacing the front of the float in agitated confusion.

"What the hell do we do now?" Margot demands.

Fuck if I know—suffering, as I seem to be, from some weird, out-of-body experience born of a potent combo of muddled exhaustion and a growing sense of the inevitable. I turn toward Adria, stock still at the edge of the float, her gaze locked on something deep in the water.

"Damn," she says quietly.

Moving to her side, I peer in. There, winking from the rocky bottom some six feet beneath the water's surface, is the metal hull of the skiff.

Margot glances from Adria, to me, to Adria again, then throws her head back and begins to laugh. Lily tries to shush her, which only makes things worse. Shrieks of laughter, Lily's tears of frustration; the whole thing getting worse by the second. I find myself vaguely wondering where that first arrow will come from, whose name will be on it. As if I didn't know.

Think, I tell myself, fighting panic. I consider diving in and trying to raise the thing, but there's no way I'd get it clear of the water, even with their help. It simply weighs too much. Not to mention it sank for a reason. Drain plugs removed at the very least, more likely Pete's holed the thing somehow.

No one says a word—Margot's laughter receding into a silence as hopeless as it is desperate—every minute that slips away bringing us that much closer to discovery.

It's then I spot the raft bobbing peacefully in the cove—afraid to hope we might have actually caught a break, that Pete had finally fucked up just enough to give us a sporting chance.

"That raft," I say, cocking my head. "What holds it in place?"

Adria turns, considers. "Just a couple lines to a cement block mooring—that's it." She gets it then, head snapping up to meet my gaze. "Margot and I can handle it," she says, a spark of that old, take-no-prisoners style back in her voice. "You go find us a paddle or two."

Right—those things that disappeared along with the kayaks days ago. Trotting back up the ramp, I squander a couple precious minutes searching for a piece of deadfall stout enough to use as a paddle but short and light enough for the chicks to manage, and find nothing. I'm so busy scanning the ground beneath the trees, I almost miss the weathered wooden oar nailed to the spruce at the head of the trail—something I vaguely remember from that first day out here. A hundred years ago at least. Thing's been there forever, too, by the look of it—the nails gone rusty and embedded deep in the trunk of the tree. I pray it won't split as I pry it loose, and for once things go our way.

Margot and Adria make short work of freeing the raft, and we quickly ease Duggan from the cart into an undignified sprawl atop the thing—Lily and Gus quickly settling beside him.

"Where are you meeting him?" Adria asks, bringing my thoughts abruptly back to the fuckhead behind all this and the various unpleasant things I have in store for him—my stomach involuntarily clenching at the thought.

"He mentioned something about Reese's Leap, so I'll head that way. I'm hours early; maybe I'll catch him off guard." Yeah, right.

I hold the raft while she and Margot climb on. "If he starts with the arrows," I tell them, "slip into the water 'til you've cleared the point. You should be out of range then." I try not to think about how vulnerable this leaves Duggan, but there's nothing for it. "You see any boats, and I mean anything at all, yell like crazy."

With that, I give the raft a long push, gazing hard at each of them as the current takes it and begins pulling them toward the mainland. Then, her face stony and resigned, Adria picks up the paddle and turns away. But it's Margot's continuing gaze that unnerves me—a combination of pity and resolve that frankly gives me the willies. As if she already knows how all this is going to end.

I must have finally twigged to Pete's psycho vibe, 'cause I feel him in my bones before I see him this time—the pillowcase hanging heavily from my hand when he steps onto the trail in front of me not twenty feet from the drop-off at Reese's Leap, knife sheathed at his waist, that fucking crossbow and quiver of arrows slung over his shoulder. For once I'm happy to see this crap; it's bound to slow him down.

He nods toward the pillowcase. "That better be the gold."

"Some of it," I tell him—his eyes tracking every move as I ease it to the ground. "There's a shitload more."

He's excited, I can tell, but careful to stay far enough away to avoid any surprises of the martial arts variety. Disappointing, really. Still, that hickory-handled knife-cum-door-bolt I snagged as we headed for the dock this morning is tucked through the back of my belt, no doubt giving me more confidence than I've any right to feel.

"Dragging this crap around isn't easy," I say huffing like I'm about to drop in my tracks—not much of a stretch. "You got any water?"

"Fuck you. Your own fault you had to do this twice." He seems distracted—glancing left, right, back over his shoulder.

"They're gone," I tell him. "Off the island. Just you and me now."

A slow grin. "And Nora."

I nod. "Why I'm here. Only I don't trust you for shit, so she comes along while we dig this stuff up. Then she and I walk out of here, and you do—you know—whatever. I don't give a fuck."

"She stays put 'til I got the gold. That don't work for you, you can try and find her on your own. Big woods out here."

"Well, since you're not that original a guy, I'd put my money on another grimy cave. That other one…Earl's little hidey-hole? Kinda grim, I gotta say. Hardly worthy of chick of Nora's quality. Sloppy work, too, all that DNA."

"Don't matter. I'll be outta here soon."

"Yeah?" I laugh. "What, you're gonna swim the gold across? 'Cause that canoe's not going anywhere. Yeah, I found it, asshole; decorated the hull with a honkin' hole not a half hour ago."

This doesn't seem to worry him, which worries me. Then I realize. "That was Earl's canoe. You came over in another you've got stowed somewhere. More likely you had someone drop you—another townie loser, right? This one with a real boat, big outboard. You get the gold, you signal him somehow. Cell phone would be my guess."

"Enough talk. Drop the bag and step back."

Fat chance. My Hail Mary play, such as it is, requires getting close enough to wing the bag of bricks at his head, then closing with the knife. A couple good jabs and he'll be begging to take me to wherever it is he's stashed Nora. And he will take me—that or bleed out right here on the path. And I'm cool with this, never mind it'll make finding Nora next to impossible without a search party of massive proportions.

"Like I said, there's a shitload of this stuff," I tell him, dragging the sack closer. I get maybe three feet, which leaves another four or five before I'm in range. "But hey," I shrug, "you want a look, that's cool." Reaching down, I let the side of the pillowcase slip just enough to reveal the single gold bar, steeling myself as I wait for him to get revved, drop his guard.

"Don't do it." And like that, a dripping Adria steps from the foliage, handgun aimed squarely at Pete's gut.

Well, fuck me.

Pete shoots me a look. "You said you got rid of her."

The gun swings my way—some Perry Mason era piece of shit, looks like. "He's full of crap. As usual. And don't point that thing at me. I told him you were all off the island, and you were. So what the hell…"

"I slipped into the water after we rounded the point, swam back," she snaps, eyeing the pillowcase. "You didn't really think I'd leave this to you?"

"Which part? Rescuing Nora or dealing with pencil-dick here?"

"The gold, you idiot. No way he's leaving with a single bar of it. No one takes what's ours. That shit ended on Malaga." She chin-nods toward the crossbow. "Take that thing off and lay it on the ground. The knife, too." Which he does—eyes boring into her, reassessing.

"And the others?" I ask, casually edging past to put myself between them, lest Pete launch himself in a sudden grab for that gun.

"On the mainland by now. Gave them Burt's cell number. Told them no police; we won't be needing them." She eyes Pete with distaste. "You killed Brit for nothing, but then you've probably figured that out by now. Let me guess. The gold wasn't where she said it was."

Huh?

"Bitch lied to me."

"Maybe, maybe not. The truth was kind of a fluid thing with Brit."

Pete considers this as I struggle to process. Brit knew about the gold?

Adria starts to edge around me for a clearer shot at Pete. "She told you Drew talked it up, right? Love that boy to death, but he can't keep a secret for shit."

"Not when he's puttin' it to somethin' like her. Me and Earl used to watch 'em goin' at it hard up at the house." A smirk as he cocks his head toward me. "Same room this one did Nora in."

That earns me another swing of the gun, an inscrutable flash of those eyes.

"But see, here's where it gets good. Earl calls me a couple weeks after he gets sprung, tells me the old man's dead. Just a bunch of women on the island now, he says. Nothin' else between us and the gold. Tit job. Last I heard from him, the dumb fuck."

"Must have made you nuts, too," I say, casually hefting the pillowcase another foot in his direction. "Being stuck in jail and knowing all that gold was just sitting out here. So you came back, tried to worm the information out of Brit. How long did you have to work her over before she gave it up?"

"No need," he says, gaze resting on Adria as I inch closer. "Gettin' dumped by your brother really pissed her off. She was just itchin' to get back at the both of you."

"Brit never loved Drew," Adria sneers. "It was the idea of the island she loved, being part of all this. Eventually he realized that."

Which explains Brit's casual cattiness toward Adria, I realize—that vein of bitterness running just beneath the surface. But if Adria so clearly disliked her, felt Drew was so much better off without her, why keep inviting her back?

Then it hits me. "You kept up the friendship with Brit so you could keep an eye on her," I say—slowly twisting the rim of the pillowcase now I'm finally within striking distance. Eyes on the prize, I remind myself. Get to Nora. "Hoping gratitude or loyalty to the group would keep her quiet about the gold, maybe. Only it didn't work." To Pete, then. "And since the money wasn't where she said it was, you figured she'd rethought the whole thing, Maybe she decided to dig it up for herself, or wanted you to split it with her. So you killed her."

"The problem," Adria tells Pete, "is even if Brit was straight with you, led you to the very spot, even fucking handed you the shovel, it still wouldn't have mattered. After Drew broke it off with her, he went to my father, admitted he'd told her where the gold was."

She pauses, waiting for him to get it. Doesn't take long.

"You moved his half," he says, his voice going dangerously quiet.

"His what?" I croak, momentarily forgetting the pillowcase. There are halves now?

"Several times, actually. But I wasn't in on it. I never even knew where it was—still don't. Dad's own, unique kind of insurance policy, I suppose, in case one of us got greedy. Each of us knows where exactly half the gold is buried, or did until Drew broke faith. Dad reburied his half alone the last time. We moved my half, too, once he realized you and your shithead brother were sniffing around again. None of it's where it was back then."

"Hold on," I say, trying to get a handle on just how many millions we're talking about here. Ten? Twenty? "You're saying there's even more than what's in the well?"

It's only as Adria's jaw drops that I realize what I've done. Together we stare in mutual disbelief at my absurd, feeble-minded slip—only it's not so much shock as surprise and a kind of muted excitement that flits through those eyes. A split second later, it's gone.

Pete's grin says it all. "Well, now. Looks like things have changed."

I'll say. Seems I was right about Adria and the gold all along. It was what Lily said yesterday at the spring that threw me off, that bit about how honest Adria was. And that if she'd really wanted the gold she could have claimed it any time. Which only works, of course, if she actually knew where it was.

I think back to yesterday morning, my outrage as I tossed that gold bar onto her bed. Ignoring her question as to where I found it; assuming she knew, that she was just being coy. Which means the night she snuck back out to the well, she really had been checking the broken pump parts like she said, had no idea the gold was mere feet away. How fucking ironic is that?

"Maybe Drew wasn't the only one Daddy didn't trust," I snarl. "He was worried you'd try and make off with the gold yourself, wasn't he?"

Adria's gaze flicks to Pete, then back to me.

"You two never buried your half together in some father-daughter Kumbaya moment; he hid it on you, just like he did with Drew. So much for all that altruistic crap about how the treasure belongs to the island. You want it as much as Pete does. Maybe more."

Christ, no wonder she didn't want the cops brought in. This way it's just the three of us—and that gun, of course. Something tells me this one's the real deal. She came back to kill Pete, then planned to force me to tell her where I found the gold. She gets rid of the two of us, she's home free.

I can see her processing—probably trying to decide which of us to shoot first now it's come down to it—the barrel of that gun drifting south as she loses focus. Just for a second, but it's long enough.

Pete lunges. He gets hold of that thing and it's over, no question, so I grab the pillowcase and swing it at his head, but it's heavy and I've got no room to build up momentum. Instead, it hits him mid-chest; and when he merely staggers and doesn't go down, I wing the bar of gold at his head without thinking, and that misses altogether.

"Shoot him!" I shout as he stoops and, in one fluid movement, snags both the gold bar and the crossbow before stumbling off into the bushes.

I whirl. "What the fuck, Adria?" I make a grab for the gun, but she holds tight. "Give it to me," I snarl, trying to wrench it from her grasp. "I have to go after him." Knowing that with every second, I stand less of a chance of ever finding Nora.

"Won't do you any good," she says, finally letting go. "It's not loaded. No ammunition," she clarifies as I struggle to take this in. "My fucking father. Look. There's plenty of gold for both of us. You help me take him and I'll split what's in the well with you."

I glare at her, at the gun, at the bushes into which Pete has now disappeared—to what—finish Nora off? No, I realize; she's nothing more than a loose end; he can take care of her later. It's the gold that's still in play here; that's where he's headed.

"First we find Nora," I say, snagging the knife he left behind on the trail and sticking it in the back of my waistband, tossing the miserable hickory-handled thing I brought from the house. "He'll have stashed her somewhere close by now things are coming to a head—another cave, maybe; he seems to like those. Less likely anyone will hear her scream. Anything this side of the island?"

"But the gold…"

"Prying those bars out won't be easy," I tell her. Especially now I've got his knife. "Trust me, he's gonna be at it a while."

She clearly doesn't like it; then again what choice does she have? She could never take him alone, and she knows it. "There's another cave about five minutes along the inland trail, very hidden."

"Take me there. Now."

Good news is the ground cover approaching this second cave's well tramped down, which means it's been used recently. Bad news comes when we peek inside. Space the size of a large closet—dank, gloomy, and empty but for a rusty lantern and another deteriorating cardboard box loaded with crap. Lots of spiders. No Nora.

The sound of someone running toward us along the trail sends us ducking for cover. Praying it's Nora, ready for it to be Pete. Only it's another wet-through island chick, Margot this time—a sight that would surprise me more if things weren't already so fucking surreal.

"Saw you two heading this way." She eyes the gun, then swings her gaze to Adria. "You weren't the only one listening when Hodge mentioned Reese's Leap. No way you're going to do this alone." Her eyes flit to me. "Any sign of Nora?"

I shake my head. "She was never here," I say quietly, pawing through the moldy box to hide my growing despair. A couple rancid-smelling shirts, a worn leather quiver with a broken strap, an aluminum camp cup missing its handle.

"He could have come here first," Adria suggests. "Taken her with him."

"She'd only slow him down," I say, the three of us digging through the box now.

"Whoa, now, what's this?" Margot crows, holding a metallic object aloft.

Adria gapes. "My fucking emergency cell phone, that's what."

"I'll take that." Snatching the thing before Margot can react, I flip it open as I head for the mouth of the cave. Looks like Pete won't be calling for that ride after all. Bummer.

"Nine-one-one work out here?" I call, praying as I wait for it to acquire a signal that there's some battery left, a couple bars of reception.

Adria follows me back into the light, trailed by Margot. "We've been through this. No police, remember? Burt knows I'm in trouble; he'll come."

Right, I think, like I'm gonna wait for Papa Jackman's lobsterman buddy to get his ass out here. I hold the thing high, watch as it sputters to life. Battery's low, reception minimal, but it'll do.

Something flits by in my peripheral vision, and just like that, Adria drops to the dirt—glancing down in surprise as blood soaks her tee shirt, begins pooling beneath her. All this in a matter of seconds. Only then do I notice the shaft protruding from her sternum.

I crouch beside her—pain and shock taking hold of her now—knowing, even as I scan the woods, I'll never see the next arrow coming. "Help me move her to the cave," I bark at a stunned Margot. "Now!"

No time to be easy or gentle. We each grab an arm, drag her inside and around the corner. "Get her down," Margot snaps. "On her back."

"This isn't good," Adria manages, eyes locked on the arrow as we ease her to the ground. "You have to pull it out."

"Can't do it, sweetie," Margot says, covering the wound with both hands, applying pressure to try and staunch the flow—plainly useless, as the stuff continues oozing freely from between her fingers. "You'll lose too much blood."

This makes no sense. Why would Pete bother circling back when he's finally about to claim the gold? Payback, maybe, only he's far too smart to waste the time. More likely a distraction—one of such massive proportion it would be sure to derail any attempt to stop him. Probably figures me for the kind of loyal wuss who wouldn't leave the side of one so grievously wounded. Goes to show how little this fucker knows me.

A sharp intake of breath as Adria struggles to sit. She's having trouble breathing now, going shocky on us.

"Goddamit, Adria," Margot snaps, swiping angrily at tears. "Lay back; save your energy."

Adria swallows hard, shuts her eyes. When they open again, they're less focused, swimming around 'til they manage to lock on mine.

"He's gone for the gold."

I nod.

"Stop him," she demands. "Promise."

I meet Margot's eyes, register the grim look, the minute shake of her head. Those eyes pleading with me: just tell her what she wants to hear.

Adria swallows again. Another sharp breath, willing each word past those lips. "Promise, damn it. Can't. Let. Mother. Fucker."

"Okay, okay. You've got it."

I give her hand a squeeze and, rising, slip from the cave—heart slamming wildly with the possibility that Pete's out here somewhere just lying in wait. Bracing for the impact, the pain, only it doesn't come. It's then I spy the gun laying in Adria's blood just outside the entrance, no doubt dropped there when I crouched beside her. I pause, consider, then grab it up as I strike off for the meadow.

This ends here. Now.

I come at the meadow from the stone wall that runs its length, creeping along behind it 'til I spy Pete dragging what's left of the ruined pump assembly off its base—the crossbow flung onto a burlap bag some six feet away.

His back is to me as he squats at the edge of the gaping shaft—staring intently for a moment, twitchy with need, before bending to the task. I creep along as the first gold bar clears the lip of the well, ducking behind the wall again as Pete turns and scans the woods above me—alerted, no doubt, by that dead-on instinct for trouble. When I poke my head up again, he's back at it. Another gold bar appears, winks from the grass beside him. I draw the useless gun, hop the wall, close on him in a crouch.

"I'm back, dickhead," I snarl from maybe twenty feet away. "Miss me?"

He whirls, glancing quickly toward the crossbow—too far away to be any use to him now. Instead he stands, grins, raising his hands in a kind of aw-shucks thing as he backs around the open shaft—putting it between us.

It's then I smell the smoke, swinging my gaze just long enough to see flames licking the sides of the shed, wherein lies what's left of Brit. Billows of smoke in the trees, too, above where the house sits. Another distraction, I figure, like shooting Adria.

His grin widens. Will I stay here and fight for the gold or put the fire out before it engulfs the entire island?

No contest. This is about Nora; it's about Duggan. It's about Adria and Brit—complicated as my feelings for those two are just now. This whole place could burn down around our ears before I'd let this murdering shit-bag win.

We circle the open maw of the well in fits and starts, a delicate dance dictated by Pete's need to keep clear of any kicks I might get in—itching, as we both know I am, to beat Nora's whereabouts out of him—and mine to keep him from that crossbow. Doubt he could get an arrow off, but that thing connects with my head and it's all over.

I lunge left and so does he, eager as he is to keep distance between us, a dumbass move on his part 'cause it brings me 'round to those gold bars he worked so hard to pry out. Mirroring his grin, I toe them one by one down the shaft—enjoying the resounding splash as they hit bottom, the way his face goes flat with displeasure. Then I toss the gun in for good measure—thinking how great a psych-out this is 'til I reach behind me for the knife tucked in my belt, only to find it's no longer there. Must have slipped out somewhere between the cave and my suddenly less than rosy-looking future.

"You ever kill a guy?" Pete growls.

"Yep," I lie. Still, the last few nights have been filled with dreams of doing just that— over and over, and in myriad ways. Painful, excruciating ways.

"Gotta commit a hundred percent," he tells me, inching toward that crossbow. "Gotta be done in your mind before it's done with your hands— know what I mean?"

Please. Martial Arts 101. Visualization is all. Not to mention that it's closing in on a week without my daily nip or two, or three, which has worked wonders for my reaction time. Better now than it's been in years. Still, I can hardly get to him with this gaping, four-foot hole between us.

The smell of smoke is stronger now. Duggan would cringe at the senseless waste, I can't help thinking—all those priceless first editions. Duggan. Man.

The thought of him sprawled shivering and vulnerable on that raft reignites my rage—helping me focus, regain my edge. "My best friend's probably dead by now, thanks to you."

Pete shrugs. "Man came here lookin' for a story; got more than he bargained for. Still," he says reasonably, "no need for you to die. You take a walk while I get what I'm after and I'm outta here."

Yeah, right. If I'm still breathing when I leave this island, he's screwed and we both know it.

"What about Nora?" I counter, my voice deceptively calm even as some visceral part of me starts analyzing vectors, angles of attack. "You won't need a hostage anymore once you've got the gold. Tell me where she is and I'll leave you to it."

"Well, now, see, changed my mind about that. Someone's gotta answer for Earl, fucked up as he was. Only fair."

Then I see it, that illusive way in—muscles tensing in anticipation just as I catch movement off to the left. I flick my gaze for just an instant, do a double take at the sight of Margot stomping toward us red-faced with fury.

"Your brother," she snarls, bloody hands balled at her sides, "was a worthless piece of shit—just like you!"

The distraction is momentary, but by the time I swing my gaze back to Pete he's launched himself from the other side of the well. And then he's on me—rearing back, trying for a head-butt. But I'm bigger and faster, and I grab him by the throat, push him off—slowly forcing him toward the edge of the shaft, Margot screaming from somewhere behind me.

Somehow in all this, Dad's Dodgers cap is knocked loose. Instinct kicks in and I make a panicked grab, watching in horror as it slips through my fingers and takes a flier down the well. All this takes two seconds, maybe—two seconds I'm left open, two seconds in which Pete could easily make his play. Instead, he flings himself left, lands flat on his back with a surprised look in his right eye, which is the only one he's got left—his other one and the entire left side of his head having vanished in a puff of red mist.

I stare, struck dumb for maybe five seconds before my brain kicks back in—my first thought that Margot's somehow come up with a gun of her own and killed the fucker, but she's busy puking in the grass, which makes that highly unlikely. Some part of me worries about what this might mean even as I step to the edge of the well and peer in, hoping against hope, but Dad's ballcap—gifted to me from his deathbed, the piece of him I've kept close ever since—is gone.

I'm still processing all this when I hear the unmistakable chambering of a round. Whirling, shooting my hands high in a palsied tremble above my head, I stumble backwards—nearly panicking into my own nasty tumble down the rabbit hole.

"Fuck that shit," the weathered-looking guy barreling toward me growls, rifle still on Pete. "I wanted you, you'd be as dead as this one here."

Burt, I realize—here in response to Lily's no doubt panicked call. I've dealt with enough lobstermen over the years to recognize the look—massive upper body earned from a lifetime of hauling traps, hands the size of oven mitts, a web of lines around the eyes that can only come from long hours in the salt air. This one has sandy hair tinged with gray and a thick scar tracking from the corner of his right eye to his ear that could have been from anything.

He steps to Pete's inert body, nudges a blue-jeaned leg with the rifle barrel. "Where's Adria at?"

"Other side of the mountain," I manage. "Gut shot by this guy."

"Damn sorry to hear it." A long, rheumy sigh as he glances skyward. "Aaron, the father, now there was a good man. 'Burt?' he'd say. 'Anything happens to me, up to you to keep an eye. My place, my kids.' Thank God the man's in his grave; would've killed him to see this day."

No kidding. Daddy Jackman might have had his suspicions about

Adria, but even he couldn't have seen this coming. So many twists in her assorted secrets and lies, I feel like I've got whiplash. I'm tempted to fill Burt in, but somehow dissing a dead woman bent on making off with the family fortune seems a hard-hearted and ultimately futile kind of revenge.

Suddenly, quite bizarrely, I'm almost preternaturally aware of the crystalline beauty of this day, this place—the kiss of sunlight on the meadow, the sigh of wind through the trees an almost obscene counterpoint to all that's happened here. For just a moment I feel plucked out of time, off kilter, as if past and present have merged for a brief span of seconds. Right now it wouldn't surprise me to turn seaward to find a cannon-firing galleon rounding the point, ready to dispatch a longboat of guys sporting tricornered hats. Here, finally, to claim the gold, and they'd be welcome to it.

"I best be gettin' on that fire," Burt says, his gaze having shifted to the smoke billowing above the trees. "House is probably gone, but we might save the rest of this place if we get lucky. Still got them extra fire extinguishers up to the outhouse?"

Nothing. "Margot?" I ask, but she's begun rocking herself like a child—Adria's blood soaking the front of her shirt.

"Missy!" Burt snaps. "Them fire extinguishers up to the outhouse; they still there?"

She flinches, manages a dull nod.

"He's torched the tool shed, too," I say, stepping over to offer a hand she ignores. "There's a body in there he won't want found—another woman he killed. And there's a third he was keeping prisoner in the woods; she's still out there somewhere." Hungry, thirsty, and in pain, I remind myself. How the hell am I going to find her now?

"We'll deal with that one later. So, here's the plan. I get on that fire; you two take care of this," he says, nudging Pete's leg with the rifle barrel. "All marsh beyond them trees," he tells us, nodding toward the arborvitaes at the far side of the meadow. "Drag him a couple hundred yards in, bury him shallow. Animals will finish him off by spring."

Margot's head snaps up at this. "What about the police?" she blurts as he starts up the trail. "We can't just bury him and walk away. What will we tell them about Adria and Brit?"

Burt stops, turns, stares her down—his hard, blank look speaking to her infinite stupidity. "Man was never here. Fire was an accident; shame that woman died. By the time we're done, it'll look like Adria died with her. Only way."

"Wait a minute," Margot says, a nervous laugh escaping. "You're not talking about putting Adria in…"

"Like I said, Aaron was a friend. Put himself on the line for me more than once—never mind what it cost him. All he asked was I help protect what he'd built here, if it ever came to it. Nothing we can do for Adria now that won't drag the man's memory through the mud. Drew and his mama, too. Woman ain't been the same since Aaron's death. And now she's lost her only girl? No way I'm gonna tell her it was murder."

Margot's eyes meet mine. Is this guy for real?

"Know what you're thinkin'," he tells us. "But ain't nobody gonna look too close at an old house got itself burned up on a island most people never heard of. 'Specially as I'm the guy investigates fires around here. All them oil lamps and candles? Accident waitin' to happen. Been telling 'em that for years."

Not a bad plan, actually, gruesome as it sounds. Not when you consider the alternative. Cops investigating three deaths? Now there's some major scrutiny for you. Raises the odds of discovery a thousand-fold. And if even the suggestion of hidden treasure gets bandied about, that'll be it. Press, treasure hunters, a small army of knuckle-dragging ex-cons duking it out while they dig the whole place up.

Burt's gaze has wandered to the broken pump. "Pete smashed it," I tell him quickly—wondering just how much, if anything, he knows about the gold. "Cutting off our water his way of making a point."

He nods, wipes sweat from his face with a dirty shirttail. "Dangerous as hell like that," he says, starting off again. "Pull it together for now," he calls over his shoulder. "Last thing we need's some hiker breakin' his leg or worse."

Margot turns to me. "I can't do this," she says thickly, clearly ready to barf again.

"Sure you can," I tell her, dragging what's left of the platform over the gaping shaft. "Island Woman, right? Fucking Amazon babe? Here." I toss her the burlap sack, glance to where the first curious flies are checking out what's left of Pete's head. "Throw this over him."

She screws up her face, averting her gaze as she moves toward Pete. "Oh, God," she says, dropping the sack onto his head, then stepping away. "It smells. Jesus."

Some jock. Stripping the belt from my jeans, I raise him enough to do a half-assed job of wrapping the burlap around what's left of his skull— ignoring the mushy feel of the whole mess as I slip the belt beneath his neck and tighten it. Good enough to see him over a couple hundred yards of grassy terrain, I figure. "We'll drag him behind us. Don't look; just grab a leg and pull."

She doesn't move. "Well, fuck, Margot," I grumble. Sighing, I take a foot in each hand and begin dragging Pete behind me, praying the sack stays put. Last thing we need is to leave a slide of bloody slurry in our wake. "Get the crossbow, at least."

"This will never work," she blurts from somewhere behind me. "I mean what are we supposed to tell people—Adria's mother, Brit's family? Sorry about this, but hey, shit happens?"

I've got no answer for this, no interest in assuring her that things will work out when they rarely do, so I ignore her and keep moving—the marshy dampness underfoot slowing our progress. Still I slog on, in full-out survival mode now.

She's mid-shin in the watery drool by the time she calls a halt to all this wandering. "Hodge. It's far enough, already. Stop."

She's right; it's not like another twenty feet's gonna keep some innocent hiker from stumbling over what's left of this guy; still, I drag him another five feet or so for no other reason than she clearly doesn't want me to, and maybe because she's the one standing here safe and sound with all her toes intact instead of Nora.

I finally drop what used to be Pete behind a thick stand of cattails, shooting her a furious glare as I snatch the crossbow and begin angrily scraping a long shallow rectangle out of the muck—while above us, smoke floats in a lazy, striated haze.

"What?" she snaps.

I stop, consider a moment, then shake my head and continue with the pseudo grave digging—flinging muck and clods of wet cord grass aside in my deepening agitation. Not her fault, I remind myself. Not. Her. Fault.

"Look," she says after a few minutes of this. "We all know you've got a thing for Nora." Her glare is almost triumphant. "Oh, don't look so surprised," she mutters, batting at a couple flies. "It was obvious your first night here."

I let that go, toss the crossbow aside. I could spend an hour out here trying to dig with this thing and still get nowhere.

"Help me roll him over," I grumble, dragging the body to the edge of the depression—the fact that this fucker's gonna eat mud into eternity the only thing cheering me just now.

"You realize it's hopeless, right?" Margot says as we're flipping him.

What am I, stupid? Of course I know it's hopeless; that's what makes her so fucking irresistible.

"Even if she wasn't married, it wouldn't work," Margot continues, watching me scrape the slurry of mud, leaves, and wet marsh grass over Pete's corpse. "You don't know her. She doesn't do relationships. She hasn't even had sex with her husband in years."

"Christ," I mutter. "We have to do this now?"

"I'm just telling you, is all."

"I don't get it," I say, glancing up. "I thought the two of you were friends."

"Not particularly. This is the first time I've seen her in ages. Any of us, actually. Technically, she shouldn't even be here. Adria made this rule a few years ago: if you miss a summer, you're dropped from the group. Nora skipped last year, so we all assumed she was done. Adria surprised us by inviting her back—but then she had her own reasons for everything, as we've all seen. It's her island; she makes the rules. And we put up with it year after year—all for a little time away."

I consider this. "She gave me this line about how the island has magical properties, that just being out here could help Nora heal."

"Which is a bunch of bullshit, since this is where it started. She was different after that."

Oh, she's different, all right. Still, this talk of Adria leads me down a path I'd rather not go just now, like how my slip of the tongue is the reason she's lying dead up there on the mountain—something that'll haunt me the rest of my days. I'm so agitated by this, it takes me a minute to realize I'm scooping and flinging the saucy goo everywhere but on Pete.

Margot's finished venting, it seems; breathes a long, weary sigh. "You think she's still alive?" All that bluster and bravado spent, crossing her arms against the fear and vulnerability left in its wake.

"Yes," I tell her. "I do."

It was Pete, ironically enough, who renewed my flagging hope. That line about changing his mind about Nora, how someone's got to answer for Earl. As in it hadn't happened yet. What's more, even wounded as she is, every time Pete left to meet me—shit, every time he went to take a piss— she'd be racking her brain for some way out of this. I have to believe she somehow managed it; the alternative is simply too grim.

More flies now. A noisy buzzing as they dance on the muddy mound that was once Pete, a shift in the wind bringing the smoke down on us. This guy's had as much burying as he's gonna get, I decide, which is far more than he deserves.

I use my last bit of energy to wing the crossbow deep into the rushes, my gaze catching on the tops of those arborvitaes at the edge of the meadow. A wink of memory, then, the glimmer of possibility, of sudden hope.

"Come on," I say, and even I can hear the exhaustion in my voice. "I think I know where she could be."

You know that feeling you get—intuition, sixth sense, whatever—when out of the blue something just reveals itself to you? Nothing to do with proof or reason or even conscious thought, just a kind of gut instinct taking you over. That's how it was when we found Nora, as I somehow knew we would, crouching—filthy, shivering, and wild-eyed—at the base of that arborvitae in Salt Marsh Cove. That first morning I surprised her there, almost a week ago now, I remember telling her she was all but invisible nestled in the crosshatch of those enormous roots. Must have sunk in.

I marvel at this as I watch Burt and Margot chatting at the edge of the float while he works to make room for us in his high-powered Zodiac, lugging tools, gas cans, and coils of rope to the bow. A shocky Nora sits beside me on the ramp—her freshly bandaged foot propped awkwardly on a toolbox.

"You okay?" I ask.

She's slow to respond—the pain pills Burt unearthed from some onboard stash, I figure—and she finally just nods, eyes locked on that gauze-wrapped foot. Mr. Tough Guy spent a good twenty minutes clucking over the thing—swearing like a sailor, hands shaking as he pried off the filthy, crusted sock she'd somehow managed to wrap it in. Must've hurt like a bitch while Margot was cleaning it; still, she never so much as winced.

I fight the urge to take her hand—touching her being the only thing I've wanted to do since we found her. So much I need to say—part of me going all macho, determined to find out what else happened out there, how she managed to escape; the other half terrified she might actually tell me.

I grab Lily's charred bag of knitting, think longingly of the wallet I left behind as identification on the off-chance things didn't go my way, my knapsack, my fucking Dodgers cap. Gone, gone, and gone.

"Just out of curiosity," I say, tossing the bag into some sooty, yellow milk crate Burt found—one of its plastic sides half-melted in a yolk-like drool, "how did you know which of us to shoot?"

He rises stiffly—his clothes, like mine, acrid smelling, covered in mud, cinders, and the blood of several people. "Little Eskimo girl described you pretty good. Besides, we got history, Pete and me. " He pauses to pick at an ear, examining the bloody scab he's pulled away before flicking it to the ground. "Only wish I could dig him up, do it again."

We stare as one toward the two women waiting in the boat, forever bonded by what we did here just a few hours ago. The less said about disposing of the bodies the better. Gruesome, ugly work. The phrase *consigning them to the fire* with all its ritualized spirituality hardly applies. No doubt about it; we were covering our asses all the way down the line—Burt as much as the rest of us, which pretty much guarantees he'll never breathe a word about how Adria and Brit really died. God knows I never will. Nightmares for years, I'm sure.

"Passable job back there in the marsh," he says. "Been chasin' that one and his brother outta these islands for years. Poachin', mostly. Had 'em in our sights for a couple break-ins on the mainland; never could nail 'em."

"The brother's dead, too," I say. "You know that, right? Died out here two years ago."

Burt nods. "Couple kayakers found his body snarled up with old nets and trash in a tidal pool below them cliffs. Not much left to the head. Whoever killed him was some pissed."

"Could be he had somebody with him," I say. "Had a disagreement of the fatal kind. Then again, Adria figured he just fell. Happens, apparently."

Burt eyes me. "That what she told you? Guess it don't matter, her bein' gone now and all, but she and her friends were out here that week, too—Island Women, she calls 'em. Scattered like rabbits soon as the body was found. Gone that same day."

I watch as Margot slides a protective arm around Nora—one of those chick looks with about twelve levels of meaning passing between them. Kinda cozy, given what she said to me back there in the marsh. A whispered word, and Nora turns my way, but doesn't return my quick smile before resting her head on Margot's shoulder.

"Never said nothin' to me, you understand, but there's no question somethin' went on out here none of 'em ever told. Cops couldn't get nothin' out of 'em neither. Nothin' in the world as silent as a bunch of women decided they ain't gonna tell you shit."

Two Weeks Later

I'm taking the stairs two at a time to my third-floor office, such as it is, after grabbing a burger and beer at an off-campus bistro—a hoppin' place this time of night. The thought of going back to the slew of academic minutia awaiting me in that small, cramped space is beyond depressing; and while I considered staying on at the bar into the wee hours and getting spectacularly drunk, hanging alone in such a place smacks too much of desperation. Besides, I've got a ton of emails to get out. Fall semester starts in just two weeks, and thanks to the last minute defection by a lecturer in my undergrad program, I'm having to pick up a Monday, Wednesday, Friday class entitled *Disease, Ectomycorrhizal, and Ethylene Effects on the Growth of Conifers*. Blah, blah, blah. Eight in the morning, no less. Happily, though, word of my pinch-hitting is beginning to make the rounds, and I've already had several young women withdraw—my dubious reputation, no doubt. Fine with me; let them all drop it. Frankly, I could give a shit.

I unlock the office door and shoulder it open, grabbing the fistful of notes stuck in the jamb and tossing them absently on the desk as I chastise myself in a vague, unfocused way for having left the gooseneck lamp on. Not like me. It's then I catch sight of those missing Ray-Ban Aviators propped open on my laptop.

Whirling, I do a panicked three-sixty, and find nothing; ditto when I peek beneath the desk, peer warily behind the door. Waste of time, really. Been here and gone, just like always.

I extend a finger, cautiously stirring the detritus that litters my desk. If true to form, one thing will have been switched for another. When she took the Ray-Bans, she left a half-eaten pear decomposing into my computer keyboard. Kissed that sucker goodbye. Another time, she filched a pile of un-graded student exams from the inbox atop my desk, replacing them with a stash of dog-eared porn mags I suspect were lifted from the office of a physics professor who shall remain nameless—a lapse I was forced to cover by giving everyone in the class an A. Sometimes, if displeased, destruction follows—in one case, a fire. In the wastebasket. A paper I'd been writing and just printed out for editing. I managed to catch it before it triggered a building-wide sprinkler meltdown, which told me two things: the locks in this building suck and, more to the point, she knew my schedule inside out—right down to my predictable trots to the pissoir.

Speaking of fires, the fiasco on the island played out just as Burt predicted, thanks to some half-assed report he cobbled together claiming Adria and Brit were alone in the house when it started—Lily and I having gone to the mainland to get the leg Duggan foolishly injured seen to, and Margot and Nora off swimming for the afternoon. Thankfully, nobody questioned why two otherwise healthy, athletic women were unable to make it out of the house before the place came down around them.

I know all this because I was in touch with Burt briefly after seeing a short bit on the late-night news—no film, thank God—about two women dying in a house fire on an island just off the coast. Careless use of candles or something. A minor tragedy that's no doubt already been forgotten by anyone who wasn't there. And those of us who were…well.

Sighing, I drop into my chair, tossing the Ray-Bans—wire ear pieces bent and mangled, I note with disgust—toward the briefcase open on the floor by my desk. Rolling my chair forward, I wake my laptop and log on, hoping for a hit on the search I've got going to replace Dad's Dodgers cap. Not some retro-looking wannabe, mind you, but the real thing—of which there might be three left on the planet. Replacing the contents of my wallet proved far less trouble than this.

Anyway, back to Burt. I'd been hoping for an update on Nora—pathetic, I know—who apparently checked herself out of Maine Medical Center a day and half after being admitted. That was all the hospital could or would say. Burt knew even less, at least that's what he told me—instead rattling off a number for Adria's brother, who'd appreciate a call, he said. I held onto it for a day or two, then simply tossed it. I mean, really, what's the point? The very idea had me in a twist. I could just see it—forced to choke back the truth about how Adria really died, her willingness to sacrifice everyone and everything to claim the gold for herself. Which may or may not have come as a surprise to the guy. Did I consider going back for it myself? Okay, yeah, for about two seconds, maybe, but considering what happened to everyone who's ever tried to claim the stuff, I'll pass. Some kind of curse the Reese kid put on it, maybe—who knows? No, it belongs to island for real now far as I'm concerned, at least 'til someone starts digging around in that well. And what a shocker that'll be.

I pull my attention back to the laptop, where I find zero hits on the ball cap—hardly a surprise. I think for a minute, then peck out another search, this one for the Zappa tee I was forced to toss. Not enough soap on the planet to get that sucker clean. I'm sure you can imagine. I figure if I can't come up with the cap, maybe a Zappa will do. Something, anything, to ground me in the here and now, jump-start the life I was living before the island. Before Nora. God knows something has to.

Duggan, who of course knows nothing about any of this, would advise patience. He's much better, by the way. And while it was touch-and-go there for a while, he's finally on the mend thanks to the quick intervention of the hospital team and Lily's loving, if bizarre, ministrations both on and off the island. Convalescing so well, in fact, he's far too busy outlining a novel based on the terrorizing exploits of the all-too-feral brothers grim to make time for me just now. Funny how coming face-to-face with death will jolt you out of writer's block.

There are times I almost convince myself I'm finally coming to grips with what happened out there, but there are a shitload more when I'm stuck obsessing about the part I played in the horror of it all. Nights are the worst. Booze helps, though even this doesn't keep Nora's image from infecting my dreams with a vague, unsettled longing, the nagging sense I've somehow gotten it all wrong.

No question somethin' went on out here none of 'em ever told. Cops couldn't get nothin' out of 'em neither. Nothin' in the world as silent as a bunch of women decided they ain't gonna tell you shit. Scattered like rabbits, Burt told me. Gone as soon as Pete's brother Earl's body was found.

I've been 'round and 'round with this, and still it gets me nowhere. It's possible they all knew about Earl's death, I suppose—not a new thought, certainly—but then why deny it unless they were involved? And if they were, where's the motive? Okay, yeah, I considered the gold—a hell of an incentive, I'll grant you, but that presupposes they all knew about it. Possible, but unlikely. Adria was far too tight-lipped for that.

Besides, even if by some miracle Earl had managed to scrape together enough brain cells to launch a plausible threat, one phone call from Adria and he'd have been quickly and permanently dispatched by the pragmatic Burt—buried fast and way deep, not left to float free and raise inconvenient questions later.

So what am I missing here?

Closing my eyes, I feel my way through those first days on the island for anything that seemed odd, felt off—my mind snagging on something about the women. About one of the women. About Nora.

I rock back in my chair, letting my thoughts find their way. Her fear of strangers, the generalized social phobia. Post-traumatic stress, Margot called it. Felt like bullshit then, feels like it now.

Then, something else she said while we were planting Pete in the marsh. Something like this being where it started, how Nora was different after that. A slip of the tongue I didn't pick up on 'til just now. So what happened to change Nora from the vibrant, creative woman she once was to one literally afraid of her own shadow?

Out of nowhere, I remember the undergrad I counseled a few years back—a young girl whose grades were slipping alarmingly, who'd become socially isolated, almost pathologically shy. It was a long three weeks of one-on-one before she trusted me enough to tell me why.

A brief flash of clarity, and my body goes leaden with realization—the twisted, unspeakable logic of it all hitting me with the heft of absolute truth.

Earl raped Nora; it's the only thing that makes any sense. And at Reese's Leap—I'm sure of it—the place Margot told me gave Nora the creeps, the final place she'd needed to go in order to get past her fear. The very spot, I realize now, that Duggan and I sat scarfing down granola bars and shooting the shit just before I stumbled across Bambi. The thought sickens me—a hot, helpless anguish blooming as the pieces slip into place. Why, I wonder, hadn't I made the connection before things spiraled so completely out of control?

Easy, comes the answer. I had help.

Margot, the others—they all knew; they had to. And yet they spent an entire week doing whatever it took to keep the truth from me. Why? To protect Nora? Okay, at first, maybe; I was a stranger after all. But when the shit hit the fan and I needed all the information I could get? No, there's more to it. Has to be.

I fight to get my mind around all this. So what do you do when your friend, this beautiful amazing woman, is savaged—beaten and raped and God only knows what else—by a moron with the I.Q. of a rock? Me, I'd scream for the cops, but this bunch? One thing I've learned, alpha chicks like these? They take care of their own.

Fuckin' A.

So who killed him—Nora? Margot? All of them in some kind of avenging angel, *Lord of the Flies* scenario? A kick in the balls, a rock to the head, roll him off the cliff and into the blue beyond. Sayonara, asshole.

And then what? Can't report the rape with a body floating free. Another reason not to acknowledge it, even after all this time. Two violent crimes in a matter of days? Cops around here might be slow, but they're not brain-dead.

So they came up with a plan. Keep their mouths shut, go back to their lives, and pray the whole thing blows over. And they got away with it, too—for a while, anyway. Until the night Pete showed up looking for answers, or so he claimed. Only one thing to do then.

Which is where I came in.

I sit bolt upright with the absolute knowledge I've been played—stroked and loved up and led to the slaughter, grinning like a fool the whole way. So infatuated with Nora, I'd no idea I was being groomed to get rid of their problem for good.

We all know you've got a thing for Nora, Margot told me. *It was obvious your first night here.*

I take a deep breath, let it out slow. Another. Feel my way through the waves of emotion. Nora—man, the chick used me from the get-go. I think of how fast and how deeply she got under my skin and how that was probably the plan all along. Using me the night she took me into her bed, gambling those few hours would ensure I'd come after her when she offered herself up to Pete the next day. That I'd rescue her and finish him off as payback. A huge risk, of course, but what other choice did they have?

So many things I should have seen. Margot explaining away Nora's panicked reaction to Pete that first night he showed up by telling me he and Earl looked alike. Sounded funny at the time, but I was too crazy with worry to wonder why, to realize there's no way she could have known such a thing if she hadn't seen him herself. Up close and very personal.

And all the mental shell games, Adria's misdirection and out-and-out lies—designed, I realize only now, to keep the attention on saving Nora and off the questions surrounding Earl's death, off the gold. I think of all the in-fighting, the mutual accusations; were they for my benefit, as well?

The connections are coming fast and furious now—soft, lethal blows to my already battered ego. Margot's sudden, inexplicable dissing of Nora back there in the marsh, her suggestion the group only put up with Adria's pseudo-patrician hogwash in hopes of a little vacation time. All of it meant to throw me off, make me believe the whole Island Women camaraderie bit was a sham. Still, it wasn't to me that a sobbing, terrified Nora ran when we found her crouched at the base of that Arborvitae but to Margot herself, their reunion as touching as any I've ever seen. Smoke and mirrors—all of it. Hell, if anything, Nora's near-death and its aftermath probably brought them closer—their bond inviolate, sealed in blood, as immutable as kryptonite. Sometimes the only way to protect something that important, I long ago realized, is to disavow it.

Another flash, this of the chicks as the raft floated off that final morning. The stillness of the air as they drifted away, the expressions on Margot's and Adria's faces as their little scheme was coming to fruition—Adria already planning to swim back and collect that gun, useless as it turned out to be, determined that no one would leave with the gold, maybe even leave at all.

Fortunately for me, it didn't quite play out that way. What was it she said that first night, how nobody ever leaves the island the same? Certainly not this time. In fact, two of them never left at all—three, if you count Pete. Then again, who'd bother?

I lace my hands behind my head, rock back in my chair—feeling suddenly old and jaded and very much alone. I should be angry; hell, I should be furious. Instead I find myself overwhelmed by the various ironies in all this, stunned by how well these women read me, how completely I was taken in.

You idiot, I murmur into the gloom—glancing wearily toward the single window as an outside security light flicks to life. You complete fucking loser, I reiterate.

It's then I notice the pert little Bonsai that normally sits on the chipped windowsill is missing from its soil-ringed saucer—the trade-off, it appears, for the return of my Ray-Bans.

Shit. I liked that thing, too.

All at once I yearn for the reassuring solitude of home, the familiar emotional territory of my urban loft with its double deadbolt locks, soft lighting, and broad selection of single malts. I could get a dog, I think—a companion who doesn't speak, whose cues I can't possibly misinterpret.

Later for this place, I decide, reaching for my briefcase. The emails can wait 'til morning; nobody reads them anyway.

I'm almost to the door when I hear the distinctive ding of an instant message, something I only ever receive from one person. I note the immediate uptick of my pulse, have to remind myself as I fight the urge to bolt from the room that ignoring her only makes things worse.

The message is short, as are they all. Four words. No greeting.

Where you been, jerkface?

Big on nicknames, this one. Dickwad, fuckhead, and my personal favorite: scum-sucking shitbag motherfucker. She's changed since that summer on Matinicus, as I prayed she would, only not in a good way.

Oddly, it's then I begin to relax. The devil you know, and all that—never mind she's by far the most dangerous of the twisted lovelies I've collected over the years, and the only one I've found it impossible to shake.

I set my briefcase down, flash again to those final weeks on Matinicus—all that I bungled and left unfinished there. I have no idea what happened to the baby. She's never said, and no, it's not mine. I'll tell you about it someday. You can buy the bottle. Trust me, it'll be worth it.

Another annoying ding and I sigh, retake my seat—the wink of the cursor taunting me as I consider my reply.

ACKNOWLEDGEMENTS

I caught the first glimmers of the story that would eventually become *Reese's Leap* while on an annual, all-female retreat on a remote island off the coast of Maine. Take five women itching to raise some hell, put them in a rambling, hundred-year-old lodge with no electricity, phone service or other connection to the outside world, throw in a three-day fog, and the imagination can't help but run a little wild.

The sad saga of Malaga Island, so central to Adria's history and character, is based on an infamous time in Maine's not-so-distant past; and while the forcible removal of the mixed-race community that made the island its home until the early twentieth century did indeed take place, the characters and scenes created in *Reese's Leap* are nothing more than the product of my imagination, and were drawn simply to suit my plot. I regret any inaccuracies in my depiction of that terrible time; no disrespect was intended. Those interested in a more thorough depiction of the entire Malaga Island fiasco might refer to the excellent radio and still-photo documentary, *Malaga Island, A Story Best Left Untold*, by Kate Philbrick and Rob Rosenthal, produced in cooperation with the Salt Institute for Documentary Studies in Portland, Maine.

Standouts among the many books and papers I read while researching *Reese's Leap* include *Lizzie Bright and the Buckminster Boy* by Gary Schmidt; *Twelve Thousand Years of American Indians in Maine* by Bruce Bourque; Miriam White's *Yarmouth Island: 100 Years*; and the issue paper titled "Aboriginal Women and Traditional Healing," prepared for the 2007 National Aboriginal Women's Summit held in Newfoundland, Canada.

I'm grateful to Tim, Marty, and Russ for sharing their knowledge of high-tech outdoor clothing; to Andrea for her stories of AnRaGo Island and Canada's northern Georgian Bay, which fueled so many of Gil's early memories; to "Gator1995"—the anonymous barista who guided me through the maze of Starbucks drink options and their questionable links to personality types; and to Sky for her patient instruction on the innumerable species of plant life indigenous to Maine's mid-coast islands.

Kudos to Mary Palmieri Gai for the terrific suggestion of the epigraph, to Anna Torborg for the fabulous book cover, and to my amazing editor, Katherine Mayfield, for her light and perceptive touch. Most of all, I'm indebted to my readers—Adair, Anita, Becca, Ben, Chuck, Ellen, Roxanne, Sarah, and my husband Cleave—none of whom held back. They never do.

Coming Soon:
Ragged Island

Gil Hodges has a thorny past he can't shake: a string of sordid, failed relationships, outrageous wrongs never put right, and a gut-wrenching moral compromise made years ago with a stone-cold killer—one who slips in and out of his life at will, taunting him, haunting his dreams. And back now with a vengeance, it seems. Question is why.

The timing couldn't be worse. At an all-time personal low after watching two people die and almost losing his own life during a harrowing week on remote Mistake Island, Gil is overwhelmed with regret, paralyzed by self-doubt, and beset by personal demons he can no longer keep at bay.

Then, out of the blue, love walks in. The real thing. A woman Gil thought he'd never find and quickly discovers he can't live without. Desperate to make a fresh start, he must first distance himself from the murderer who relentlessly shadows him, obsessed with one terrifying goal and bent on Gil's helping to achieve it, no matter the cost.

Determined to cut this tie once and for all, Gil risks everything by going back to where it all started—back to Matinicus.

ABOUT THE AUTHOR

DARCY SCOTT is a live-aboard sailor and experienced ocean cruiser who's sailed to Grenada and back on a whim, island-hopped through the Caribbean, and been struck by lightning in the middle of the Gulf Stream. Her favorite cruising ground remains the coast of Maine, however, and her appreciation of the history and rugged beauty of its sparsely populated out-islands serves as inspiration for her Maine Island Mystery Series, which includes 2012's award-winning *Matinicus* and the newly released *Reese's Leap*. Book three, *Ragged Island*, is currently in the works. Her debut novel, *Hunter Huntress*, was published in June, 2010 by Snowbooks, Ltd., UK. Learn more at www.Darcyscott.net.